Stories

All-New Tales Edited By

Neil Gaiman
and
Al Sarrantonio

Volume 1

W F HOWES LTD

This large print edition published in 2011 by
W F Howes Ltd
Unit 4, Rearsby Business Park, Gaddesby Lane,
Rearsby, Leicester LE7 4YH

1 3 5 7 9 10 8 6 4 2

First published in the United Kingdom in 2010
by Headline Review

A CIP catalogue record for this book is available
from the British Library

ISBN 978 1 40746 746 7

Typeset by Palimpsest Book Production Limited,
Falkirk, Stirlingshire
Printed and bound in Great Britain
by MPG Books Ltd, Bodmin, Cornwall

For all the storytellers and tale spinners who entertained the public and kept themselves alive, for Alexandre Dumas and Charles Dickens, for Mark Twain and Baroness Orczy and the rest, and most of all, for Scheherazade, who was the storyteller and the story told.

CONTENTS

Many loving thanks to Jennifer Brehl and Merrilee Heifetz, dual rudders on a long boat, for steering us safely to shore.

INTRODUCTION

JUST FOUR WORDS

Al Sarrantonio and I were discussing anthologies of short stories. He had edited a huge anthology of cutting-edge horror, and another of cutting-edge fantasy, each book, in its way, definitive. And in talking, we realised that we had something in common: that all we cared about, really, were the stories. What we missed, what we wanted to read, were stories that made us care, stories that forced us to turn the page. And yes, we wanted good writing (why be satisfied with less?). But we wanted more than that. We wanted to read stories that used a lightning flash of magic as a way of showing us something we have already seen a thousand times as if we have never seen it before. Truly, we wanted it all.

And slowly, the wish becomes the deed . . .

When I was a child, I pestered my elders for stories. My family would improvise, or read me stories from books. As soon as I was old enough to read, I was one of those children who needed to have a book within reach. I would read a book a day, or more. I wanted stories, and I wanted

1

them always, and I wanted the experience that only fiction could give me: I wanted to be inside them.

Television and cinema were all very well, but these stories happened to other people. The stories I found in books happened inside my head. I was, in some way, there.

It's the magic of fiction: you take the words and you build them into worlds.

As time passed, I became a more discriminating reader (I remember the first time I realised I did not have to finish reading a book; the first time I realised that the way a story was told was getting in the way of the story). But even as I became more discriminating as a reader I started to feel that the thing that kept me reading, the place the magic occurred, the driving force of narrative was sometimes being overlooked. I would read beautiful prose, and I would simply not care.

It came down to four words.

There are the kind of readers who read only non-fiction: who read biographies, perhaps, or travel writing. Readers who read nothing but concrete poetry. There are those who read things that will improve them and their lot, who only read books that tell them how to survive the coming financial crisis, or have confidence in themselves, or play poker, or build beehives. I myself can sometimes be found reading books about beekeeping and, because I write fiction, am always happy to read strange factual things.

Whatever we read, we are part of the community of the story.

There are nonreaders, of course. I knew a man in his nineties who, when he learned that I was a writer, admitted to me that he had tried to read a book, once, long before I was born, but he had been unable to see the point of it, and had never tried again. I asked him if he remembered the name of the book, and he told me, in the manner of someone who tried to eat a snail once and did not care for it, and who does not need to remember the breed of the snail, that one was much like another, surely.

Still. Four words.

And I didn't realise it until a couple of days ago, when someone wrote in to my blog:

Dear Neil,

If you could choose a quote – either by you or another author – to be inscribed on the wall of a public library children's area, what would it be?

Thanks!
Lynn

I pondered for a bit. I'd said a lot about books and kids' reading over the years, and other people had said things pithier and wiser than I ever could. And then it hit me, and this is what I wrote:

I'm not sure I'd put a quote up, if it was me, and I had a library wall to deface. I think I'd just remind people of the power of stories, of why they exist in the first place. I'd put up the four words that anyone telling a story wants to hear. The ones that show that it's working, and that pages will be turned:

'. . . and then what happened?'

The four words that children ask, when you pause, telling them a story. The four words you hear at the end of a chapter. The four words, spoken or unspoken, that show you, as a story-teller, that people care.

The joy of fiction, for some of us, is the joy of the imagination, set free from the world and able to imagine.

Talking to Al Sarrantonio I realised that I was not alone in finding myself increasingly frustrated with the boundaries of genre: the idea that categories which existed only to guide people around bookshops now seemed to be dictating the kind of stories that were being written. I love the word *fantasy*, for example, but I love it for the almost infinite room it gives an author to play: an infinite playroom, of a sort, in which the only boundaries are those of the imagination. I do not love it for the idea of commercial fantasy. Commercial fantasy, for good or for ill, tends to drag itself through already existing furrows, furrows dug by

J.R.R. Tolkien or Robert E. Howard, leaving a world of stories behind it, excluding so much. There was so much fine fiction, fiction allowing free rein to the imagination of the author, beyond the shelves of genre. That was what we wanted to read.

It seemed to us that the fantastic can be, can do, so much more than its detractors assume: it can illuminate the real, it can distort it, it can mask it, it can hide it. It can show you the world you know in a way that makes you realise you've never looked at it, not *looked* at it. G.K. Chesterton compared fantastic fiction to going on holiday – that the importance of your holiday is the moment you return, and you see the place you live through fresh eyes.

And so the call went out from Mr Sarrantonio and from me, and the stories began to come back to us. Writers rose to the challenge. We learned to expect only the unexpected.

'. . . and then what happened?'

The real magic of this little invocation is that it has inspired hundreds of millions of words, has made people who never imagined themselves as storytellers into tale-tellers who could have given Scheherazade or Dunsany's Joseph Jorkens a run for their money or their whiskey or their lives. We turn the page, and the adventure begins.

There is something waiting for you. So turn the page.

Neil Gaiman
December 2009

5

BLOOD

RODDY DOYLE

He grew up in Dracula's City. He'd walked past Bram Stoker's house every day on his way to school. But it had meant nothing to him. He'd never felt a thing, not the hand of a ghost or a shiver, not a lick on his neck as he passed. In fact, he was nearly eighteen, in his last year at school, before he'd even noticed the plaque beside the door. He'd never read the book, and probably never would. He'd fallen asleep during Coppola's *Dracula*. One minute his wife was screaming, grabbing his knee; the next, she was grabbing the same knee, trying to wake him up. The cinema lights were on and she was furious.

-How can you do that?

-What?

-Sleep during a film like that.

-I always fall asleep when the film's shite.

-We're supposed to be out on a date.

-That's a different point, he said. –For that, I apologise. How did it end, anyway?

-Oh, fuck off, she said, affectionately – that was possible in Dublin.

So the whole thing, the whole Dracula business, meant absolutely nothing to him.

Nevertheless, he wanted to drink blood.

Badly.

The *badly* was recent, and dreadful. The itch, the urge, the leaking tongue – it was absolutely dreadful.

He wasn't sure when it had started. He was, though – he knew when he'd become aware.

-How d'you want your steak?

-Raw.

His wife had laughed. But he'd been telling her the truth. He wanted the slab of meat she was holding over the pan, raw and *now* – fuck the pan, it wasn't needed. He could feel muscles holding him back, and other muscles fighting for him – neck muscles, jaw muscles.

Then he woke.

But he was awake already, still standing in the kitchen, looking at the steak, and looking forward to it.

-Rare, so, he said.

She smiled at him.

-You're such a messer, she said.

He hid behind that, the fact that he acted the eejit, that it was *him*, as he bent down to the charred meat on the plate a few minutes later, and licked it. The kids copied him and they all ended up with brown gravy on their noses. He made himself forget about his aching jaws and the need to bite and growl. They all watched a DVD after dinner, and everything was grand.

And it was; it was fine. Life was normal. For a while. For quite a while. Weeks – he thought. He opened the fridge one day. There were two fillet steaks on a plate, waiting. It must have been weeks later because she – her name was Vera – she wouldn't have bought steak all that frequently. And it wasn't the case that Vera did all the shopping, or even most of it; she just went past the butcher's more often than he did. She bought the food; he bought the wine. She bought the soap and toilet paper – and he bought the wine. *You're such a messer.*

He grabbed one of the steaks and took it over to the sink. He looked behind him, to make sure he was alone, and then devoured it as he leaned over the sink. But he didn't *devour* it. He licked it first, like an ice-pop; it was cold. He heard the drops of blood hit the aluminium beneath him, and he felt the blood running down his chin, as if it – the blood – was coming from him. And he started to suck it, quickly, to drink it. It should have been warm. He knew that, and it disgusted him, the fact that he was already planting his disappointment, setting himself up to do it again – *this* – feeding a need, an addiction he suddenly had and accepted. He growled – he fuckin' growled. He looked behind him – but he didn't care. *You're such a messer.* He chewed till it stopped being meat and spat the pulp into the bin. He rubbed his chin; he washed his hands. He looked at his shirt. It was clean. He ran the hot tap and watched the black drops turn red, pink, then nothing. He took the remaining fillet from the fridge and slid it off the plate, into the bin. He tied the plastic liner and brought it out to the wheelie bin.

-Where's the dinner? Vera wanted to know, later.

-What?

-I bought fillet steaks for us. There.

She stood in front of the fridge's open door.

-They were off, he said.

-They were not.

-They were, he said. –They were minging. I threw them out.

-They were perfect, she said. –Are they in here?

She was at the bin.

-The wheelie, he said.

He hadn't expected this; he hadn't thought ahead.

-I'm bringing them back, she said, as she moved to the back door. –The fucker.

She was talking about the butcher.

-Don't, he said.

He didn't stand up, he didn't charge to block her. He stayed sitting at the table. He could feel his heart – his own meat – hopping, thumping.

-He's always been grand, he said. –If we complain, it'll – I don't know – change the relationship. The customer-client thing.

He enjoyed listening to himself. He was winning.

-We can have the mince, he said.

-It was for the kids, she said. –Burgers.

-I like burgers, he said. –You like burgers.

The back door was open. It was a hot day, after a week of hot days. He knew: she didn't want to

9

open the wheelie and shove her face into a gang of flies.

They had small burgers. The kids didn't complain. That was that.

Out of his system. He remembered – he saw himself – attacking the meat, hanging over the sink. He closed his eyes, snapped them shut – the idea, the thought, of being caught like that. By a child, by his wife. The end of his life.

He'd killed it – the urge. But it came back, days later. And he killed it again. The fridge again – lamb chops this time. He sent his hand in over the chops, and grabbed a packet of chicken breasts, one of those polystyrene trays, wrapped in cling-film. He put a finger through the film, pulled it away. He slid the breasts onto a plate – and drank the pink, the near-white blood. He downed it, off the tray. And vomited.

Cured. Sickened – revolted. Never again. He stayed home from work the next day. Vera felt his forehead.

-Maybe it's the swine flu.

-Chicken pox, he said. *You're such a messer.*

-You must have had the chicken pox when you were a boy, she said.

-Did you?

-I think so, he said.

She looked worried.

-It can make adult males sterile, she said.

-I had a vasectomy, he told her. –Three years ago.

-I forgot, she said.

-I didn't.

But he was cured; he'd sorted himself out. The thought, the memory – the taste of the chicken blood, the polystyrene tray – it had him retching all day. He wouldn't let it go. He tortured himself until he knew he was fixed.

It was iron he was after. He decided that after he'd done a bit of Googling when he went back to work. It made sense; it was fresh air across his face. Something about the taste, even the look, of the cow's deep red blood – it was metal, rusty. That was what he'd craved, the iron, the metal. He'd been looking pale; he'd been falling asleep in front of the telly, like an old man. Anaemia. Iron was all he needed. So he bought himself a carton of grapefruit juice – he knew the kids would never touch it – and he went into a chemist on his way home from work, for iron tablets. He regretted it when the woman behind the counter looked at him over her specs and asked him if they were for his wife.

-We share them, he said.

She wasn't moving.

-I'd need to see a letter from your GP, she said.

-For iron?

-Yes.

He bought condoms and throat lozenges, and left. By the time he got home he knew his iron theory was shite and he'd pushed the grapefruit juice into a hedge, with the condoms. The kids were right; grapefruit juice was disgusting. There

11

was nothing wrong with him, except he wanted to drink blood.

He had kids. That was the point. A boy and a girl. He had a family, a wife he loved, a job he tolerated. He worked in one of the banks, not high enough up to qualify for one of the mad bonuses they'd been handing out in the boom days, but high enough to have his family held hostage while he went to the bank with one of the bad guys and opened the safe – although that event had never occurred. The point was, he was normal. He was a forty-one-year-old heterosexual man who lived in Dublin and enjoyed the occasional pint with his friends – Guinness, loads of iron – played a game of indoor football once a week in a leaking school hall, had sex with his wife often enough to qualify as regularly, just about, and would like to have had sex with other women, many other women, but it was just a thought, never a real ambition or anything urgent or mad. He was normal.

He took a fillet steak into the gents' toilet at work, demolished it, and tried to flush the plastic bag down the toilet. But it stayed there like a parachute, on top of the water. He fished it out and put it in his pocket. He checked his shirt and tie in the mirror, even though he'd been careful not to let himself get carried away as he went at the meat in the cubicle. He was clean, spotless, his normal self. He checked his teeth for strings of flesh, put his face right up to the mirror. He was grand. He went back to his desk and ate his lunch with his colleagues, a sandwich he'd made himself that morning, avocado and tomato – no recession in his fridge. He felt good, he felt great.

He was controlling it, feeding it. He was his own doctor, in very good hands. He'd soon be ironed up and back to his even more normal self.

So he was quite surprised when he went over the wall, even as he went over. *What the fuck am I doing?* He knew exactly what he was doing. He was going after the next-door neighbours' recession hens. At three in the morning. He was going to bite the head off one of them. He'd seen the hens – he wasn't sure if you called them hens or chickens – from one of the upstairs windows. He saw them every night when he was closing his daughter's curtains, after he'd read to her. (See? He's normal.) There were three of them, scrabbling around in the garden. He hated them, the whole idea of them. The world economy wobbled and the middle classes immediately started growing their own spuds and carrots, buying their own chickens, and denying they had property portfolios in Eastern Europe. And they stopped talking to him because he'd become the enemy, and evil, because he worked in a bank. The shiftless bitch next door could pretend she was busy all day looking after the hens. Well, she'd have one less to look after, because he was over the wall. He'd landed neatly and quietly – he was fit; he played football – and he was homing in on the hens.

He knew what he was up to. He was hoping a

light would go on, upstairs – or better, down-stairs – or next door, in his own house. Frighten the shite out of him, send him scrambling back over the wall. *I was just looking to see if I could see the space shuttle. It's supposed to be coming over Ireland tonight.* He'd bluff his way out of it – *Although it won't be stopping* – while his heart thumped away at his ribs. It would sort him out for another few days, a week; it would get him over the weekend.

But no light went on.

And the chickens cluck-clucked: *We're over here.*

He grabbed one. It was easy, too easy. It was a lovely night; they were as clear there as they could have been, standing in a row, like a girl band, the Supremes. Shouldn't they have been cooped up – was that the phrase? – and let out again in the morning? The city's foxes were famous; everyone had seen one. He'd seen one himself, strolling down the street when he was walking home from the station a few months before.

He grabbed his hen, expected the protest, the pecks. But no, the hen settled into his arms like a fuckin' kitten. The little head in one hand, the hard, scrawny legs in the other, he stretched it out like a rubber band and brought it up to his mouth. And he bit – kind of. There was no burst of blood or even a clean snap. The neck was still in his mouth. He could feel a pulse on his tongue. The hen was terrified; he could feel that in the legs. But he didn't want to terrify the bird – he wasn't a cruel man.

14

He just wanted to bite its head off and hold his mouth under its headless neck. But he knew: he didn't have it in him. He wasn't a vampire or a werewolf. And he needed a filling – he could feel that. *I was biting the head off a chicken, Doctor.* He'd put the hen down now and get back over the wall.

But a light went on – and he bit. Downstairs, right in front of him – and the head came clean off. There was no blood, not really, just – well – bone, gristle, something wet. He wouldn't vomit. They'd be staring out at him, the neighbours, him or her or him *and* her – Jim and Barbara. But he was quick, he was calm. He knew they couldn't see him because the light was on in the kitchen and it was dark out here. Although, now that he thought of it – and he *was* thinking – they might have seen him before they turned on the light.

And now the chicken, the headless, dead chicken, decided to protest. A squawk came out of something that couldn't have been its beak, because the head, detached or at least semi-detached, was in one of his hands. He was holding the body by the neck and it was wriggling. *Let me down, let me down.*

He dropped the hen, heard it running away, and he charged. He ran at the wall. Not his own wall – he was *thinking*. The wall on the other side, two houses down from his own. He was up, no sweat, and he was over. He sat down for a while, to get his breath back, to work out his route home. He

15

listened. He hadn't heard the kitchen door being opened and the hen seemed to have accepted that it was dead. The other two hadn't noticed, or they were in mourning. It was very quiet.

He was safe – he thought he was safe. He was stupid, exhilarated, appalled, ashamed, fuckin' delighted, and safe. He looked up at the sky. And he saw it, the shuttle. The brightest star, moving steadily across the night. The *Endeavour* – he remembered the name.

He was back in the bed.

She woke – half woke. His cold feet, his weight on the mattress.

-What's wrong?

-Nothing, he said. –I got up to see the shuttle.

-Great.

She was asleep already.

-It was amazing, he said, addressing her back. –Amazing.

He kissed her neck.

He actually slept. It was Friday night, Saturday morning.

The bed was empty when he woke. It was a long time since that had happened, since she'd been awake before him. He felt good – he felt great. He'd flossed and brushed before he'd got back into bed, no trace of the hen between his teeth. He'd gargled quietly till his eyes watered. No bad taste, and no guilt. He shouldn't have done what he'd done, but a more important consideration quickly smothered any guilt. It was the thought

16

he'd fallen asleep with, clutching it like a teddy bear, just after he'd kissed his wife's neck.

Necks.

It was as simple as that.

The blood was a red herring, so to speak, sent to distract him – by his psyche or whatever, his conscience – to stop him from seeing the much healthier obvious. It was necks he'd been craving, not blood. He didn't want to drink blood and he was no more anaemic than a cow's leg. The simple, dirty truth was, he wanted to bite necks. It was one of those midlife things. And that was grand, it was fine, because he was in the middle of his life, give or take a few years.

Sex.

Simple.

He wanted to have sex with everything living. Not literally. He wanted to have sex with most things. Some things – most women. He was a normal man, slipping into middle age. His days were numbered. He knew this, but he didn't *think* it. A year was 365 days. Ten years was 3,650. Thirty years gave him 14,600. *You have 14,600 days to live. That's fine, thanks.* As he lay on the bed, he felt happy. The urge was gone, because he understood. His mind was fine, but something in him had been running amok. His biology, or something like that. Not long ago, only a few generations back, he'd have been dead already or at least drooling and toothless. Middle age and the autumn years were modern concepts. His brain understood them, but his biology – his manhood – didn't. He only had a few years of riding left – that was what biology thought. More to the point, a few years of reproducing. And maybe the vasectomy had made things worse, or more drastic, sent messages haywire – he didn't know.

The human mind was a funny thing. He'd been dying for a ride, so he bit the head off a neighbour's chicken.

He went downstairs.

-A fox got one of Barbara's hens last night, said Vera.

-Well, that was kind of inevitable, wasn't it?

-That's a bit heartless.

-It's what foxes do, he said. –When?

-What?

-Did the fox strike?

-Last night, she said. –Did you hear anything when you were looking at the shuttle?

-Not a thing, he said. –Just the astronauts chatting.

She smiled. *You're such a messer.*

-About what?

-Oh, just about how much they love Ireland. How's Barbara?

-In bits.

-Did she say she felt violated?

-She did, actually, but you're such a cynical bastard.

She was laughing. And he knew: he was home and dry.

It was later now, night again, and he kissed her neck. He bit her neck. They were a pair of kids for half an hour, and still giddy half an hour after that.

-Well, she said. –I'm ready for afters.

Her hand went exploring.

-Back in a minute, he said.

He went downstairs, went to the fridge – two mackerel on a plate. He looked in the freezer, pulled out a likely bag. A couple of pork chops. He put the bag under the hot tap, till the plastic loosened. Then he tore away the plastic and went at one of the chops. But it was too hard, too cold. He gave it thirty seconds in the microwave and hoped – and dreaded – that the ding would bring her down-stairs. He stood at the kitchen window and nibbled at the edges of the chop and hoped – and dreaded – that she'd come in and see his reflection – the blind was up – before she saw him, that he'd turn and reveal himself, some kind of vampire having a snack, and she'd somehow find it sexy or at least reasonable, and forgive him, and put her hands through his hair, like she did, and maybe even join him in the chop, and he'd bring her over the wall so they could get Barbara's last two hens, one each.

He binned the rest of the chop, shook the bin so it would disappear under the other rubbish.

He'd wait for the right moment. The visuals were important; there was a huge difference between being caught devouring raw steak and licking a frozen pork chop, or inviting your life partner to do the same. There was no hurry, no mad rush. No madness at all; he was normal.

He went back upstairs.

She was waiting for him. But not in the bed, or *on* the bed. She was standing far away from the bed.

-What's this? she asked.

She turned on the light.

She was holding a head on the palm of her open hand. A small head.

-A chicken's head, he said.

-Where did you get it?

-I found it.

He was a clown, an eejit; he'd hidden it under his socks.

-It's Barbara's, she said. –Isn't it?

-Barbara's head would be a bit bigger, he said.

It didn't work; she didn't smile.

-Did the fox drop it in the garden? she asked.

She was giving him an escape route, offering him a reasonable story. But it was the wrong one. He'd found a chicken's head and hidden it? He wasn't going to admit to the lie. It was sad, perverse.

-No, he said.

-Well, she said, and looked away. –What happened?

-I bit it off, he said.

She looked at him again. For quite a while.

-What was that like?

-Great, he said. –Great.

FOSSIL-FIGURES

JOYCE CAROL OATES

1.

I nside the great belly where the *beat beat beat* of the great heart pumped life blindly. Where there should have been one, there were two: the demon brother, the larger, ravenous with hunger, and the other, the smaller brother, and in the liquidy darkness a pulse between them, a beat that quivered and shuddered, now strong, now lapsing, now strong again, as the demon brother grew even larger, took the nourishment as it pulsed into the womb, the heat, the blood, the mineral strength, kicked and shuddered with life so the mother, whose face was not known, whose existence could only be surmised, winced in pain, tried to laugh but went deathly pale, trying to smile gripping a railing *Ah! My baby. Must be a boy.* For in her ignorance the mother did not yet know that inside her belly there was not one but two. Flesh of my flesh and blood of my blood and yet not one but two. And yet not two equally, for the demon brother was the larger of the two, with but a single wish to suck suck suck into his being the

21

life of the other, the smaller brother, all of the nourishment of the liquidy-dark womb, to suck into himself the smaller brother about whom he was hunched as if embracing him, belly to curving spine and the forehead of the demon brother pressed against the soft bone of the back of the head of the smaller brother. The demon brother had no speech but was purely appetite. *Why there be this other here – this thing! Why this, when there is me! There is me, me, me, there is only me.* The demon brother did not yet feed by mouth, had not yet sharp teeth to tear, chew, devour and so could not swallow up the smaller brother into his gut, and so the smaller brother survived inside the swollen belly where the *beat beat beat* of the great heart pumped life blindly and in ignorance until the very hour of the birth, when the demon brother forced his way out of the womb headfirst, a diver, a plunger, eager for oxygen, thrusting, squawling, struggling to declare himself, drew his first breath in a shudder of astonishment and began to bawl loudly, hungrily, kicking his small legs, flailing his small arms, a furious purple-flushed face, half-shut glaring eyes, strands of startlingly dark and coarse hair on the flushed infant scalp *A boy! Nine-pound boy! A beautiful – perfect – boy!* Swathed in mother's oily blood, glistening like pent-up fire, a sharp scream and frenzied kicking as the umbilical cord attached to his navel was deftly severed. And what shock then – was it possible? – there was yet another baby inside the mother, but this was not a perfect baby, a runt, cloaked in oily blood, a tiny aged man with a wizened face expelled from the mother after fourteen grunting minutes in a final spasm of waning contractions *Another! There is another boy* yet so tiny, malnourished, five pounds nine ounces, most of this weight in the head, bulbous blue-veined head, purple-flushed skin, the skull forceps dented at the left temple, eyelids stuck together with bloody pus, tiny fists weakly flailing, tiny legs weakly kicking, tiny lungs weakly drawing breath inside the tiny rib cage *Oh but the poor thing won't live – will he?* Tiny caved-in chest, something twisted about the tiny spine, and only faintly, as if at a distance, came the choked bleating cries. In contempt the demon brother laughed. From his place at the mother's breast suck suck sucking the mother's rich milk yet the demon brother laughed in contempt and anger for *Why there be this other here, why this, why 'brother,' why 'twin,' when there is me. Only be one of me.*

Yet not one: two.

At a fever pitch childhood passed for the demon brother who was first in all things. At a glacial pace childhood passed for the smaller brother who trailed behind his twin in all things. The demon brother was joyous to behold, pure infant fire, radiant thrumming energy, every molecule of his being quivering with life, appetite, *me me me.* The smaller brother was often sick, lungs filled with fluids, a tiny valve in his heart fluttered, soft bones of his curving spine, soft bones of his bowed legs, anemia, weak appetite, and the skull subtly misshapen from the forceps delivery, his cries were breathy, bleating, nearly inaudible *me? me?* For the demon brother was first in all things. In the twins' crib the first to roll onto his stomach, and the first to roll onto his back. The first to crawl. The first to rise on shaky baby legs. The first to toddle about wide eyed in triumph at being vertical. The first to speak: *Mama.* The first to drink in, to swallow up, to suck nourishment from all that he encountered, eyes widened in wonder, in greed, his first word *Mama* not an appeal or a plea but a command: *Mama!* Belatedly the smaller brother followed the demon brother, uncertain in his movements, poorly coordinated in his legs, his arms, the very tilt of his head questionable, and his head quivering on frail shoulders, the eyes rapidly blinking, watery, seemingly weak as the facial features were less defined than those of the demon brother of whom it was claimed proudly *He's all boy!* while of the smaller brother it was murmured *Poor thing! But he is growing.* Or it was murmured *Poor thing! But what a sweet sad smile.* In these early years the smaller brother was often sickly and several times had to be hospitalized (anemia, asthma, lung congestion, heart-valve flutter, sprained bones) and in these interims the demon brother did not seem to miss the smaller brother but basked in the full attention of their parents and grew yet taller and

24

stronger and soon it could scarcely be claimed that the brothers were twins – even 'fraternal' twins – for observers would react with baffled smiles *Twins? How can that be possible?* For by the age of four, the demon brother was several inches taller than the smaller brother whose spine curved, and whose chest caved in upon itself, and whose eyes blinked, teary and vaguely focused, and it came to seem that the brothers were not twins but, simply, brothers: the one older than the other by two or three years, and much healthier. *We love the boys equally. Of course.* At bedtime the demon brother sank into sleep with the abruptness of a rock sinking into dark water, come to rest in the soft dark mud below. At bedtime the smaller brother lay with opened eyes and stem-thin limbs twitching, for he feared sleep as one might fear sinking into infinity *Even as a young child I understood that infinity is a vast fathomless chasm inside the brain into which we fall and fall through our lives, fall and fall unnamed, faceless and unknown where even, in time, the love of our parents is lost. Even the love of our mothers is lost. And all memory* waking from a thin tormented sleep like frothy water spilled across his face and he's struggling to breathe, choking and coughing, for the demon brother has sucked up most of the oxygen in the room, how can the demon brother help it, his lungs are so strong, his breath so deep and his metabolism so heated, naturally the demon brother will suck up the oxygen in the brothers' room where each night at bedtime their parents tuck the boys in, in twin beds, kissing each, declaring their love for each, and in the night the smaller brother is wakened from a nightmare of suffocation, his weak lungs unable to breathe, panicked and whimpering, in a plea for help managing to crawl from his bed and out of the room and into the hall, collapsed partway between the brothers' room and their parents' room where in the early morning the parents will discover him.

Such meager life, yet such life struggles to save itself! – so the demon brother would recall, in contempt.

Of course we love Edgar and Edward equally. They are both our sons.
This declaration the demon brother knew to be a lie. Yet was angered by the thought that, when the parents uttered the lie, as they did frequently, those who heard it might believe. And the smaller brother, the sickly brother, with his caved-in chest, crooked spine, wheezy asthmatic breath, yearning teary eyes and sweet smile wished to believe. To rebuke him, the demon brother had a way of turning on him when they were alone, for no (evident) reason pushing him, shoving him, wrestling him to the floor, as the smaller brother drew breath to protest straddling him with his knees, gripping the breakable rib cage like a vise, thump-thump-thumping the little freak's head against the floor, the moist hard

palm of a hand clamped over the little freak's mouth to prevent him from crying for help *Mama mama mama* faint as a dying lamb's bleating and so unheard by the mother in another part of the house downstairs in her bliss of ignorance not hearing the thump-thump-thump of the smaller brother's head against the carpeted floor of the boys' room until at last the smaller brother goes limp, ceases to struggle, ceases to struggle for breath, his pinched little face has turned blue, and the demon brother relents, releases him panting and triumphant.

Could've killed you, freak. And I will, if you tell.

For why were there two and not one? As in the womb, the demon brother felt the injustice, and the illogic.

School! So many years. Here the demon brother, who was called Eddie, was first in all things. As the smaller brother, who was called Edward, lagged behind. Immediately in elementary school the brothers were not perceived to be twins but only just brothers, or relatives sharing a last name.

Eddie Waldman. Edward Waldman. But you never saw them together.

At school, Eddie was one of the popular boys. Adored by girls, emulated and admired by boys. He was a big boy. A husky boy. He was a natural leader, an athlete. Waved his hand, and the teachers called upon him. His grades were never less than a B. His smile was a dimpled smile, sly-sincere. He had a way of looking you frankly in the eye. By the age of ten Eddie had learned to shake hands with adults and to introduce himself *Hi! I'm Eddie* provoking smiles of admiration *What a bright precocious child!* and, to demon brother's parents *How proud you must be of your son* as if in fact there was but one son, and not two. In sixth grade, Eddie ran for president of his class and was elected by a wide margin.

I am your brother, remember me!
You are nothing of mine. Go away!
But I am in you. Where can I go?

Already in elementary school the smaller brother Edward had dropped behind his twin. The problem wasn't his schoolwork – for Edward was a bright, intelligent, inquisitive boy – his grades were often As, when he was able to complete his work – but his health. So frequently absent from his fifth-grade classes, he'd had to repeat the year. His lungs were weak, he caught respiratory infections easily. His heart was weak, in eighth grade he was hospitalized for weeks following surgery to repair the faulty heart valve. In tenth grade he suffered a 'freak accident' – observed only by his brother Eddie, in their home – falling down a flight of stairs, breaking his right leg and kneecap and his right arm and several ribs and injuring his spine and thereafter he had to hobble about stricken with shyness, wincing in pain, on crutches. His teachers were aware of him, the younger Waldman boy. His teachers regarded him with sympathy, pity. In high school, his grades became ever more erratic: sometimes As but more often Cs, Ds, Incompletes. The smaller brother seemed to have difficulty concentrating in his classes, he fidgeted with pain, or stared open eyed in a haze of painkillers, scarcely aware of his surroundings. When he was fully awake, he had a habit of hunching over his notebooks, which were unusually large, spiral notebooks with unlined pages, like sketchbooks, and in these notebooks he appeared to be constantly drawing, or writing; he frowned and bit his lower lip, lost in concentration, ignoring the teacher and the rest of the class *Slipping into infinity, a pleat in time and a twist of the pen and there's freedom!* The pen had to be a black felt-tip with a fine point. The notebooks had to have marbled black-and-white covers. The teacher had to call upon 'Edward' several times to get the boy's full attention and in his eyes then, a quick flaring up, like a match lighted, shyness supplanted by something like resentment, fury. *Leave me alone why can't you, I am not one of you.*

By the time the brothers were eighteen, Eddie was a senior bound for college, president of his class and captain of the football team and in the school yearbook 'most likely to succeed' and Edward was trailing behind by a year, with poor grades. He'd begun to arrive at school with a wheelchair, brought by his mother, now in the throes of spinal pain from a slipped disk, and in this wheelchair he was positioned at the front, right-hand corner of his classes, near the teacher's desk, a broken, freaky figure with a small pinched boy's face, waxy skin and slack lips, drowsy from painkillers, or absorbed in his spiral notebooks in which he only pretended to take notes while in fact drawing bizarre figures – geometrical, humanoid – that seemed to spring from the end of his black felt-tip pen.

In the spring of his junior year, stricken with bronchitis, Edward didn't complete his courses and never returned to school: his formal education had ended. In that year, Eddie Waldman was recruited by a dozen universities offering sports scholarships and, shrewdly, he chose the most academically prestigious of the universities, for his goal beyond the university was law school.

Resembling each other as a shadow can be said to resemble its object. Edward was the shadow.

By this time the brothers no longer shared a room. The brothers never longer shared – even! – the old, cruel childish custom of the demon brother's wish to harm his smaller twin; the demon brother's wish to suck all the oxygen out of the air, to swallow up his smaller twin entirely. *Why be this other here – this thing! Why this, when there is me!*

Here was the strange thing: the smaller brother was the one to miss the bond between them. For he had no other so deeply imprinted in his soul as his brother, no bond so fierce and intimate. *I am in you, I am your brother, you must love me.*

But Eddie laughed, backing away. Shook hands with his sickly brother for whom he felt only a

30

mild repugnance, the mildest pang of guilt, and he said good-bye to his parents, allowed himself to be embraced and kissed and went away, smiling in anticipation of his life he went away with no plan to return to his hometown and to his boyhood house except for expediency's sake as a temporary visitor who would be, within hours of his return, restless, bored, eager to escape again to his 'real' life elsewhere.

2.

Now in their twenties the brothers rarely saw each other. Never spoke on the phone.

Eddie Waldman graduated from law school. Edward Waldman continued to live at home.

Eddie excelled, recruited by a prominent New York City law firm. Edward suffered a succession of 'health crises.'

The father divorced the mother, abruptly and mysteriously it seemed for the father, too, had a 'real' life elsewhere.

Eddie entered politics, under the tutelage of a prominent conservative politician. Edward, suffering spinal pain, spent most days in a wheelchair. Inside his head calculating numbers, imagining equations in which the numerical, the symbolic, and the organic were combined, inventing music, rapidly filling large sheets of construction paper with bizarre yet meticulously detailed geometrical and humanoid figures in settings resembling those of the surrealist

31

painter de Chirico and the visionary artist M. C. Escher. *Our lives are Möbius strips, misery and wonder simultaneously. Our destinies are infinite, and infinitely recurring.*

In the affluent suburb of the great American city, on a residential street of large, expensive houses, the Waldman house, a clapboard colonial on a two-acre lot, began by degrees to fall into disrepair, decline. The front lawn was unmowed and spiky, moss grew on the rotting shingle boards of the roof and newspapers and flyers accumulated on the front walk. The mother, once a sociable woman, began to be embittered, suspicious of neighbors. The mother began to complain of ill health. Mysterious 'hexes.' The mother understood that the father had divorced her as a way of divorcing himself from the misshapen broke-backed son with the teary yearning eyes who would never grow up, would never marry, would spend the rest of his life in the fevered execution of eccentric and worthless 'art.'

Frequently the mother called the other son, the son of whom she was so proud, whom she adored. But Eddie seemed always to be traveling, and rarely returned his mother's messages.

In time, within a decade, the mother would die. In the now derelict house (visited, infrequently, by a few concerned relatives) Edward would live as a recluse in two or three downstairs rooms, one of which he'd converted into a makeshift studio. The embittered mother had left him enough money to enable him to continue to live alone and to devote himself to his work; he hired help to come to the house from time to time to clean it, or to attempt to clean it; to shop for him, and to prepare meals. *Freedom! Misery and wonder!* On large canvases Edward transcribed his bizarre dream-images, among galaxies of hieroglyphic shapes in a sequence titled *Fossil-Figures*. For it was Edward's belief, which had come to him in a paroxysm of spinal pain, that misery and wonder are interchangeable and that one must not predominate. In this way time passed in a fever heat for the afflicted brother, who was not afflicted but blessed. Time was a Möbius strip that looped back upon itself, weeks, months and years passed and yet the artist grew no older in his art. (In his physical being, perhaps. But Edward had turned all mirrors to the wall and had not the slightest curiosity about what Edward now 'looked like.')

The father, too, died. Or disappeared, which is the same thing.

Relatives ceased to visit, and may have died.

Into infinity, which is oblivion. But it is out of that infinity we have spring: why?

It began to be, as if overnight, the era of the Internet. No man need be a recluse now. However alone and cast off by the world.

Via the Internet E.W. communicated with companions – soul mates – scattered in cyberspace, of whom, at any given time, there were invariably a few – but E.W.'s needs were so minimal, his ambition for his art so modest, he required only a few – fascinated by the *Fossil-Figures* he displayed on the Web, who negotiated to buy them. (Sometimes, bidding against one another, for unexpectedly high sums.) And there were galleries interested in exhibiting the works of E.W. – as the artist called himself – and small presses interested in publishing them. In this way, in the waning years of the twentieth century, E.W. became something of an underground cult figure, rumored to be impoverished, or very wealthy; a crippled recluse living alone in a deteriorating old house, in a deteriorating body, or, perversely, a renowned public figure who guarded his privacy as an artist.

Alone yet never lonely. For is a twin lonely?

Not so long as his twin-self continues to exist.

The brothers were never in contact now, yet, on TV, by chance as sometimes Edward flicked through channels like one propelling himself through the chill of intergalactic space, he came upon images of his lost brother: giving impassioned speeches ('sanctity of life' – 'prolife' – 'family values' – 'patriotic Americans') to adoring crowds, being interviewed, smiling into the camera with the fiery confidence of one ordained by God. There was the demon brother elected to the U.S. Congress from a district in a neighboring state the smaller brother hadn't known he was living in; there, the demon brother beside an attractive young woman, gripping the young woman's hand, a wife, a Mrs Edgar Waldman, the smaller brother hadn't known he had married. The demon brother had been taken up by rich, influential elders. In a political party, such elders look to youth to further their political heritage, their 'tradition.' In this political party the 'tradition' was identical with economic interests. This was the triumphant politics of the era. This was the era of the self. *Me, me, me! There is me, me, me there is only me.* Cameras panned rapturous audiences, fervently applauding audiences. For in *me*, there is the blind wish to perceive *we*. As in the most primitive, wrathful, and soulless of gods, humankind will perceive *we*. In the most distant galaxies, infinities of mere emptiness, the ancient yearning *we*.

So Edward, the left-behind brother, hunched in his wheelchair, regarded the demon brother glimpsed on TV with no bitterness nor even a sense of estrangement as one might feel for a being of another species but with the old, perverse yearning *I am your brother, I am in you. Where else can there be, that I am?*

Here was the inescapable fact: the brothers shared a single birthday. Even beyond their deaths, that fact would never change.

January 26. The dead of winter. Each year on that day the brothers thought of each other with such vividness, each might have imagined that the other was close beside him, or behind him, a breath on his cheek, a phantom embrace. *He is alive, I can feel him* Edward thought with a shiver of anticipation. *He is alive, I can feel him* Edgar thought with a shiver of revulsion.

3.

There came a January 26 that marked the brothers' fortieth birthday. And a few days later there came to an exhibit of E.W.'s new exhibit *Fossil-Figures* in a storefront gallery in the warehouse district near the Hudson River at West and Canal streets, New York City, U.S. Congressman Edgar Waldman, who'd given a political speech that afternoon in midtown, alone now, a limousine with U.S. federal plates waiting at the curb. Noting with satisfaction that the exhibit rooms were nearly deserted. Noting with disgust how the old, cracked linoleum stuck against the bottom of his expensive shoes. The handsome congressman wore very dark glasses, he looked at no one, in dread of being recognized in this sordid place. Especially he was in dread of seeing the crippled brother – 'E.W' – whom he had not seen in nearly twenty years but believed that he would recognize immediately though by this time the twins – 'fraternal twins' – looked nothing alike. Edgar anticipated the stunted broken figure in a wheelchair, yearning teary eyes and wistful smile that maddened, made you want to strike with your fists, that offer of forgiveness where forgiveness was not wanted. *I am your brother, I am in you. Love me!* But there was no one.

Only E.W.'s work, pretentiously called by the gallery 'collage paintings.' These *Fossil-Figures* lacked all beauty, even the canvases upon which they were painted looked soiled and battered and the walls upon which they were (unevenly) hung were streaked as if the hammered-tin ceiling leaked rust. What were these artworks covered in dream/nightmare shapes, geometrical, yet humanoid, shifting into and out of one another like translucent guts, deeply offensive to the congressman who sensed 'subterfuge' – 'perversion' – 'subversion' in such obscure art, and what was obscure was certain to be 'soulless' – even 'traitorous.' Most upsetting, the *Fossil-Figures* seemed to be taunting the viewer, anyway this viewer, like riddles, and he had no time for God-damned riddles, the rich man's daughter he'd married to advance his career was awaiting him at the St Regis, this visit to West and Canal streets was an (unmarked) stop in Congressman Waldman's itinerary for the day. Wiping his eyes to better see an artwork depicting the night sky, distant galaxies, and constellations, almost there was beauty here, suns like bursting egg yolks swallowing up smaller suns, comets shaped like – was it male sperm? – blazing male sperm? – colliding with luminous bluish-watery planets; and, protruding from the rough surface of the canvas, a thing so unexpected, so ugly, the congressman stepped back in astonishment: was it a nestlike growth of some kind? a tumor? composed of plasticine flesh and dark crinkly hairs and – could it be baby teeth? arranged in a smile? – and a scattering of baby bones?

A fossil, it was. A thing removed from the human body. Something very ugly discovered a cavity of a surviving twin's body. The fossil-soul of the other, which had never breathed life.

Stunned, quivering with disgust, the congressman turned away.

Walked on, in a haze of denunciations, denials. Seeing that some of the canvases were beautiful – were they? – or were they all ugly, obscene, if you knew how to decode them? – he was made to think that he was endangered, something was going to happen to him, there was a blunt statistical fact that in the last election he'd been reelected to his seat in Congress by a smaller majority than in any of the preceding elections, in such victory there is the presentiment of defeat. Through the maze of rooms circling back to the start of the exhibit and at a glass-topped counter there was a bored-looking girl with dead-white skin and a face glittering with piercings who seemed to be working for the gallery and he asked of her in a voice that quavered with indignation if these ridiculous 'fossil-figures' were considered 'art' and she told him politely yes of course, everything the gallery exhibited was art and he asked if the exhibit was supported by public funds and seemed but partly mollified to learn that it was not. He asked who the 'so-called artist' E.W. was and the girl spoke vaguely saying nobody knew

38

E.W. personally, only the proprietor of the gallery had ever seen him, he lived by himself outside the city and never came into the city, not even to oversee the exhibit, didn't seem to care if his artworks sold, or what prices they were sold for.

'He's got some "wasting-away" disease, like muscular dystrophy, or Parkinson's, but last we knew, E.W. is alive. He's alive.'

And I won't go away. You will come to me instead.

Each year: January 26. One year, one insomniac night, Edward is flicking restlessly through TV channels and is surprised to see a sudden close-up of – is it Edgar? The demon brother Edgar? TV news footage from earlier in the day, rerun now in the early hours of the morning, suddenly this magnification of a man's head, thick-jawed face, an aging face obscured by dark glasses, skin gleaming with oily sweat, an arm lifted to shield the disgraced congressman from a pack of pursuing reporters, photographers and TV camera crews, there's Congressman Edgar Waldman being briskly walked into a building by plainclothes police officers. *Indicted on multiple charges of bribe-taking, violations of federal campaign laws, perjury before a federal grand jury.* Already the rich man's daughter has filed for divorce, there's a quick smile, a suggestion of bared teeth. In the brothers' childhood house in which Edward lives in a few downstairs rooms Edward stares at the TV screen from which his lost brother has faded, uncertain if the thumping sensation in his head is a profound shock, a pang of hurt that must beat within the brother, or his own excitement, eagerness. *He will come to me now. He will not deny me, now.*

Epilogue

It was so. The demon brother would return home, to his twin who awaited him.

For he knew himself now *Not one but two*. In the larger world he'd gambled his life and lost his life and would retreat now, to the other. In retreat a man sets aside pride, disgraced, divorced, bankrupt and a glisten of madness in the washed-out blue eyes. His heavy jaws were silvery-dark with stubble, a tremor in his right hand that had been lifted in a federal court to swear that Edgar Waldman would tell the truth the whole truth and nothing but the truth *Yes I swear* and in that heartbeat it was all over for him, a taste like bile rising at the back of his mouth.

Still the wonder. Disbelief. The corroded ruin of a face like clay that has been worn down by rivulets of water, wind. And that glisten of madness in the eyes: *Me?*

In retreat now returning to his childhood home he had shunned for years. The left-behind, broke-backed younger brother who'd been living alone since their mother's death, now many years ago. As a young man he'd never considered time as anything other than a current to bear him aloft, propel him into his future, now he understood that time is a rising tide, implacable inexorable unstoppable rising tide, now at the ankles, now the knees, rising to the thighs, to the groin and the torso and to the chin, ever rising, a dark water of utter mystery propelling us forward not into the future but into infinity, which is oblivion.

Returning to the suburban town of his birth and to the house he's shunned for decades, seeing now with a pang of loss how the residential neighborhood had changed, many of the large houses converted to apartment buildings and commercial sites, and most of the plane trees lining the street severely trimmed or removed altogether. And there was the old Waldman home that had once been their mother's pride, once so splendidly white, now a weatherworn gray with sagging shutters and a rotting roof and a lush junglelike front lawn awash in litter as if no one had lived there for a long time. Edgar had been unable to contact Edward by phone, there was no directory listing for a phone under the name Edward Waldman, now his heart pounded in his chest, he felt a wave of dread *He has died, it is too late.* Hesitantly knocking at the front door and listening for a response from within and knocking again, more loudly, hurting his knuckles, and at last there came from within a faint bleating sound, a voice asking who it was and he called out *It's me.*

Slowly as if with effort the door opened. And there, in his wheelchair, as Edgar had imagined him,

41

but not so ravaged as Edgar has imagined him, was his brother Edward whom he hadn't seen in more than two decades: a shrunken individual of no obvious age with a narrow, pale, pinched yet unlined face, a boy's face, and his hair threaded with gray like Edgar's, and one bony shoulder higher than the other. Pale blue eyes filling with moisture he swiped at with the edges of both hands and in a scratchy voice that sounded as if it hadn't been used in some time he said *Eddie. Come in.*

. . . When it happened could never be determined precisely since the bodies were frozen and preserved from decay found together on a leather sofa made up as a bed pulled up to within a foot of a fireplace heaped with ashes in a downstairs room of the old clapboard colonial crowded with furniture and what appeared to be the accumulated debris of decades but which may have been materials for artworks or the very artworks themselves of the eccentric artist known as E. W., the elderly Waldman brothers in layers of bulky clothing must have fallen asleep in front of a fire in the otherwise unheated house, the fire must have burnt out in the night and the brothers died in their sleep in a protracted January cold spell: the brother to be identified as Edgar Waldman, eighty-seven, embracing his brother Edward Waldman, also eighty-seven, from behind, protectively fitting his body to his brother's crippled body, forehead tenderly pressed to the back of the other's head, the two figures coiled together like a gnarled organic material that has petrified to stone.

WILDFIRE IN MANHATTAN

JOANNE HARRIS

I t's not my name – well, not *quite* – but you can call me Lucky. I live right here in Manhattan, in the penthouse suite of a hotel just off Central Park. I'm a model citizen in every way, punctual, polite and orderly. I wear sharp suits. I wax my chest hair. You'd never think I was a god.

It's a truth often overlooked that old gods – like old dogs – have to die sometime. It just takes longer, that's all; and in the meantime citadels may fall, empires collapse, worlds end and folk like us end up on the pile, redundant and largely forgotten.

In many ways, I've been fortunate. My element is fire, which never quite goes out of style. There are Aspects of me that still wield power – there's too much of the primitive left in you Folk for it to be otherwise, and although I don't get as many sacrifices as I used to, I can still get obeisance if I want it (who doesn't?) – after dark, when the campfires are lit. And the dry lightning strikes across the plains – yes, they're mine – and the forest fires; and the funeral pyres and the random sparks and the human torches – all mine.

But here, in New York, I'm Lukas Wilde, lead singer in the rock band Wildfire. Well, I say *band*. Our only album, *Burn It Up*, went platinum when the drummer was tragically killed on stage by a freakish blast of lightning.

Well, maybe not so freakish. Our only U.S. tour was stalked by lightning from beginning to end; of fifty venues, thirty-one suffered a direct hit; in just nine weeks we lost three more drummers, six roadies and a truckload of gear. Even I was beginning to feel I'd taken it just a *little* too far.

Still, it was a great show.

Nowadays, I'm semi-retired. I can afford to be; as one of only two surviving band members I have a nice little income, and when I'm feeling bored I play piano in a fetish bar called the Red Room. I'm not into rubber myself (too sweaty), but you can't deny it makes a terrific insulator.

By now you may have gathered – I'm a night person. Daylight rather cramps my style; and besides, fire needs a night sky to show to best advantage. An evening in the Red Room, playing piano and eyeing the girls, then downtown for rest and recreation. *Not* a scene that my brother frequents; and so it was with some surprise that I ran smack into him that night, as I was checking out the nicely flammable back streets of the Upper East Side, humming 'Light My Fire' and contemplating a spot of arson.

I didn't say? Yes, in this present Aspect, I have a brother. Brendan. A twin. We're not close;

44

Wildfire and Hearth Fire have little in common, and he rather disapproves of my flamboyant lifestyle, preferring the more domestic joys of baking and grilling. Imagine that. A firegod running a restaurant – it makes me burn with shame. Still, it's his funeral. Each of us goes to hell in his own way, and besides, his flame-grilled steaks are the best in the business.

It was past midnight, I was a little light-headed from the booze – but not so drunk that you'd have noticed – and the streets were as still as they get in a city that only ever shuts one eye. A huddle of washouts sleeping in cardboard boxes under a fire escape; a cat raiding a Dumpster. It was November; steam plumed from the sewer grates and the sidewalks were shiny with cold sweat.

I was just crossing the intersection of Eighty-First and Fifth, in front of the Hungarian meat market when I saw him, a familiar figure with hair the colour of embers tucked into the collar of a long grey coat. Tall, slim and ballet quick; you might almost have been forgiven for thinking it was me. Close scrutiny, however, reveals the truth. *My* eyes are red and green; his, on the other hand, are green and red. Anyway, I wouldn't be seen dead wearing those shoes.

I greeted him cheerily. 'Do I smell burning?'

He turned to me with a hunted expression. 'Shh! Listen!'

I was curious. I know there's never been much love between us, but he usually greets me, at least,

45

before he starts with the recriminations. He called me by my true name. Put a finger to his lips, then dragged me into a side alley that stank of piss.

'Hey, Bren. What gives?' I whispered, correcting my lapels.

His only reply was a curt nod in the direction of the near-deserted alley. In the shadows, two men, boxy in their long overcoats, hats pulled down over narrow, identical faces. They stopped for a second on the kerb, checked left, checked right and crossed over with swift, effortless choreography before vanishing, wolfish, into the night.

'I see.' And I did. I'd seen them before. I could feel it in my blood. In another place, in another Aspect, I knew them, and they knew me. And believe me, they were men in form alone. Beneath those cartoon-detective overcoats they were all teeth. 'What d'you think they're doing here?'

He shrugged. 'Hunting.'

'Hunting who?'

He shrugged again. He's never been a man of words, even when he wasn't a man. Me, I'm on the wordy side. I find it helps.

'So you've seen them here before?'

'I was following them when you came along. I doubled back – I didn't want to lead them home.'

Well, I could understand that. 'What are they?' I said. 'Aspects of what? I haven't seen anything like this since Ragnarók, but as I recall—'

'Shh—'

I was getting kinda sick of being shoved and

shushed. He's the elder twin, you know, and some-times he takes liberties. I was about to give him a heated reply when I heard a sound coming from nearby, and something swam into rapid view. It took me a while to figure it out; derelicts are hard to see in this city, and he'd been hiding in a card-board box under a fire escape, but now he shifted quick enough, his old overcoat flapping like wings around his bony ankles.

I knew him, in passing. Old man Moony, here as an Aspect of Mani, the Moon, but mad as a coot, poor old sod (it often happens when they've been at the juice, and the mead of poetry is a heady brew). Still, he could run, and was running now, but as Bren and I stepped out of his way, the two guys in their long overcoats came to inter-cept him at the mouth of the alley.

Closer this time – I could smell them. A rank and feral smell, half rotted. Well, you know what they say. You can't teach a carnivore oral hygiene.

At my side I could feel my brother trembling. Or was it me? I wasn't sure. I was scared, I knew that – though there was still enough alcohol carousing in my veins to make me feel slightly removed from it all. In any case I stayed put, tucked into the shadows, not quite daring to move. The two guys stood there at the mouth of the alley, and Moony stopped, wavering now between fight and flight. And –

Fight it was. Okay, I thought. Even a rat will turn when cornered. That didn't mean I had to get involved. I could smell him too, the underpinning stench of him, like booze and dirt and that stinky sickly poet smell. He was scared, I knew that. But he was also a god – albeit a beat-up Aspect of one – and that meant he'd *fight* like a god, and even an old alky god like Moony has his tricks.

Those two guys might yet have a shock coming.

For a moment they held their position, two over-coats and a mad poet in a dark triangle under the single streetlight. Then they moved – the guys with that slick, fluid motion I'd seen before, Moony with a lurch and a yell and a flash from his finger-tips. He'd cast Týr – a powerful rune – and I saw it flicker through the dark air like a shard of steel, hurtling towards the two not-quite-men. They dodged – no pas de deux could have had more grace – parting, then coming together again as the missile passed, moving in a tight axe-head forma-tion towards the old god.

But throwing Týr had thrown Moony. It takes strength to cast the runes of the Elder Script, and most of his glam was already gone. He opened his mouth – to speak a cantrip, I thought – but before he could, the overcoats moved in with that spooky superhuman speed and I could smell their rankness once more, but so much stronger, like the inside of a badger's sett. They closed in, unbut-toning their coats as they ran – but *were* they running? Instead they seemed to *glide*, like boats, unfurling their long coats like sails to hide and envelop the beleaguered moongod.

He began to chant – the mead of poetry, you know – and for a second the drunken voice cracked and changed, becoming that of Mani in his full Aspect. A sudden radiance shone forth – the predators gave a single growl, baring their teeth – and for a moment I heard the chariot chant of the mad moongod, in a language you could never learn, but of which a single word could drive a mortal crazy with rapture, bring down the stars, strike a man dead – or raise him back to life again.

He chanted, and for a beat the hunters paused – and was that a single trace of a tear gleaming in the shadow of a black fedora? – and Mani sang a glamour of love and death, and of the beauty that is desolation and of the brief firefly that lights up the darkness – for a wing's beat, for a breath – before it gutters, burns and dies.

But the chant did not halt them for more than a second. Tears or not, these guys were *hungry*. They glided forward, hands outstretched, and now I could see *inside* their unbuttoned coats, and for a moment I was sure there was no body beneath their clothes, no fur or scale, no flesh or bone. There was just *the shadow*; the blackness of Chaos; a blackness beyond colour or even its absence; a hole in the world, all-devouring, all-hungry.

Brendan took a single step, and I caught him by the arm and held him back. It was too late anyway; old Moony was already done for. He went down – not with a crash, but with an eerie sigh, as if he'd been punctured – and the creatures that

49

now no longer even *looked* like men were on him like hyenas, fangs gleaming, static hissing in the folds of their garments.

There was nothing human in the way they moved. Nothing superfluous. They Hoovered him up from blood to brain – every glamour, every spark, every piece of kith and kindling – and what they left looked less like a man than a cardboard cutout of a man left lying in the dirt of the alleyway.

Then they were gone, buttoning up their overcoats over the terrible absence beneath.

A silence. Brendan was crying. He always was the sensitive one. I wiped something (sweat, I think) from my face and waited for my breathing to return to normal.

'That was nasty,' I said at last. 'Haven't seen anything quite like that since the End of the World.'

'Did you hear him?' said Brendan.

'I heard. Who would have thought the old man had so much glam in him?'

My brother said nothing, but hid his eyes.

I suddenly realized I was hungry, and thought for a moment of suggesting a pizza, but decided against it. Bren was so touchy nowadays, he might have taken offence.

'Well, I'll see you later, I guess,' and sloped off rather unsteadily, wondering why brothers are always so damned hard, and wishing I'd been able to ask him home.

I wasn't to know, but I wish I had – I'd never see that Aspect of him again.

I slept till late the next day. Awoke with a headache and a familiar post-cocktail nauseous feeling, then remembered – the way you remember doing something to your back when you were in the gym, but didn't realize how bad it was going to be until you'd slept on it – and sat bolt upright.

The guys, I thought. *Those two guys.*

I must have been drunker than I'd thought last night, because this morning the memory of them froze me to the core. Delayed shock; I know it well, and to combat its effects I called room service and ordered the works. Over coffee, bacon, pancakes and rivers of maple syrup, I worked on my recovery, and though I did pretty well, given the circumstances, I found I couldn't quite get the death of old Moony out of my mind, or the slick way the two overcoats had crawled over him, gobbling up his glam before buttoning up and back to business. Poetry in motion.

I pondered my lucky escape – well, I guessed that if they hadn't sniffed out Moony first, then it would have been Yours Truly and Brother Bren for a double serving of Dish of the Day – but my heart was far from light as it occurred to me that if these guys were really after our kind, this was at best a reprieve, not a pardon, and that sooner or later those overcoats would be sharpening their teeth at my door.

So I finished breakfast and called Bren. But all I got was his answering machine, so I looked up the number of his restaurant and dialled it. The line was dead.

I would have tried his mobile, but, like I said, we're not close. I didn't know it, or the name of his girl, or even the number of his house. Too late now, right? Just goes to show. Carpe diem, and all that. And so I showered and dressed and went off in haste under gathering clouds to the Flying Pizza, Bren's place of work (but what a dumb name!), in the hope of getting some sense out of my twin.

It was there that I realized something was amiss. Ten blocks away I knew it already, and the sirens and the engines and the shouting and the smoke were just confirmation. There was something ominous about those gathering thunderclouds, and the way they sat like a Russian hat all spiky with needles of lightning above the scene of devastation. My heart sank lower the closer I got. Something was amiss, all right.

Looking around to ensure that I was unobserved, I cast the visionary rune Bjarkán with my left hand, and squinted through its spyglass shape. Smoke I saw; and lightning from the ground; my brother's face looking pale and strained; then fire; darkness; then, as I'd feared, the Shadow – and its minions, the wolves, the shadow hunters, boxed into their heavy overcoats.

Those guys, I thought, and cursed. *Again.*

And now I knew where I'd known them before – and they were pretty bad in that Aspect, too, though I had more on my plate at that time than I do nowadays, and I'll admit I didn't give them my full attention. I did now, though, casting runes of concealment about me as I skirted the funnel of black smoke, the funeral pyre of my brother's restaurant – and for all I knew, of Brendan himself, who had looked pretty wasted in my vision.

I got there at last, keeping an eye out for over-coats, to find fire engines and cop cars everywhere. A line had been cordoned off at the end of the road, and there were men trying to spray water over the great fizzing spume of fire that had already dug its roots deep into the Flying Pizza.

I could have told them they were wasting their time. You can't put out the work of a firegod – even a god of hearth fire – like it was just a squib. The flames sheeted up, thirty, forty, fifty feet high, clean and yellow and shot through with glamours that would probably have looked like dancing sparks to your kind, but which, if they'd touched you, would have stripped you, flesh to bone, in one.

And Brendan? I thought. *Could he still be alive somewhere?*

Well, if he was, he must have run. There was no way anyone could have survived that blaze. And it wasn't like Bren to flee the scene. He had turned and fought; I'd seen as much in my vision, and my brother was so dead set against the use of glamours among the Folk that he wouldn't have used them if he'd had any kind of choice.

I used Ós – the rune of mystery – to scry my brother's fate. I saw their faces, thin and wolfish; saw his smile, teeth bared, so that for a second in my vision he could have been me, wild and furious and filled with killing rage. He could be okay, my brother, you know; it just took more time to fire him up. I saw him draw his mindsword – flaming, it was, with an edge that shivered translucent light. A sword that could have cut through granite or silk with the same easy slice; a sword I hadn't seen since the last time the world ended, a flickering flame of a firegod's sword that just *touched* the shadow inside an unbuttoned overcoat and went out like a puff of smoke.

Then, in the dark, they were on him. Question answered. Well, at least my brother went out in style.

I wiped my face and pondered the points. Point one: I was now an only twin. Point two: unless he'd taken his assailants with him (which I doubted), by now the two coats would be on my tail. Point three –

I was just embarking on point three when a heavy hand fell onto my shoulder, another grasped my arm just above the elbow and then both applied a painful pressure, which soon became excruciating as the joint locked and a low, familiar voice rasped in my ear.

'Lucky. I should have known you were in this

somehow. This shambles has got your mark all over it.'

I yelped and tried to free my arm. But the other bastard was holding me too tight.

'Move, and I'll break it,' snarled the voice. 'Hell, perhaps I ought to break it anyway. Just for old times' sake.'

I indicated to him that I'd rather he didn't. He locked my arm a little further – I felt it begin to go and screamed – then he shoved me hard towards the alley wall. I hit it, bounced, spun round with mindsword ready, half drawn, and found myself staring into a pair of eyes as grim and colourless as a rainy day. Just my luck – a friend with a grievance, which is the only kind I tend to have nowadays.

Well, I say *friend*. He's one of our kind, but you know how it is. Fire and rainstorm – we don't get along. Besides, in his present Aspect he stood taller, weighed heavier, hit harder than me. His face was a thundercloud, and any thought I had of fighting the guy evaporated like cheap perfume. I sheathed the sword and took the better part of valour.

'Hey,' I said. 'It's Our Thor.'

He sniffed. 'Try anything, and I'll douse you cold,' he said. 'I've got an army of stormclouds ready to roll. You'll be out like a light before you can blink. Want to try it?'

'Did I ever? Nice greeting, friend. It's been a long time.'

55

He grunted. 'Arthur's the name in this present Aspect. Arthur Pluviôse – and *you're* dead.' He made it sound like some weird kind of naming ceremony.

'Wrong,' I said. *'Brendan's* dead. And if you think I'd be a party to the murder of my own brother—'

'Wouldn't put it past you,' Arthur said, though I could tell the news had shaken him. 'Brendan's *dead?*' he repeated.

''Fraid so.' I was touched – I'd always thought he hated us both.

'Then this wasn't you?'

'My, you're fast.'

He glowered. 'Then how?'

'How else?' I shrugged. 'The Shadow, of course. Chaos. Black Surt. Choose your own damn metaphor.'

Arthur gave a long, soft sigh. As if it had preyed on his mind for such a long time that any news – even bad news – even *terrible* news – could come as a relief. 'So it's true,' he said. 'I was beginning to think—'

'Finally—'

He ignored the gibe and turned on me once more, his rainy-day eyes gleaming. 'It's the wolves, Lucky. The wolves are on the trail again.'

I nodded. Wolves, demons, no word exists in any tongue of the Folk to describe exactly what they were. I call them *ephemera,* though I had to admit there was nothing ephemeral about their present Aspect.

'Skól and Haiti, the Sky-Hunters, servants of the Shadow, Devourers of the Sun and Moon. And of anything else that happens to be in their way, for that matter. Brendan must have tried to tackle them. He never did have any sense.'

But I could tell he was no longer listening. 'The Sun and—'

'Moon.' I gave him the abridged version on the events of last night. He listened, but I could tell he was distracted.

'So, after the Moon, the Sun. Right?'

'I guess.' I shrugged. 'That is, assuming there's an Aspect of Sol in Manhattan, which, if there is—'

'There is,' said Arthur grimly. 'Her name's Sunny.' And there was something about his eyes as he said it, something even more ominous than the rain-swelled clouds above us, or his hand on my shoulder, horribly pally and heavy as lead, that made me think I was in for an even lousier day than I'd had so far.

'Sunny,' I said. 'Then she'll be next.'

'Over my dead body,' said Arthur. 'And yours,' he added, almost as an afterthought, keeping his hand hard on my shoulder and smiling that dangerous, stormy smile.

'Sure. Why not?' I humoured him. I could afford to – I'm used to running, and I knew that at a pinch, Lukas Wilde could disappear within an hour, leaving no trace.

He knew it too. His eyes narrowed, and above us the clouds began to move softly, gathering momentum like wool on a spindle. A dimple appeared at its nadir – soon, I knew, to become a funnel of air, stitched and barbed with deadly glamours.

'Remember what they say,' said Arthur, addressing me by my true name. 'Everywhere you go, you always take the weather with you.'

'You wrong me.' I smiled, though I'd never felt less like it. 'I'll be only too happy to help your friend.'

'Good,' said Arthur. He kept that hand on my shoulder, though, and his smile was all teeth. 'We'll keep to the shadows. No need to involve the Folk any more than we have to. Right?'

It was a dark and stormy afternoon. I had an idea that it was going to be the first of many.

Sunny lived in Brooklyn Heights, in a loft apartment on a quiet street. Not a place I visit often, which accounts for my not having spotted her sooner. Most of our kind take the discreet approach; gods have enemies too, you know, and we find it pays to keep our glam to ourselves.

But Sunny was different. For a start, according to Arthur (what a dumb name!), she didn't know what she was any more. It happens sometimes; you just forget. You get all wrapped up in your present Aspect; you start to think you're like everyone else. Perhaps that's what kept her safe for so long; they say gods look after drunks and half-wits and little children, and Sunny certainly qualified. Transpires that my old pal Arthur had been looking after her for nearly a year without her knowing it, making sure that she got the sunshine she needed to be happy, keeping sniffers and prowlers away from her door.

Because even the Folk start getting suspicious when someone like Sunny lives nearby. It wasn't just the fact that it hadn't rained in months; that sometimes all of New York City could be under a cloud but for the two or three streets surrounding her block; or the funny northern lights that sometimes shone in the sky above her apartment. It was *her*, just *her*, with her face and her smile, turning heads wherever she went. A man – a *god* – could fall in love.

Arthur had dropped his raingod Aspect, and was now looking more or less like a regular citizen, but I could tell he was making a hell of an effort. As soon as we crossed the Brooklyn Bridge I could see him beginning to hold it in, the way a fat man holds in his gut when a pretty girl comes into the room. Then I saw her colours – from afar, like lights in the sky, and the look on his face – that look of truculent yearning – intensified a little.

He gave me the critical once-over. 'Tone it down a bit, will you?' he said.

Well, *that* was offensive. I'd looked a lot flashier as Lukas Wilde, but looking at Arthur right then I thought it a bad time to say so. I turned down the volume on my red coat, but kept my hair as it was, hiding my mismatched eyes behind a pair of snappy shades.

'Better?'

'You'll do.'

We were standing outside the place now. A standard apartment at the back of a lot of others; black fire escape, small windows, little roof garden throwing down wisps of greenery into the guttering. But at the window there was a light, something rather like sunlight, I guess, occasionally strobing here and there – following her movements as she wandered about her flat.

Some people have no idea of how to go unnoticed. In fact, it was astonishing that the wolves hadn't seized on her before. She'd not even tried to hide her colours, which was frankly beyond unwise, I thought – hell, she hadn't even pulled the drapes.

Arthur gave me one of his looks. 'We're going to protect her, Lucky,' he said. 'And *you're* going to be nice. Okay?'

I made a face. 'I'm always nice. How could you possibly doubt me?'

She invited us in straightaway. No checking of credentials; no suspicious glance from behind the open drapes. I'd had her down as pretty, but dumb; now I saw she was a genuine innocent, a little-girl-lost in the big city. Not my type, naturally, but I could see what Arthur saw in her.

She offered us a cup of ginseng tea. 'Any friend of Arthur's,' she said, and I saw his painful grimace as he tried to fit his big fingers around the little china cup, all the while trying to hold himself in so that Sunny could have her sunshine . . .

Finally, it was too much for him. He let it out with a gasp of release, and the rain started to come down in snakes, hissing into the gutters.

Sunny looked dismayed. 'Damn *rain!*'

Arthur looked like someone had punched him hard, right in the place where thunder gods keep their ego. He gave that feeble smile again. 'It doesn't make you feel safe?' he said. 'You don't think there's a kind of poetry in the sound, like little hammers beating down onto the rooftops?'

Sunny shook her head. 'Yuck.'

I lit the fire with a discreet cantrip and a fingering of the rune Kaen. Little flames shot out of the grate and danced winsomely across the hearth. It was a good trick, though I say it myself – especially as it was an electric fire.

'Neat,' said Sunny, smiling again.

Arthur gave a low growl.

'So – have you seen anything strange around here lately?' Stupid damn question, I told myself. Move a sun goddess onto the third floor of a Manhattan brownstone, and you're apt to see more than the occasional pyrotechnics. 'No guys in suits?' I went on. 'Dark overcoats and fedora hats, like someone from a bad fifties comic strip?'

'Oh, *those* guys.' She poured more tea. 'Yeah, I saw them yesterday. They were sniffing around in the alleyway.' Sunny's blue eyes darkened a little. 'They didn't look friendly. What do they want?'

I was going to tell her about Bren, and what had happened to Old Man Moony, but Arthur stopped me with a glance. Sunny has that effect, you know; makes guys want to do stupid things. Stupid, noble, self-sacrificing things – and I was beginning to understand that I was going to be a part of it, whether or not I wanted to be.

'Nothing *you* need to worry about,' Arthur said with a big smile, clamping a hand on my upper arm and marching me onto the balcony. 'They're just some guys we're looking for. We'll camp out here tonight and keep an eye out for them for you. Any trouble, we'll be here. No need for you to worry. Okay?'

'Okay,' said Sunny.

'Okay,' I said between gritted teeth (my arm felt like it had been pounded several times with a hammer). I waited until we were alone, and Sunny had drawn the curtains, then I turned on him. 'What's the deal?' I said. 'We can't hold back the Shadow-wolves. You must know that by now, right? You saw what they did to Moony and Bren. Our only chance is to outrun them, to take your lady friend with you and to run like the blazes to another city, to another continent if we can, where the Shadow has less influence—'

Arthur looked stubborn. 'I won't run.'

'Fine. Well, it's been a blast – *Ow! My arm!*'

'And neither will you,' said Our Thor.

'Well, if you put it *that* way—'

I may be a trifle impetuous, but I know when

62

to surrender to force majeure. Arthur had his mind set on both of us being heroes. My only remaining choice was whether to set *my* mind to helping him, thereby possibly saving both our hides, or to make a run for it as soon as the bastard's guard was down –

Well, I might have gone down either path, but just then I caught sight of our boys in the alleyway, sniffing and snarling like wolves in suits, and I was down to no choice at all. I drew my mindsword, he drew his. Glamours and runes distressed the night air. Not that *they* would help us, I thought; they hadn't helped my brother Bren, or the mad old moongod. And Shadow – or Chaos, if you prefer – had plenty of glamours of its own with which to strike down three renegade gods, fugitives left over from the End of the World –

'Hey! Up here!' yelled Our Thor.

Two pairs of eyes turned up towards us. A hiss like static as the ephemera tuned into our whereabouts. A glint of teeth as they grinned – and then they were crawling up the fire escape, all pretence of humanity gone, slick beneath those boxy black coats, nothing much in there but tooth and claw, like poetry with an appetite.

Oh, great, I thought. Way to keep a low profile, Our Thor. Was it an act of self-sacrifice, a ploy to attract their attention, or could he possibly have a plan? If he did, then it would be a first. Mindless self-sacrifice was about his level. I wouldn't have minded *that* much, but it was clear that in his boundless generosity he also meant to sacrifice *me*.

'Lucky!' It was raining again. Great ropes and coils of thunderous rain that thrashed down onto our bowed heads, all gleaming in the neon lights in shades of black and orange – from the static-ridden sky, great flakes of snow lumbered down. Well, that's what happens around a raingod under stress; but that didn't stop me getting soaked, and wishing I'd brought my umbrella. It didn't stop the ephemera though. Even the bolts of lightning that crashed like stray missiles into the alleyway (I have skills too, and I was using them like the blazes by then) had no effect on the wolves of Chaos, whose immensely slick and somehow snakelike forms were now poised on the fire escape beneath us, ten feet away and ready to pounce.

One did – a mindbolt flew. I recognized the rune Hagall. One of my colleague's most powerful, and yet it passed right through the ephemera with a squeal of awesome feedback, then the creature was on us again, unbuttoning its overcoat, and now I was sure there were *stars* in there, stars and the mindless static of space –

'Look,' I said. 'What do you want? Girls, money, power, fame – I can get all those things for you, no problem. I've got influence in this world. Two handsome, single guys like yourselves – hey, you could make a killing in showbiz.'

Perhaps not the wisest choice of words.

The first wolf leered. '*Killing*,' it said. By then

I could smell it again, and I knew that words couldn't save me. First, the thing was ravenous. Second, *nothing* with that level of halitosis could possibly hope to make it in the music business. Some guys, I knew, had come pretty close. My daughter Hel, for instance, has, in spite of her – shall we say *alternative* – looks, a serious fan base in certain circles. But not these guys. I mean, *Ew.*

I flung a handful of mindrunes then: Tý; Kaen; Hagall; Ýr – but none of them even slowed it down. The other wolf was onto us now, and Arthur was wrestling with it, caught in the flaps of its black coat. The balcony was pulling away from the wall; sparks and shards of runelight hissed into the torrential rain.

Damn it, I thought. *I'm going to die wet.* And I flung up a shield using the rune Sól, and with the last, desperate surge of my glam I cast *all* the fire-runes of the First Aettir at the two creatures that once had been wolves but were now grim incarnations of revenge, because nothing escapes from Chaos, not Thunder, not Wildfire, not even the Sun—

'Are you guys okay out there?' It was Sunny, peering through a gap in the curtains. 'Do you want some more ginseng tea?'

'Ah – no thanks,' said Arthur, now with a demon wolf in each hand and that stupid grin on his face again. 'Look, ah, Sunny, go inside. I'm kinda busy right now—'

The thing that Our Thor had been holding at

bay finally escaped his grasp. It didn't go far, though; it sprang at me and knocked me backwards against the rail. The balcony gave way with a screech, and we all fell together, three floors down. I hit the deck – damned hard – with the ephemera on top of me, and all the fight knocked out of me and I knew that I was finished.

Sunny peered down from her window. 'Do you need help?' she called to me.

I could see right *into* the creature now, and it was grim – like those fairy tales where the sisters get their toes chopped off and the bad guys get pecked to death by crows and even the little mermaid has to walk on razor blades for the rest of her life for daring to fall in love . . . Except that I knew Sunny had got the Disney version instead, with all the happy endings in it, and the chipmunks and rabbits and the goddamned squirrels (I hate squirrels!) singing in harmony, where even the wolves are good guys and no one ever *really* gets hurt –

I gave her a sarcastic smile. 'Yeah, wouldya?' I said.

'Okay,' said Sunny, and pulled the drapes and stepped out onto the balcony.

And then something very weird happened.

I was watching her from the alleyway, my arms pinned to my sides now and the ephemera straddling me with its overcoat spread like a vulture about to spear an eyeball. The cold was so intense that I couldn't feel my hands at all, and the stench of the thing made my head swim, and the rain was pounding into my face and my glam was bleeding out so fast that I knew I had seconds, no more –

So the first thing she did was put her umbrella up.

Ignored Arthur's desperate commands – besides, he was still wrestling with the second ephemera. His colours were flaring garishly; runelight whirled around them both, warring with the driving rain.

And then she smiled.

It was as if the sun had come out. Except that it was night, and the light was, like, sixty times more powerful than the brightest light you've ever known, and the alley lit up a luminous white, and I screwed my eyes shut to prevent them from being burnt there and then out of their sockets, and all these things happened at once.

First of all, the rain stopped. The pressure on my chest disappeared, and I could move my arms again. The light, which had been too intense even to see when it first shone out, diffused itself to a greenish-pink glow. Birds on the rooftops began to sing. A scent of something floral filled the air – strangest of all in that alleyway, where the smell of piss was predominant – and someone put a hand on my face and said:

'It's okay, sweetie. They've gone now.'

Well, that was it. I opened my eyes. I figured that either I'd taken more concussion than I'd thought, or there was something Our Thor hadn't told me. He was standing over me, looking self-conscious and bashful. Sunny was kneeling at my side, heedless of the alleyway dirt, and her blue dress was shining like the summer sky, and her bare feet were like little white birds, and her sugar blond hair fell over my face and I was glad she really wasn't my type, because that lady was nothing but trouble. And she gave me a smile like a summer's day, and Arthur's face went dangerously red, and Sunny said:

'Lucky? Are you okay?'

I rubbed my eyes. 'I think so. What happened to Skól and Haiti?'

'Those guys?' she said. 'Oh, they had to go. I sent them back into Shadow.'

Now Arthur was looking incredulous. 'How do you know about Shadow?' he said.

'Oh, Arthur, you're so *sweet*.' Sunny pirouetted to her feet and planted a kiss on Our Thor's nose. 'As if I could have lived here this long and not have known I was different—' She looked at the illuminated sky. 'Northern lights,' she said happily. 'We ought to have them more often here. But I really do appreciate it,' she went on. 'You guys looking out for me, and everything. If things had been different, if we hadn't been made from such different elements, then maybe you and I could have – you know—'

Arthur's face went, if possible, even redder.

'So, what are you going to do now?' she said. 'I guess we're safe – for a while, at least. But Chaos knows about us now. And the Shadow never really gives up . . .'

I thought about it for a while. And then an idea came to me. I said: 'Have you ever thought of a career in entertainment? I could find a job for you with the band . . .' I wondered if she could sing. Most celestial spheres can, of course, and anyway, she'd light up the place just by stepping onto the stage – we'd save a fortune on pyrotechnics . . .

She gave that megawatt smile of hers. 'Is Arthur in the band, too?'

I looked at him. 'He could be, I guess. There's always room for a drummer.'

Come to think of it, there's a lot to be said for going on the road right now. New people, new line-up, new places to go –

'That would be nice.' Her face was wistful. His was like that of a sick puppy, and it made me even more relieved that I'd never been the romantic type. I tried to imagine the outcome: sun goddess and thunder god on stage together, every night –

I could see it now, I thought. Wildfire, on tour again. I mean, we're talking rains of fish, equatorial northern lights; hurricanes, eclipses, solar flares, flash floods – and lightning. Lots of lightning. Might be a little risky, of course.

But all the same – a hell of a show.

THE TRUTH IS A CAVE IN THE BLACK MOUNTAINS

NEIL GAIMAN

You ask me if I can forgive myself? I can forgive myself for many things. For where I left him. For what I did. But I will not forgive myself for the year that I hated my daughter, when I believed her to have run away, perhaps to the city. During that year I forbade her name to be mentioned, and if her name entered my prayers when I prayed, it was to ask that she would one day learn the meaning of what she had done, of the dishonour that she had brought to my family, of the red that ringed her mother's eyes.

I hate myself for that, and nothing will ease that, not even what happened that night, on the side of the mountain.

I had searched for nearly ten years, although the trail was cold. I would say that I found him by accident, but I do not believe in accidents. If you walk the path, eventually you must arrive at the cave.

But that was later. First, there was the valley on the mainland, the whitewashed house in the gentle meadow with the burn splashing through it, a house that sat like a square of white sky against the green of the grass and the heather just beginning to purple.

And there was a boy outside the house, picking wool from off a thorn-bush. He did not see me approaching, and he did not look up until I said, 'I used to do that. Gather the wool from the thorn-bushes and twigs. My mother would wash it, then she would make me things with it. A ball, and a doll.'

He turned. He looked shocked, as if I had appeared out of nowhere. And I had not. I had walked many a mile, and had many more miles to go. I said, 'I walk quietly. Is this the house of Calum MacInnes?'

The boy nodded, drew himself up to his full height, which was perhaps two fingers bigger than mine, and he said, 'I am Calum MacInnes.'

'Is there another of that name? For the Calum MacInnes that I seek is a grown man.'

The boy said nothing, just unknotted a thick clump of sheep's wool from the clutching fingers of the thorn-bush. I said, 'Your father, perhaps? Would he be Calum MacInnes as well?'

The boy was peering at me. 'What are you?' he asked.

'I am a small man,' I told him. 'But I am a man, nonetheless, and I am here to see Calum MacInnes.'

'Why?' The boy hesitated. Then, 'And why are you so small?'

71

I said, 'Because I have something to ask your father. Man's business.' And I saw a smile start at the tips of his lips. 'It's not a bad thing to be small, young Calum. There was a night when the Campbells came knocking on my door, a whole troop of them, twelve men with knives and sticks, and they demanded of my wife, Morag, that she produce me, as they were there to kill me, in revenge for some imagined slight. And she said, "Young Johnnie, run down to the far meadow, and tell your father to come back to the house, that I sent for him." And the Campbells watched as the boy ran out the door. They knew that I was a most dangerous person. But nobody had told them that I was a wee man, or if that had been told them, it had not been believed.'

'Did the boy call you?' said the lad.

'It was no boy,' I told him, 'but me myself, it was. And they'd had me, and still I walked out the door and through their fingers.'

The boy laughed. Then he said, 'Why were the Campbells after you?'

'It was a disagreement about the ownership of cattle. They thought the cows were theirs. I maintained the Campbells' ownership of them had ended the first night the cows had come with me over the hills.'

'Wait here,' said young Calum MacInnes.

I sat by the burn and looked up at the house. It was a good-sized house: I would have taken it for the house of a doctor or a man of law, not of a border reaver. There were pebbles on the ground and I made a pile of them, and I tossed the pebbles, one by one, into the burn. I have a good eye, and I enjoyed rattling the pebbles over the meadow and into the water. I had thrown a hundred stones when the boy returned, accompanied by a tall, loping man. His hair was streaked with grey, his face was long and wolfish. There are no wolves in those hills, not any longer, and the bears have gone too.

'Good day to you,' I said.

He said nothing in return, only stared; I am used to stares. I said, 'I am seeking Calum MacInnes. If you are he, say so, I will greet you. If you are not he, tell me now, and I will be on my way.'

'What business would you have with Calum MacInnes?'

'I wish to hire him, as a guide.'

'And where is it you would wish to be taken?'

I stared at him. 'That is hard to say,' I told him. 'For there are some who say it does not exist. There is a certain cave on the Misty Isle.'

He said nothing. Then he said, 'Calum, go back to the house.'

'But da—'

'Tell your mother I said she was to give you some tablet. You like that. Go on.'

Expressions crossed the boy's face – puzzlement, hunger, happiness – and then he turned and ran back to the white house.

Calum MacInnes said, 'Who sent you here?'

I pointed to the burn as it splashed its way between us on its journey down the hill. 'What's that?' I asked.

'Water,' he replied.

'And they say there is a king across it,' I told him.

I did not know him then at all, and never knew him well, but his eyes became guarded, and his head cocked to one side. 'How do I know you are who you say you are?'

'I have claimed nothing,' I said. 'Just that there are those who have heard that there is a cave on the Misty Isle, and that you might know the way.'

He said, 'I will not tell you where the cave is.'

'I am not here asking for directions. I seek a guide. And two travel more safely than one.'

He looked me up and down, and I waited for the joke about my size, but he did not make it, and for that I was grateful. He just said, 'When we reach the cave, I will not go inside. You must bring out the gold yourself.'

I said, 'It is all one to me.'

He said, 'You can take only what you carry. I will not touch it. But yes, I will take you.'

I said, 'You will be paid well for your trouble.' I reached into my jerkin, handed him the pouch I had in there. 'This for taking me. Another, twice the size, when we return.'

He poured the coins from the pouch into his huge hand, and he nodded. 'Silver,' he said. 'Good.' Then, 'I will say good-bye to my wife and son.'

'Is there nothing you need to bring?'

He said, 'I was a reaver in my youth, and reavers travel light. I'll bring a rope, for the mountains.' He patted his dirk, which hung from his belt, and went back into the whitewashed house. I never saw his wife, not then, nor at any other time. I do not know what colour her hair was.

I threw another fifty stones into the burn as I waited, until he returned, with a coil of rope thrown over one shoulder, and then we walked together away from a house too grand for any reaver, and we headed west.

The mountains between the rest of the world and the coast are gradual hills, visible from a distance as gentle, purple, hazy things, like clouds. They seem inviting. They are slow mountains, the kind you can walk up easily, like walking up a hill, but they are hills that take a full day and more to climb. We walked up the hill, and by the end of the first day we were cold.

I saw snow on the peaks above us, although it was high summer.

We said nothing to each other that first day. There was nothing to be said. We knew where we were going.

We made a fire, from dried sheep dung and a dead thorn-bush: we boiled water and made our porridge, each of us throwing a handful of oats and a fingerpinch of salt into the little pan I carried. His handful was huge, and my handful was small, like my hands, which made him smile and say, 'I hope you will not be eating half of the porridge.'

I said I would not and indeed, I did not, for my appetite is smaller than that of a full-grown man. But this is a good thing, I believe, for I can keep going in the wild on nuts and berries that would not keep a bigger person from starving.

A path of sorts ran across the high hills, and we followed it and encountered almost nobody: a tinker and his donkey, piled high with old pots, and a girl leading the donkey, who smiled at me when she thought me to be a child, and then scowled when she perceived me to be what I am, and would have thrown a stone at me had the tinker not slapped her hand with the switch he had been using to encourage the donkey; and, later, we overtook an old woman and a man she said was her grandson, on their way back across the hills. We ate with her, and she told us that she had attended the birth of her first great-grandchild, that it was a good birth. She said she would tell our fortunes from the lines in our palms, if we had coins to cross her palm. I gave the old biddy a clipped lowland groat, and she looked at my palm.

She said, 'I see death in your past and death in your future.'

'Death waits in all our futures,' I said.

She paused, there in the highest of the high lands, where the summer winds have winter on their breath, where they howl and whip and slash the air like knives. She said, 'There was a woman in a tree. There will be a man in a tree.'

I said, 'Will this mean anything to me?'

'One day. Perhaps.' She said, 'Beware of gold. Silver is your friend.' And then she was done with me.

To Calum MacInnes she said, 'Your palm has been burned.' He said that was true. She said, 'Give me your other hand, your left hand.' He did so. She gazed at it, intently. Then, 'You return to where you began. You will be higher than most other men. And there is no grave waiting for you, where you are going.'

He said, 'You tell me that I will not die?'

'It is a left-handed fortune. I know what I have told you, and no more.'

She knew more. I saw it in her face.

That was the only thing of any importance that occurred to us on the second day.

We slept in the open that night. The night was clear and cold, and the sky was hung with stars that seemed so bright and close I felt as if I could have reached out my arm and gathered them, like berries.

We lay side by side beneath the stars, and Calum MacInnes said, 'Death awaits you, she said. But death does not wait for me. I think mine was the better fortune.'

'Perhaps.'

'Ah,' he said. 'It is all nonsense. Old-woman talk. It is not truth.'

I woke in the dawn mist to see a stag, watching us curiously.

The third day we crested those mountains, and we began to walk downhill.

My companion said, 'When I was a boy, my father's dirk fell into the cooking fire. I pulled it out, but the metal hilt was as hot as the flames. I did not expect this, but I would not let the dirk go. I carried it away from the fire, and plunged the sword into the water. It made steam. I remember that. My palm was burned, and my hand curled, as if it was meant to carry a sword until the end of time.'

I said, 'You, with your hand. Me, only a little man. It's fine heroes we are, who seek our fortunes on the Misty Isle.'

He barked a laugh, short and without humour. 'Fine heroes,' was all he said.

The rain began to fall then, and did not stop falling. That night we passed a small croft house. There was a trickle of smoke from its chimney, and we called out for the owner, but there was no response.

I pushed open the door and called again. The place was dark, but I could smell tallow, as if a candle had been burning and had recently been snuffed.

'No one at home,' said Calum, but I shook my head and walked forward, then leaned my head down into the darkness beneath the bed.

'Would you care to come out?' I asked. 'For we

are travellers, seeking warmth and shelter and hospitality. We would share with you our oats and our salt and our whisky. And we will not harm you.'

At first the woman, hidden beneath the bed, said nothing, and then she said, 'My husband is away in the hills. He told me to hide myself away if the strangers come, for fear of what they might do to me.'

I said, 'I am but a little man, good lady, no bigger than a child, you could send me flying with a blow. My companion is a full-sized man, but I do swear that we shall do nothing to you, save partake of your hospitality, and dry ourselves. Please do come out.'

All covered with dust and spiderwebs she was when she emerged, but even with her face all begrimed, she was beautiful, and even with her hair all webbed and greyed with dust it was still long and thick, and golden red. For a heartbeat she put me in the mind of my daughter, but that my daughter would look a man in the eye, while this one glanced only at the ground fearfully, like something expecting to be beaten.

I gave her some of our oats, and Calum produced strips of dried meat from his pocket, and she went out to the field and returned with a pair of scrawny turnips, and she prepared food for the three of us.

I ate my fill. She had no appetite. I believe that Calum was still hungry when his meal was done.

He poured whisky for the three of us: she took but a little, and that with water. The rain rattled on the roof of the house, and dripped in the corner, and, unwelcoming though it was, I was glad that I was inside.

It was then that a man came through the door. He said nothing, only stared at us, untrusting, angry. He pulled off his cape of oiled sacking, and his hat, and he dropped them on the earth floor. They dripped and puddled. The silence was oppressive.

Calum MacInnes said, 'Your wife gave us hospitality, when we found her. Hard enough she was in the finding.'

'We asked for hospitality,' I said. 'As we ask it of you.'

The man said nothing, only grunted.

In the high lands, people spend words as if they were golden coins. But the custom is strong there: strangers who ask for hospitality must be granted it, though you have a blood feud against them and their clan or kind.

The woman – little more than a girl she was, while her husband's beard was grey and white, so I wondered if she was his daughter for a moment, but no: there was but one bed, scarcely big enough for two – the woman went outside, into the sheep pen that adjoined the house, and returned with oatcakes and a dried ham she must have hidden there, which she sliced thin, and placed on a wooden trencher before the man.

Calum poured the man whisky, and said, 'We seek the Misty Isle. Do you know if it is there?'

The man looked at us. The winds are bitter in the high lands, and they would whip the words from a man's lips. He pursed his mouth, then he said, 'Aye. I saw it from the peak this morning. It's there. I cannot say if it will be there tomorrow.'

We slept on the hard-earth floor of that cottage. The fire went out, and there was no warmth from the hearth. The man and his woman slept in their bed, behind the curtain. He had his way with her, beneath the sheepskin that covered that bed, and before he did that, he beat her for feeding us and for letting us in. I heard them, and could not stop hearing them, and sleep was hard in the finding that night.

I have slept in the homes of the poor, and I have slept in palaces, and I have slept beneath the stars, and would have told you before that night that all places were one to me. But I woke before first light, convinced we had to be gone from that place, but not knowing why, and I woke Calum by putting a finger to his lips, and silently we left that croft on the mountainside without saying our farewells, and I have never been more pleased to be gone from anywhere.

We were a mile from the place when I said, 'The island. You asked if it would be there. Surely, an island is there, or it is not there.'

Calum hesitated. He seemed to be weighing his words, and then he said, 'The Misty Isle is not as other places. And the mist that surrounds it is not like other mists.'

We walked down a path worn by hundreds of years of sheep and deer and few enough men.

He said, 'They also call it the Winged Isle. Some say it is because the island, if seen from above, would look like butterfly wings. And I do not know the truth of it.' Then, '"And what is truth?" said jesting Pilate.'

It is harder coming down than it is going up.

I thought about it. 'Sometimes I think that truth is a place. In my mind, it is like a city: there can be a hundred roads, a thousand paths, that will all take you, eventually, to the same place. It does not matter where you come from. If you walk toward the truth, you will reach it, whatever path you take.'

Calum MacInnes looked down at me and said nothing. Then, 'You are wrong. The truth is a cave in the black mountains. There is one way there, and one only, and that way is treacherous and hard, and if you choose the wrong path you will die alone, on the mountainside.'

We crested the ridge, and we looked down to the coast. I could see villages below, beside the water. And I could see high black mountains before me, on the other side of the sea, coming out of the mist.

Calum said, 'There's your cave. In those mountains.'

The bones of the earth I thought, seeing them.

And then I became uncomfortable, thinking of bones, and to distract myself, I said, 'And how many times is it you have been there?'

'Only once.' He hesitated. 'I searched for it all my sixteenth year, for I had heard the legends, and I believed if I sought I should find. I was seventeen when I reached it, and came back with all the gold coins I could carry.'

'And were you not frightened of the curse?'

'When I was young, I was afraid of nothing.'

'What did you do with your gold?'

'A portion I buried and I alone know where. The rest I used as brideprice for the woman I loved, and I built a fine house with it.'

He stopped as if he had already said too much.

There was no ferryman at the jetty. Only a small boat, hardly big enough for three full-sized men, tied to a tree trunk on the shore, twisted and half dead, and a bell beside it.

I sounded the bell, and soon enough a fat man came down the shore.

He said to Calum, 'It will cost you a shilling for the ferry, and your boy, three pennies.'

I stood tall. I am not as big as other men are, but I have as much pride as any of them. 'I am also a man,' I said. 'I'll pay your shilling.'

The ferryman looked me up and down, then he scratched his beard. 'I beg your pardon. My eyes are not what they once were. I shall take you to the island.'

I handed him a shilling. He weighed it in his

hand, 'That's ninepence you did not cheat me out of. Nine pennies are a lot of money in this dark age.' The water was the colour of slate, although the sky was blue, and whitecaps chased one another across the water's surface. He untied the boat and hauled it, rattling, down the shingle to the water. We waded out into the cold water, and clambered inside.

The splash of oars on seawater, and the boat propelled forward in easy movements. I sat closest to the ferryman. I said, 'Ninepence. It is good wages. But I have heard of a cave in the mountains on the Misty Isle, filled with gold coins, the treasure of the ancients.'

He shook his head dismissively.

Calum was staring at me, lips pressed together so hard they were white. I ignored him and asked the man again, 'A cave filled with golden coins, a gift from the Norsemen or the Southerners or from those who they say were here long before any of us: those who fled into the West as the people came.'

'Heard of it,' said the ferryman. 'Heard also of the curse of it. I reckon that the one can take care of the other.' He spat into the sea. Then he said, 'You're an honest man, dwarf. I see it in your face. Do not seek this cave. No good can come of it.'

'I am sure you are right,' I told him, without guile.

'I am certain I am,' he said. 'For not every day is it that I take a reaver and a little dwarfy man to the Misty Isle.' Then he said, 'In this part of the world, it is not considered lucky to talk about those who went to the West.' We rode the rest of the boat journey in silence, though the sea became choppier, and the waves splashed into the side of the boat, such that I held on with both hands for fear of being swept away.

And after what seemed like half a lifetime the boat was tied to a long jetty of black stones. We walked the jetty as the waves crashed around us, the salt spray kissing our faces. There was a humpbacked man at the landing selling oatcakes and plums dried until they were almost stones. I gave him a penny and filled my jerkin pockets with them.

We walked on into the Misty Isle.

I am old now, or at least, I am no longer young, and everything I see reminds me of something else I've seen, such that I see nothing for the first time. A bonny girl, her hair fiery red, reminds me only of another hundred such lasses, and their mothers, and what they were as they grew, and what they looked like when they died. It is the curse of age, that all things are reflections of other things.

I say that, but my time on the Misty Isle, that is also called, by the wise, the Winged Isle, reminds me of nothing but itself.

It is a day from that jetty until you reach the black mountains.

Calum MacInnes looked at me, half his size or

less, and he set off at a loping stride, as if challenging me to keep up. His legs propelled him across the ground, which was wet, and all ferns and heather.

Above us, low clouds were scudding, grey and white and black, hiding each other and revealing and hiding again.

I let him get ahead of me, let him press on into the rain, until he was swallowed by the wet, grey haze. Then, and only then, I ran.

This is one of the secret things of me, the things I have not revealed to any person, save to Morag, my wife, and Johnnie and James, my sons, and Flora, my daughter (may the Shadows rest her poor soul): I can run, and I can run well, and, if I need to I can run faster and longer and more sure-footedly than any full-sized man; and it was like this that I ran then, through the mist and the rain, taking to the high ground and the black-rock ridges, yet keeping below the skyline.

He was ahead of me, but I spied him soon, and I ran on and I ran past him, on the high ground with the brow of the hill between us. Below us was a stream. I can run for days without stopping. That is the first of my three secrets, and one secret I have revealed to no man.

We had discussed already where we would camp that first night on the Misty Isle, and Calum had told me that we would spend the night beneath the rock that is called Man and Dog, for it is said that it looks like an old man with his dog by his side, and I reached it late in the afternoon. There was a shelter beneath the rock, which was protected and dry, and some of those who had been before us had left firewood behind, sticks and twigs and branches. I made a fire and dried myself in front of it and took the chill from my bones. The woodsmoke blew out across the heather.

It was dark when Calum loped into the shelter and looked at me as if he had not expected to see me that side of midnight. I said, 'What took you so long, Calum MacInnes?'

He said nothing, only stared at me. I said, 'There is trout, boiled in mountain water, and a fire to warm your bones.'

He nodded. We ate the trout, drank whisky to warm ourselves. There was a mound of heather and of ferns, dried and brown, piled high in the rear of the shelter, and we slept upon that, wrapped tight in our damp cloaks.

I woke in the night. There was cold steel against my throat – the flat of the blade, not the edge. I said, 'And why would you ever kill me in the night, Calum MacInnes? For our way is long, and our journey is not yet over.'

He said, 'I do not trust you, dwarf.'

'It is not me you must trust,' I told him, 'but those that I serve. And if you left with me but return without me, there are those who will know the name of Calum MacInnes, and cause it to be spoken in the shadows.'

The cold blade remained at my throat. He said, 'How did you get ahead of me?'

'And here was I, repaying ill with good, for I made you food and a fire. I am a hard man to lose, Calum MacInnes, and it ill becomes a guide to do as you did today. Now, take your dirk from my throat and let me sleep.'

He said nothing, but after a few moments, the blade was removed. I forced myself neither to sigh nor to breathe, hoping he could not hear my heart pounding in my chest; and I slept no more that night.

For breakfast, I made porridge, and threw in some dried plums to soften them.

The mountains were black and grey against the white of the sky. We saw eagles, huge and ragged of wing, circling above us. Calum set a sober pace and I walked beside him, taking two steps for every one of his.

'How long?' I asked him.

'A day. Perhaps two. It depends upon the weather. If the clouds come down then two days, or even three . . .'

The clouds came down at noon and the world was blanketed by a mist that was worse than rain: droplets of water hung in the air, soaked our clothes and our skin; the rocks we walked upon became treacherous and Calum and I slowed in our ascent, stepped carefully. We were walking up the mountain, not climbing, up goat paths and craggy sharp ways. The rocks were black and slippery: we walked, and climbed and clambered and clung, we slipped and slid and stumbled and staggered, and even in the mist, Calum knew where he was going, and I followed him.

He paused at a waterfall that splashed across our path, thick as the trunk of an oak. He took the thin rope from his shoulders, wrapped it about a rock.

'This was not here before,' he told me. 'I'll go first.' He tied one end of the rope about his waist and edged out along the path, into the falling water, pressing his body against the wet rock face, edging slowly, intently through the sheet of water.

I was scared for him, scared for both of us: holding my breath as he passed, only breathing when he was on the other side of the waterfall. He tested the rope, pulled on it, motioned me to follow him, when a rock gave way beneath his foot, and he slipped on the wet rock, and fell into the abyss.

The rope held, and the rock beside me held. Calum MacInnes dangled from the end of the rope. He looked up at me, and I sighed, anchored myself by a slab of crag, and I wound and pulled him up and up. I hauled him back onto the path, dripping and cursing.

He said, 'You're stronger than you look,' and I cursed myself for a fool. He must have seen it on my face for, after he shook himself (like a dog, sending droplets flying), he said, 'My boy Calum told me the tale you told him about the Campbells

89

coming for you, and you being sent into the fields by your wife, with them thinking she was your ma, and you a boy.'

'It was just a tale,' I said. 'Something to pass the time.'

'Indeed?' he said. 'For I heard tell of a raiding party of Campbells sent out a few years ago, seeking revenge on someone who had taken their cattle. They went, and they never came back. If a small fellow like you can kill a dozen Campbells . . . well, you must be strong, and you must be fast.'

I must be *stupid*, I thought ruefully, telling that child that tale.

I had picked them off one by one, like rabbits, as they came out to piss or to see what had happened to their friends: I had killed seven of them before my wife killed her first. We buried them in the glen, built a small cairn of stacking stones above them, to weigh them down so their ghosts would not walk, and we were sad: that Campbells had come so far to kill me, that we had been forced to kill them in return.

I take no joy in killing: no man should, and no woman. Sometimes death is necessary, but it is always an evil thing. That is something I am in no doubt of, even after the events I speak of here.

I took the rope from Calum MacInnes, and I clambered up and up, over the rocks, to where the waterfall came out of the side of the hill, and it was narrow enough for me to cross. It was slippery there, but I made it over without incident, tied the rope in place, came down it, threw the end of it to my companion, walked him across.

He did not thank me, neither for rescuing him, nor for getting us across; and I did not expect thanks. I also did not expect what he actually said, though, which was: 'You are not a whole man, and you are ugly. Your wife: is she also small and ugly, like yourself?'

I decided to take no offence, whether offence had been intended or no. I simply said, 'She is not. She is a tall woman, almost as tall as you, and when she was young – when we were both younger – she was reckoned by some to be the most beautiful girl in the lowlands. The bards wrote songs praising her green eyes and her long red-golden hair.'

I thought I saw him flinch at this, but it is possible that I imagined it, or more likely, wished to imagine I had seen it.

'How did you win her, then?'

I spoke the truth: 'I wanted her, and I get what I want. I did not give up. She said I was wise and I was kind, and I would always provide for her. And I have.'

The clouds began to lower, once more, and the world blurred at the edges, became softer.

'She said I would be a good father. And I have done my best to raise my children. Who are also, if you are wondering, normal-sized.'

'I beat sense into young Calum,' said older Calum. 'He is not a bad child.'

'You can only do that as long as they are there with you,' I said. And then I stopped talking, and I remembered that long year, and also I remembered Flora when she was small, sitting on the floor with jam on her face, looking up at me as if I were the wisest man in the world.

'Ran away, eh? I ran away when I was a lad. I was twelve. I went as far as the court of the King over the Water. The father of the current king.'

'That's not something you hear spoken aloud.'

'I am not afraid,' he said. 'Not here. Who's to hear us? Eagles? I saw him. He was a fat man, who spoke the language of the foreigners well, and our own tongue only with difficulty. But he was still our king.' He paused. 'And if he is to come to us again, he will need gold, for vessels and weapons and to feed the troops that he raises.'

I said, 'So I believe. That is why we go in search of the cave.'

He said, 'This is bad gold. It does not come free. It has its cost.'

'Everything has its cost.'

I was remembering every landmark – climb at the sheep skull, cross the first three streams, then walk along the fourth until the five heaped stones and find where the rock looks like a seagull and walk on between two sharply jutting walls of black rock, and let the slope bring you with it . . .

I could remember it, I knew. Well enough to find my way down again. But the mists confused me, and I could not be certain.

We reached a small loch, high in the mountains, and drank fresh water, caught huge white creatures that were not shrimps or lobsters or crayfish, and ate them raw like sausages, for we could not find any dry wood to make our fire, that high.

We slept on a wide ledge beside the icy water and woke into clouds before sunrise, when the world was grey and blue.

'You were sobbing in your sleep,' said Calum.

'I had a dream,' I told him.

'I do not have bad dreams,' Calum said.

'It was a good dream,' I said. It was true. I had dreamed that Flora still lived. She was grumbling about the village boys, and telling me of her time in the hills with the cattle, and of things of no consequence, smiling her great smile and tossing her hair the while, red-golden like her mother's, although her mother's hair is now streaked with white.

'Good dreams should not make a man cry out like that,' said Calum. A pause, then, 'I have no dreams, not good, not bad.'

'No?'

'Not since I was a young man.'

We rose. A thought struck me: 'Did you stop dreaming after you came to the cave?'

He said nothing. We walked along the mountainside, into the mist, as the sun came up.

The mist seemed to thicken and fill with light, in the sunshine, but did not fade away and I realized that it must be a cloud. The world glowed. And then it seemed to me that I was staring at a man of my size, a small, humpty man, his shadow, standing in the air in front of me, like a ghost or an angel, and it moved as I moved. It was haloed by the light, and shimmered, and I could not have told you how near it was or how far away. I have seen miracles and I have seen evil things, but never have I seen anything like that.

'Is it magic?' I asked, although I smelled no magic on the air.

Calum said, 'It is nothing. A property of the light. A shadow. A reflection. No more. I see a man beside me, as well. He moves as I move.' I glanced back, but I saw nobody beside him.

And then the little glowing man in the air faded, and the cloud, and it was day, and we were alone.

We climbed all that morning, ascending. Calum's ankle had twisted the day before, when he had slipped at the waterfall. Now it swelled in front of me, swelled and went red, but his pace did not ever slow, and if he was in discomfort or in pain, it did not show upon his face.

I said, 'How long?' as the dusk began to blur the edges of the world.

'An hour, less, perhaps. We will reach the cave, and then we will sleep for the night. In the morning you will go inside. You can bring out as much gold as you can carry, and we will make our way back off the island.'

I looked at him, then: grey-streaked hair, grey eyes, so huge and wolfish a man, and I said, 'You would sleep outside the cave?'

'I would. There are no monsters in the cave. Nothing that will come out and take you in the night. Nothing that will eat us. But you should not go in until daylight.'

And then we rounded a rockfall, all black rocks and grey half-blocking our path, and we saw the cave mouth. I said, 'Is that all?'

'You expected marble pillars? Or a giant's cave from a gossip's fireside tales?'

'Perhaps. It looks like nothing. A hole in the rock face. A shadow. And there are no guards?'

'No guards. Only the place, and what it is.'

'A cave filled with treasure. And you are the only one who can find it?'

Calum laughed then, like a fox's bark. 'The islanders know how to find it. But they are too wise to come here, to take its gold. They say that the cave makes you evil: that each time you visit it, each time you enter to take gold, it eats the good in your soul, so they do not enter.'

'And is that true? Does it make you evil?'

'. . . No. The cave feeds on something else. Not good and evil. Not really. You can take your gold, but afterwards, things are,' he paused, 'things are *flat*. There is less beauty in a rainbow, less meaning in a sermon, less joy in a kiss . . .' He looked at the cave mouth and I thought I saw fear in his eyes. 'Less.'

I said, 'There are many for whom the lure of gold outweighs the beauty of a rainbow.'

'Me, when young, for one. You, now, for another.'

'So we go in at dawn.'

'You will go in. I will wait for you out here. Do not be afraid. No monster guards the cave. No spells to make the gold vanish, if you do not know some cantrip or rhyme.'

We made our camp, then; or rather we sat in the darkness, against the cold rock wall. There would be no sleep there.

I said, 'You took the gold from here, as I will do tomorrow. You bought a house with it, a bride, a good name.'

His voice came from the darkness. 'Aye. And they meant nothing to me, once I had them, or less than nothing. And if your gold pays for the King over the Water to come back to us and rule us and bring about a land of joy and prosperity and warmth, it will still mean nothing to you. It will be as something you heard of that happened to a man in a tale.'

'I have lived my life to bring the king back,' I told him.

He said, 'You take the gold back to him. Your king will want more gold, because kings want more. It is what they do. Each time you come back, it will mean less. The rainbow means nothing. Killing a man means nothing.'

Silence then, in the darkness. I heard no birds: only the wind that called and gusted about the peaks like a mother seeking her babe.

I said, 'We have both killed men. Have you ever killed a woman, Calum MacInnes?'

'I have not. I have killed no woman, no girls.'

I ran my hands over my dirk in the darkness, seeking the wood and centre of the hilt, the steel of the blade. It was there in my hands. I had not intended to ever tell him, only to strike when we were out of the mountains, strike once, strike deep, but now I felt the words being pulled from me, would I or never-so. 'They say there was a girl,' I told him. 'And a thorn-bush.'

Silence. The whistling of the wind. 'Who told you?' he asked. Then, 'Never mind. I would not kill a woman. No man of honour would kill a woman . . .'

If I said a word, I knew, he would be silent on the subject, and never talk about it again. So I said nothing. Only waited.

Calum MacInnes began to speak, choosing his words with care, talking as if he was remembering a tale he had heard as a child and had almost forgotten. 'They told me the kine of the lowlands were fat and bonny, and that a man could gain honour and glory by adventuring off to the south-lands and returning with the fine red cattle. So I went south, and never a cow was good enough, until on a hillside in the lowlands I saw the finest, reddest, fattest cows that ever a man has seen. So I began to lead them away, back the way I had come.

'She came after me with a stick. The cattle were her father's, she said, and I was a rogue and a knave and all manner of rough things. But she was beautiful, even when angry, and had I not already a young wife, I might have dealt more kindly to her. Instead I pulled a knife, and touched it to her throat, and bade her to stop speaking. And she did stop.

'I would not kill her – I would not kill a woman, and that is the truth – so I tied her, by her hair, to a thorn tree, and I took her knife from her waistband, to slow her as she tried to free herself, and pushed the blade of it deep into the sod. I tied her to the thorn tree by her long hair, and I thought no more of her as I made off with her cattle.

'It was another year before I was back that way. I was not after cows that day, but I walked up the side of that bank – it was a lonely spot, and if you had not been looking, you might not have seen it. Perhaps nobody searched for her.'

'I heard they searched,' I told him. 'Although some believed her taken by reavers, and others believed her run away with a tinker, or gone to the city. But still, they searched.'

'Aye. I saw what I did see – perhaps you'd have to have stood where I was standing, to see what I did see. It was an evil thing I did, perhaps.'

'Perhaps?'

He said, 'I have taken gold from the cave of the mists. I cannot tell any longer if there is good or there is evil. I sent a message, by a child, at an inn, telling them where she was, and where they could find her.'

I closed my eyes but the world became no darker. 'There is evil,' I told him.

I saw it in my mind's eye: her skeleton picked clean of clothes, picked clean of flesh, as naked and white as anyone would ever be, hanging like a child's puppet against the thorn-bush, tied to a branch above it by its red-golden hair.

'At dawn,' said Calum MacInnes, as if we had been talking of provisions or the weather, 'you will leave your dirk behind, for such is the custom, and you will enter the cave, and bring out as much gold as you can carry. And you will bring it back with you, to the mainland. There's not a soul in these parts, knowing what you carry or where it's from, would take it from you. Then send it to the King over the Water, and he will pay his men with it, and feed them, and buy their weapons. One day, he will return. Tell me on that day that there is evil, little man.'

When the sun was up, I entered the cave. It was damp in there. I could hear water running down one wall, and I felt a wind on my face, which was strange, because there was no wind inside the mountain.

In my mind, the cave would be filled with gold. Bars of gold would be stacked like firewood, and bags of golden coins would sit between them. There would be golden chains and golden rings, and golden plates, heaped high like the china plates in a rich man's house.

I had imagined riches, but there was nothing like that here. Only shadows. Only rock.

Something was here, though. Something that waited.

I have secrets, but there is a secret that lies beneath all my other secrets, and not even my children know it, although I believe my wife suspects, and it is this: my mother was a mortal woman, the daughter of a miller, but my father came to her from out of the West, and to the West he returned when he had had his sport with her. I cannot be sentimental about my parentage: I am sure he does not think of her, and doubt that he ever knew of me. But he left me a body that is small, and fast, and strong; and perhaps I take after him in other ways – I do not know. I am ugly, and my father was beautiful, or so my mother told me once, but I think that she might have been deceived.

I wondered what I would have seen in that cave if my father had been an innkeeper from the lowlands.

You would be seeing gold, said a whisper that was not a whisper, from deep in the heart of the mountain. It was a lonely voice, and distracted, and bored.

'I would see gold,' I said aloud. 'Would it be real, or would it be an illusion?'

The whisper was amused. *You are thinking like a mortal man, making things always to be one thing or another. It is gold they would see, and touch. Gold they would carry back with them, feeling the weight of it the while, gold they would trade with other mortals for what they needed. What does it matter if it is there or no if they can see it, touch it, steal it, murder for it? Gold they need and gold I give them.*

'And what do you take, for the gold you give them?'

Little enough, for my needs are few, and I am old; too old to follow my sisters into the West. I taste their pleasure and their joy. I feed, a little, feed on what they do not need and do not value. A taste of heart, a lick and a nibble of their fine consciences, a sliver of soul. And in return a fragment of me leaves this cave with them and gazes out at the world through their eyes, sees what they see until their lives are done and I take back what is mine.

'Will you show yourself to me?'

I could see, in the darkness, better than any man born of man and woman could see. I saw something move in the shadows, and then the shadows congealed and shifted, revealing formless things at the edge of my perception, where it meets imagination. Troubled, I said the thing it is proper to say at times such as this: 'Appear before me in a form that neither harms nor is offensive to me.'

Is that what you wish?

The drip of distant water. 'Yes,' I said.

From out of the shadows it came, and it stared down at me with empty sockets, smiled at me with wind-weathered ivory teeth. It was all bone, save its hair, and its hair was red and gold, and wrapped about the branch of a thorn-bush.

'That offends my eyes.'

I took it from your mind, said a whisper that surrounded the skeleton. Its jawbone did not move. *I chose something you loved. This was your daughter, Flora, as she was the last time you saw her.*

I closed my eyes, but the figure remained.

It said, *The reaver waits for you at the mouth of the cave. He waits for you to come out, weaponless and weighed down with gold. He will kill you, and take the gold from your dead hands.*

'But I'll not be coming out with gold, will I?'

I thought of Calum MacInnes, the wolf-grey in his hair, the grey of his eyes, the line of his dirk. He was bigger than I am, but all men are bigger than I am. Perhaps I was stronger, and faster, but he was also fast, and he was strong.

He killed my daughter, I thought, then wondered if the thought was mine or if it had crept out of the shadows and into my head. Aloud, I said, 'Is there another way out of this cave?'

You leave the way you entered, through the mouth of my home.

I stood there and did not move, but in my mind I was like an animal in a trap, questing and darting from idea to idea, finding no purchase and no solace and no solution.

I said, 'I am weaponless. He told me that I could not enter this place with a weapon. That it was not the custom.'

It is the custom now, to bring no weapon into my

place. It was not always the custom. Follow me, said the skeleton of my daughter.

I followed her, for I could see her, even when it was so dark that I could see nothing else.

In the shadows it said, *It is beneath your hand.*

I crouched and felt it. The haft felt like bone – perhaps an antler. I touched the blade cautiously in the darkness, discovered that I was holding something that felt more like an awl than a knife. It was thin, sharp at the tip. It would be better than nothing.

'Is there a price?'

There is always a price.

'Then I will pay it. And I ask one other thing. You say that you can see the world through his eyes.'

There were no eyes in that hollow skull, but it nodded.

'Then tell me when he sleeps.'

It said nothing. It melded into the darkness, and I felt alone in that place.

Time passed. I followed the sound of the dripping water, found a rock pool, and drank. I soaked the last of the oats and I ate them, chewing them until they dissolved in my mouth. I slept and woke and slept again, and dreamed of my wife, Morag, waiting for me as the seasons changed, waiting for me just as we had waited for our daughter, waiting for me for ever.

Something, a finger I thought, touched my hand: it was not bony and hard. It was soft, and humanlike, but too cold. *He sleeps.*

I left the cave in the blue light, before dawn. He slept across the cave-mouth, catlike, I knew, such that the slightest touch would have woken him. I held my weapon in front of me, a bone handle and a needlelike blade of blackened silver, and I reached out and took what I was after, without waking him.

Then I stepped closer, and his hand grasped for my ankle and his eyes opened.

'Where is the gold?' asked Calum MacInnes.

'I have none.' The wind blew cold on the mountainside. I had danced back, out of his reach, when he had grabbed at me. He stayed on the ground, pushed himself up onto one elbow.

Then he said, 'Where is my dirk?'

'I took it,' I told him. 'While you slept.'

He looked at me, sleepily. 'And why ever would you do that? If I was going to kill you I would have done it on the way here. I could have killed you a dozen times.'

'But I did not have gold then, did I?'

He said nothing.

I said, 'If you think you could have got me to bring the gold from the cave, and that not bringing it out would have saved your miserable soul, then you are a fool.'

He no longer looked sleepy. 'A fool, am I?'

He was ready to fight. It is good to make people who are ready to fight angry.

I said, 'Not a fool. No. For I have met fools and idiots, and they are happy in their idiocy, even with straw in their hair. You are too wise for foolishness. You seek only misery and you bring misery with you and you call down misery on all you touch.'

He rose then, holding a rock in his hand like an axe, and he came at me. I am small, and he could not strike me as he would have struck a man of his own size. He leaned over to strike. It was a mistake.

I held the bone haft tightly, and stabbed upward, striking fast with the point of the awl, like a snake. I knew the place I was aiming for, and I knew what it would do.

He dropped his rock, clutched at his right shoulder. 'My arm,' he said. 'I cannot feel my arm.'

He swore then, fouling the air with curses and threats. The dawn light on the mountaintop made everything so beautiful and blue. In that light, even the blood that had begun to soak his garments was purple. He took a step back, so he was between me and the cave. I felt exposed, the rising sun at my back.

'Why do you not have gold?' he asked me. His arm hung limply at his side.

'There was no gold there for such as I,' I said.

He threw himself forward, then, ran at me and kicked at me. My awl blade went flying from my hand. I threw my arms around his leg, and I held on to him as together we tumbled off the mountainside.

His head was above me, and I saw triumph in

it, and then I saw sky, and then the valley floor was above me and I was rising to meet it and then it was below me and I was falling to my death.

A jar and a bump, and now we were turning over and over on the side of the mountain, the world a dizzying whirligig of rock and pain and sky, and I knew I was a dead man, but still I clung to the leg of Calum MacInnes.

I saw a golden eagle in flight, but below me or above me I could no longer say. It was there, in the dawn sky, in the shattered fragments of time and perception, there in the pain. I was not afraid: there was no time and no space to be afraid in, no space in my mind and no space in my heart. I was falling through the sky, holding tightly to the leg of a man who was trying to kill me; we were crashing into rocks, scraping and bruising and then . . .

. . . .we stopped. Stopped with force enough that I felt myself jarred, and was almost thrown off Calum MacInnes and to my death beneath. The side of the mountain had crumbled, there, long ago, sheared off, leaving a sheet of blank rock, as smooth and as featureless as glass. But that was below us. Where we were, there was a ledge, and on the ledge there was a miracle: stunted and twisted, high above the treeline, where no trees have any right to grow, was a twisted hawthorn tree, not much larger than a bush, although it was old. Its roots grew into the side of the mountain, and it was this hawthorn that had caught us in its grey arms.

I let go of the leg, clambered off Calum MacInnes's body, and onto the side of the mountain. I stood on the narrow ledge and looked down at the sheer drop. There was no way down from here. No way down at all.

I looked up. It might be possible, I thought, climbing slowly, with fortune on my side, to make it up that mountain. If it did not rain. If the wind was not too hungry. And what choice did I have? The only alternative was death.

A voice: 'So. Will you leave me here to die, dwarf?'

I said nothing. I had nothing to say.

His eyes were open. He said, 'I cannot move my right arm, since you stabbed it. I think I broke a leg in the fall. I cannot climb with you.'

I said, 'I may succeed, or I may fail.'

'You'll make it. I've seen you climb. After you rescued me, crossing that waterfall. You went up those rocks like a squirrel going up a tree.'

I did not have his confidence in my climbing abilities.

He said, 'Swear to me by all you hold holy. Swear by your king, who waits over the sea as he has since we drove his subjects from this land. Swear by the things you creatures hold dear – swear by shadows and eagle feathers and by silence. Swear that you will come back for me.'

'You know what I am?' I said.

'I know nothing,' he said. 'Only that I want to live.'

I thought. 'I swear by these things,' I told him. 'By shadows and by eagle feathers and by silence. I swear by green hills and standing stones. I will come back.'

'I would have killed you,' said the man in the hawthorn bush, and he said it with humour, as if it was the biggest joke that ever one man had told another. 'I had planned to kill you, and take the gold back as my own.'

'I know.'

His hair framed his face like a wolf-grey halo. There was red blood on his cheek where he had scraped it in the fall. 'You could come back with ropes,' he said. 'My rope is still up there, by the cave mouth. But you'd need more than that.'

'Yes,' I said. 'I will come back with ropes.' I looked up at the rock above us, examined it as best I could. Sometimes good eyes mean the difference between life and death, if you are a climber. I saw where I would need to be as I went, the shape of my journey up the face of the mountain. I thought I could see the ledge outside the cave, from which we had fallen as we fought. I would head for there. Yes.

I blew on my hands, to dry the sweat before I began to climb. 'I will come back for you,' I said. 'With ropes. I have sworn.'

'When?' he asked, and he closed his eyes.

'In a year,' I told him. 'I will come here in a year.'

I began to climb. The man's cries followed me

as I stepped and crawled and squeezed and hauled myself up the side of that mountain, mingling with the cries of the great raptors; and they followed me back from the Misty Isle, with nothing to show for my pains and my time, and I will hear him screaming, at the edge of my mind, as I fall asleep or in the moments before I wake, until I die.

It did not rain, and the wind gusted and plucked at me but did not throw me down. I climbed, and I climbed in safety.

When I reached the ledge, the cave entrance seemed like a darker shadow in the noonday sun. I turned from it, turned my back on the mountain, and from the shadows that were already gathering in the cracks and the crevices and deep inside my skull, and I began my slow journey away from the Misty Isle. There were a hundred roads and a thousand paths that would take me back to my home in the lowlands, where my wife would be waiting.

UNBELIEF

MICHAEL MARSHALL SMITH

It happened in bryant park, a little after six o'clock in the evening. He was sitting by himself in lamp shadow amongst the trees, at one of the rickety green metal tables along the north side, close to where the Barnes & Noble library area is during the day. He was warmly dressed in nondescript, casual clothing and sipping from a Starbucks in a seasonally red cup, acquired from the outlet on the corner of Sixth, right opposite one of the entrances to the park. He queued, just like any normal person: watching through the window you'd have no idea of who he was, or the power he wielded over this and other neighbourhoods.

He had done exactly the same on the preceding two evenings. I'd followed him down from Times Square both times, watched him buy the same drink from the same place and then spend half an hour sitting in the same chair, or near enough, watching the world go by. Evidently, as I had been assured, it was what this man always did at this time of day and this time of year. Habit and ritual are some of our greatest comforts, but they're a gift to people like me.

He might as well have tied himself up with a bow.

On the previous occasions I had merely observed, logged his actions, and walked on by. The thing had been booked for a specific date, for reasons I neither knew nor cared about.

That day had come, and so I entered the park by the next entrance along, by the restrooms, strolling in casually and without evident intent.

I paused for a moment on the steps. He didn't appear to be there with protection. There were other people sparsely spread over the park, perched at tables or walking in the very last of the twilight, but there was no indication they were anything more than standard-issue New Yorkers, taking a little time before battling the subway or bridges and tunnels or airports, heading home to their families or friends or real partners for the holidays. Grabbing a last few seconds' blessed solitude, an unwitnessed cigarette, or an illicit kiss and a promise not to forget, before entering a day or two of enforced incarceration with the people who populated their real lives.

Their presence in the park did not concern me. They were either absorbed in their companions or in something within themselves, and none would notice me until it was too late. I have done harder jobs under more difficult conditions. I could have just taken the shot from twenty feet away, kept on walking, but I found I didn't want it to happen like that. Not with this guy. He deserved less.

I watched him covertly as I approached his position. He appeared relaxed, at ease, as if savoring his own few private moments of peace before tackling some great enterprise. I knew what he thought that was going to be. I also knew it wasn't going to happen.

There was an empty chair on the other side of his table. I sat down on it.

He ignored me for a couple minutes, peering in a vaguely benign way at the skeletal branches of the tall trees that stand all around the park's central grassy area: at them, or perhaps at all the buildings around the square revealed by the season's dearth of leaves. Being able to see these monoliths makes the park seem both bigger and yet more intimate, stripped.

Defenseless.

'Hello, Kane,' he said, finally.

I'd never actually seen him before – not in the flesh at least, only in pictures – so I have no idea how he'd managed to make me straightaway. I guess it's his job to know things about people.

'You don't seem surprised,' I said.

He glanced at me finally, then away again, seemingly to watch a young couple perched at a table twenty yards up the path. They were bundled up in thick coats and scarves and necking with cautious optimism. After a few minutes they separated, tentatively smiling, still with their arms around each other's shoulders, and turned to look at the lights strung in the trees, to listen to the sound of cars honking, to savour being where they were. A recent liaison, the legacy of an office party, perhaps, destined to be a source of embarrassed silences in the office by Valentine's Day. Either that, or pregnancy and marriage and all the silences after that.

'I knew it could happen,' the man said, taking the lid off his coffee and peering inside, as if gauging how long he had left. 'I'm not surprised it's you sitting there.'

'Why's that?'

'Accepting a job for this evening? That's cold. Takes a certain kind of person. Who else they going to call?'

'That supposed to be a compliment? You think if you butter me up then I won't do it?'

The man looked calmly at me through the steam of what smelt like a gingerbread latte.

'Oh, you'll do it. I have no doubt of that.'

I didn't like his tone, and I felt the thing start to uncurl inside me. If you've ever tried to give up smoking, you'll have felt something like it – the sudden, lurid desire to lay waste to the world and everything in it, starting right here, right now, and with the person physically closest to you.

I don't know what this thing is. It doesn't have a name. I just know it's there, and I feel it when it wakes. It has always been a very light sleeper.

'No, really,' I said. 'Just because I live in a big house these days, and I got a wife and a child, you think I can't do what I do?'

'You've still got it. You'll always have it.'

'Fucking right I will.'

'And that's something to be proud of?' He shook his head. 'Shame of it is, you were a good kid.'

'Isn't everyone?'

'No. Some people come out of the womb broken. You can nurture all you want, sooner or later they're going to pass the damage on. With you, it could have been different. That makes it worse, somehow.'

'I am who I chose to be.'

'Really? Everyone in the neighbourhood knows the kind of person your father was.'

My hands twitched, involuntarily.

'He had no faith in anything,' the man said. 'He was a hater. And a hurter. I remember watching him when he was young, knowing how he'd grow up. Either dead inside, or affectionate in inappropriate ways. Maybe both. Am I right?'

'If you'd like this to play out in a civilised fashion,' I said, my voice tight, 'you want to drop this line of discussion.'

'Forgive me. But you've come here to kill me, Kane. That's pretty personal too, wouldn't you say?'

I knew I should get on with it. But I was also aware that this was the biggest job of my career, and when it was done, it would be over.

I was also simply curious. 'What the fuck makes

114

you think you're better than me?' I said. 'What you do isn't so different.'

'You really think so?'

'You put yourself in a position of power, made it so you get to choose who gets what. Who prospers, who gets nothing. And then you point the finger and lives get fucked up forever. Same as me.'

'I don't see it that way.' He looked into his cup again. The habit was beginning to get on my nerves.

'Yeah, drink up,' I said. 'Time's running out.'

'One question.'

'How'd I find you?'

He nodded.

'People talk.'

'My people?'

I shook my head, irritably. The truth was, his own soldiers had held the line. I'd tracked down a couple of them (one slurping pho in a noodle bar under a bridge in Queens, the other sleeping in a tree deep in Central Park) and leaned on them hard – to the point where one of them would not be working for him, or anyone else, ever again. Both had merely looked up at me with their cold, strange eyes and waited for whatever I was going to do. It was not they who'd told me to go and stand in Times Square at the end of any December afternoon, and wait there until this man appeared, arriving there from directions unknown.

'So, who, then?'

'It's too late for you to be taking names,' I said, with some satisfaction. 'That's all over now.'

He smiled again, but more coldly, and I saw something in his face that had not been there before – not on the surface, at least. The steady calm of a man who was used to making judgment calls, decisions upon which the lives of others had hung. A man who had measured, assayed, and who was now about to pay the price, at the behest of people who had fallen on the wrong side of the line he had believed it was his God-given right to draw.

'You think you're this big, bountiful guy,' I said. 'Everybody's old man. But some understand the real truth. They realise it's all bullshit.'

'Have I not made my rules clear? Have I not looked out for the people who deserved it?'

'Only to make them do what you want.'

'And what do *you* want? Why are you really here tonight, Kane?'

'Someone paid me to be. More than one, in fact. A syndicate. People saying that enough is enough. Getting back for what you did to them.'

'I know about that,' he interrupted, as if bored. 'I can even guess who these people are. But I asked why *you're* here.'

'For the money.'

'No. Otherwise you'd have done it from ten yards away and be on your way home by now.'

'So you tell me why, if you're so fucking wise.'

'It's personal,' he said. 'And that's a mistake.

116

You've made a good living out of what you do, and have something of a life. On your terms. That's because you've merely been for hire. But you want this one for yourself. Admit it. You hate me on your own account.'

This man was smart enough to know a lie when he heard it, so I said nothing.

'Why, Kane? Did something happen, some night, when there was snow on the ground outside and everything should have been carols and fairy lights? Did your presents come with conditions, or costs? Payments that came due in the middle of the night, when Mom was asleep?'

'That's enough.'

'How many people have you killed, Kane? Can you even remember?'

'I remember,' I said, though I could not.

'When you let it get personal, the cost becomes personal too. You're opening your own heart here. You sure you want to do that?'

'I'd do it for free. For the bullshit you are, and have always been.'

'Disbelief is easy, Kane. It's faith that takes courage, and character.'

'You're out of time,' I said.

He sighed. Then he tipped the cup, drained the last of his coffee, and set it down on the table between us.

'I'm done,' he said.

In the fifteen minutes we'd been talking, nearly half the people had left the park. The necking

117

couple had been amongst them, departing hand in hand. The nearest person was now about sixty yards away. I stood up, reached in my jacket.

'Anything you want to say?' I asked, looking down at his mild, rosy face. 'People do, sometimes.'

'Not to you,' he said.

I pulled out the gun and placed the silenced end in the middle of his forehead. He didn't try to move. I took hold of his right shoulder with my other hand, and pulled the trigger once.

With all the traffic around the square, I barely even heard the sound. His head jerked back.

I let go of his shoulder and he sagged slowly around the waist, until the weight of his big, barrel chest pulled his body down off the chair to slump heavily onto the path, nearly face-first.

A portion of the back of his head was gone, but his eyes were still open. His beard scratched against the pavement as he tried to say something. After a couple of times I realised it was not words he was forcing out, but a series of sounds. I put the barrel to his temple and pulled the trigger again. A portion of the opposite temple splatted out onto the stones.

Yet still he was trying to push out those three short syllables, each the same.

I pulled the trigger a final time, and he was quiet. I bent down close to make sure, and to whisper in the remains of his ear.

'Check it twice, right, asshole?'

Then I walked out of the park. A few blocks away I found a cab, and started the long, slow journey home to New Jersey.

I woke early the next morning, like most fathers, to the sound of my son hurrying past our bedroom and down the stairs. On his way to the fireplace, no doubt.

Good luck with that, I thought, though I knew his stocking would be full nonetheless.

A few minutes later Lauren levered herself into a sitting position. She pulled on her robe and went to the window, yanking aside the drapes.

She smiled at something she saw out there, then turned and quickly left the room.

By the time I'd got my own robe on and gone down to the kitchen to make coffee, I knew what she'd seen through the window. It had snowed overnight, covering the yard and hanging off the trees. The whole nine yards of Winter Wonderland set dressing. Probably I would have to help build a snowman later, whether I felt like it or not.

In the living room my wife and child were sitting together Indian style in the middle of the floor, cooing over the stockings they'd already taken down from the fireplace. Candy, little gifts, pieces of junk that were supposed to mean something just because they'd been found in a sock. I noticed that the cookie left on the table near the hearth had a large bite taken out of it. Lauren has always been good with detail.

'Happy Christmas, guys,' I said, but neither of them seemed to hear.

I stepped around them and went to the fire-place. I took down the remaining stocking. I knew something was different before it was even in my hand.

It was empty.

'Lauren?'

She looked up at me. 'Ho, ho, ho,' she said. There was nothing in her face.

Then she smiled, briefly, before going back to chattering with our son, watching for the third or fifth time as he excitedly repacked and then unpacked his stocking. Her smile went straight through me. But then they always have.

I left the stocking on the arm of one of the chairs and walked out into the kitchen.

I opened the back door, and went to stand outside in the snow.

It was very quiet, and it was nothing but cold.

THE STARS ARE FALLING

JOE R. LANSDALE

Before Deel Arrowsmith came back from the dead, he was crossing a field by late moonlight in search of his home. His surroundings were familiar, but at the same time different. It was as if he had left as a child and returned as an adult to examine old property only to find the tree swing gone, the apple tree cut down, the grass grown high, and an outhouse erected over the mound where his best dog was buried.

As he crossed, the dropping moon turned thin, like cheap candy licked too long, and the sun bled through the trees. There were spots of frost on the drooping green grass and on the taller weeds, yellow as ripe corn. In his mind's eye he saw not the East Texas field before him or the dark rows of oaks and pines beyond it, or even the clay path that twisted across the field toward the trees like a ribbon of blood.

He saw a field in France where there was a long, deep trench, and in the trench were bloodied bodies, some of them missing limbs and with bits of brains scattered about like spilled oatmeal. The air filled with the stinging stench of rotting meat and wafting gun smoke, the residue of poison gas, and the buzz of flies. The back of his throat tasted of burning copper. His stomach was a knot. The trees were like the shadowy shades of soldiers charging toward him, and for a moment, he thought to meet their charge, even though he no longer carried a gun.

He closed his eyes, breathed deeply, shook his head. When he opened them the stench had passed and his nostrils filled with the nip of early morning. The last of the moon faded like a melting snowflake. Puffy white clouds sailed along the heavens and light tripped across the tops of the trees, fell between them, made shadows run low along the trunks and across the ground. The sky turned light blue and the frost dried off the drooping grass and it sprang to attention. Birds began to sing. Grasshoppers began to jump.

He continued down the path that crossed the field and split the trees. As he went, he tried to remember exactly where his house was and how it looked and how it smelled, and most important, how he felt when he was inside it. He tried to remember his wife and how she looked and how he felt when he was inside her, and all he could find in the back of his mind was a cipher of a woman younger than he was in a long, colorless dress in a house with three rooms. He couldn't even remember her nakedness, the shape of her breasts and the length of her legs. It was as if they had met only once, and in passing.

When he came through the trees and out on the other side, the field was there as it should be, and it was full of bright blue and yellow flowers. Once it had been filled with tall corn and green bursts of beans and peas. It hadn't been plowed now in years, most likely since he left. He followed the trail and trudged toward his house. It stood where he had left it. It had not improved with age. The chimney was black at the top and the unpainted lumber was stripping like shedding snakeskin. He had cut the trees and split them and made the lumber for the house, and like everything else he had seen since he had returned, it was smaller than he remembered. Behind it was the smokehouse he had made of logs, and far out to the left was the outhouse he had built. He had read many a magazine there while having his morning constitutional.

Out front, near the well, which had been built up with stones and now had a roof over it supported on four stout poles, was a young boy. He knew immediately it was his son. The boy was probably eight. He had been four years old when Deel had left to fight in the Great War, sailed across the vast dark ocean. The boy had a bucket in his hand, held by the handle. He set it down and raced toward the house, yelling something Deel couldn't define.

A moment later she came out of the house and his memory filled up. He kept walking, and the closer he came to her, standing framed in the doorway, the tighter his heart felt. She was blond and tall and lean and dressed in a light-colored dress on which were printed flowers much duller than those in the field. But her face was brighter than the sun, and he knew now how she looked naked and in bed, and all that had been lost came back to him, and he knew he was home again.

When he was ten feet away the boy, frightened, grabbed his mother and held her, and she said, 'Deel, is that you?'

He stopped and stood, and said nothing. He just looked at her, drinking her in like a cool beer. Finally he said, 'Worn and tired, but me.'

'I thought . . .'

'I didn't write cause I can't.'

'I know . . . but . . .'

'I'm back, Mary Lou.'

They sat stiffly at the kitchen table. Deel had a plate in front of him and he had eaten the beans that had been on it. The front door was open and they could see out and past the well and into the flower-covered field. The window across the way was open too, and there was a light breeze ruffling the edges of the pulled-back curtains framing it. Deel had the sensation he'd had before when crossing the field and passing through the trees, and when he had first seen the outside of the house. And now, inside, the roof felt too low and the room was too small and the walls were too close. It was all too small.

But there was Mary Lou. She sat across the table from him. Her face was clean of lines and her shoulders were as narrow as the boy's. Her eyes were bright, like the blue flowers in the field.

The boy, Winston, was to his left, but he had pulled his chair close to his mother. The boy studied him carefully, and in turn, Deel studied the boy. Deel could see Mary Lou in him, and nothing of himself.

'Have I changed that much?' Deel said, in response to the way they were looking at him. Both of them had their hands in their laps, as if he might leap across the table at any moment and bite them.

'You're very thin,' Mary Lou said.

'I was too heavy when I left. I'm too skinny now. Soon I hope to be just right.' He tried to smile, but the smile dripped off. He took a deep breath. 'So, how you been?'

'Been?'

'Yeah. You know. How you been?'

'Oh. Fine,' she said. 'Good. I been good.'

'The boy?'

'He's fine.'

'Does he talk?'

'Sure he talks. Say hello to your daddy, Winston.'

The boy didn't speak.

'Say hello,' his mother said.

The boy didn't respond.

'That's all right,' Deel said. 'It's been a while. He doesn't remember me. It's only natural.'

'You joined up through Canada?'

'Like I said I would.'

'I couldn't be sure,' she said.

'I know. I got in with the Americans, a year or so back. It didn't matter who I was with. It was bad.'

'I see,' she said, but Deel could tell she didn't see at all. And he didn't blame her. He had been caught up in the enthusiasm of war and adventure, gone up to Canada and got in on it, left his family in the lurch, thinking life was passing him by and he was missing out. Life had been right here and he hadn't even recognized it.

Mary Lou stood up and shuffled around the table and heaped fresh beans onto his plate and went to the oven and brought back cornbread and put it next to the beans. He watched her every move. Her hair was a little sweaty on her forehead and it clung there, like wet hay.

'How old are you now?' he asked her.

'How old?' she said, returning to her spot at the table. 'Deel, you know how old I am. I'm twenty-eight, older than when you left.'

'I'm ashamed to say it, but I've forgotten your birthday. I've forgotten his. I don't hardly know how old I am.'

She told him the dates of their births.

'I'll be,' he said. 'I don't remember any of that.'

'I . . . I thought you were dead.'

She had said it several times since he had come home. He said, 'I'm still not dead, Mary Lou. I'm in the flesh.'

'You are. You certainly are.'

She didn't eat what was on her plate. She just sat there looking at it, as if it might transform.

Deel said, 'Who fixed the well, built the roof over it?'

'Tom Smites,' she said.

'Tom? He's a kid.'

'Not anymore,' she said. 'He was eighteen when you left. He wasn't any kid then, not really.'

'I reckon not,' Deel said.

After dinner, she gave him his pipe the way she used to, and he found a cane rocker that he didn't remember being there before, took it outside and sat and looked toward the trees and smoked his pipe and rocked.

He was thinking of then and he was thinking of now and he was thinking of later, when it would be nighttime and he would go to bed, and he wasn't certain how to approach the matter. She was his wife, but he hadn't been with her for years, and now he was home, and he wanted it to be like before, but he didn't really remember how it was before. He knew how to do what he wanted to do, but he didn't know how to make it love. He feared she would feel that he was like a mangy cat that had come in through the window to lie there and expected petting.

He sat and smoked and thought and rocked.

The boy came out of the house and stood to the side and watched him.

The boy had the gold hair of his mother and he was built sturdy for a boy so young. He had a bit of a birthmark in front of his right ear, on the jawline, like a little strawberry. Deel didn't remember that. The boy had been a baby, of course, but he didn't remember that at all. Then again, he couldn't remember a lot of things, except for the things he didn't want to remember. Those things he remembered. And Mary Lou's skin. That he remembered. How soft it was to the touch, like butter.

'Do you remember me, boy?' Deel asked.

'No.'

'Not at all?'

'No.'

''Course not. You were very young. Has your mother told you about me?'

'Not really.'

'Nothing.'

'She said you got killed in the war.'

'I see . . . Well, I didn't.'

Deel turned and looked back through the open door. He could see Mary Lou at the washbasin pouring water into the wash pan, water she had heated on the stove. It steamed as she poured. He thought then he should have brought wood for her to make the fire. He should have helped make the fire and heat the water. But being close to her made him nervous. The boy made him nervous.

'You going to school?' he asked the boy.

'School burned down. Tom teaches me some

128

readin' and writin' and cipherin'. He went eight years to school.'

'You ever go fishin'?'

'Just with Tom. He takes me fishin' and huntin' now and then.'

'He ever show you how to make a bow and arrow?'

'No.'

'No, sir,' Deel said. 'You say, no, sir.'

'What's that?'

'Say yes, sir or no, sir. Not yes and no. It's rude.'

The boy dipped his head and moved a foot along the ground, piling up dirt.

'I ain't gettin' on you none,' Deel said. 'I'm just tellin' you that's how it's done. That's how I do if it's someone older than me. I say no, sir and yes, sir. Understand, son?'

The boy nodded.

'And what do you say?'

'Yes, sir.'

'Good. Manners are important. You got to have manners. A boy can't go through life without manners. You can read and write some, and you got to cipher to protect your money. But you got to have manners too.'

'Yes, sir.'

'There you go . . . About that bow and arrow. He never taught you that, huh?'

'No, sir.'

'Well, that will be our plan. I'll show you how to do it. An old Cherokee taught me how. It ain't as easy as it might sound, not to make a good one. And then to be good enough to hit somethin' with it, that's a whole nuther story.'

'Why would you do all that when you got a gun?'

'I guess you wouldn't need to. It's just fun, and huntin' with one is real sportin', compared to a gun. And right now, I ain't all that fond of guns.'

'I like guns.'

'Nothin' wrong with that. But a gun don't like you, and it don't love you back. Never give too much attention or affection to somethin' that can't return it.'

'Yes, sir.'

The boy, of course, had no idea what he was talking about. Deel was uncertain he knew himself what he was talking about. He turned and looked back through the door. Mary Lou was at the pan, washing the dishes; when she scrubbed, her ass shook a little, and in that moment, Deel felt, for the first time, like a man alive.

That night the bed seemed small. He lay on his back with his hands crossed across his lower stomach, wearing his faded red union suit, which had been ragged when he left, and had in his absence been attacked by moths. It was ready to come apart. The window next to the bed was open and the breeze that came through was cool. Mary Lou lay beside him. She wore a long white nightgown that had been patched with a variety of colored cloth patches. Her hair was undone and it was long. It had been long when he left. He wondered how often she had cut it, and how much time it had taken each time to grow back.

'I reckon it's been a while,' he said.

'That's all right,' she said.

'I'm not sayin' I can't, or I won't, just sayin' I don't know I'm ready.'

'It's okay.'

'You been lonely?'

'I have Winston.'

'He's grown a lot. He must be company.'

'He is.'

'He looks some like you.'

'Some.'

Deel stretched out his hand without looking at her and laid it across her stomach. 'You're still like a girl,' he said. 'Had a child, and you're still like a girl . . . You know why I asked how old you was?'

''Cause you didn't remember.'

'Well, yeah, there was that. But on account of you don't look none different at all.'

'I got a mirror. It ain't much of one, but it don't make me look younger.'

'You look just the same.'

'Right now, any woman might look good to you.' After she said it, she caught herself. 'I didn't mean it that way. I just meant you been gone a long time . . . In Europe, they got pretty women, I hear.'

'Some are, some ain't. Ain't none of them pretty as you.'

'You ever . . . you know?'

'What?'

'You know . . . While you was over there.'

'Oh . . . Reckon I did. Couple of times. I didn't know for sure I was comin' home. There wasn't nothin' to it. I didn't mean nothin' by it. It was like filling a hungry belly, nothin' more.'

She was quiet for a long time. Then she said, 'It's okay.'

He thought to ask her a similar question, but couldn't. He eased over to her. She remained still. She was as stiff as a corpse. He knew. He had been forced at times to lie down among them. Once, moving through a town in France with his fellow soldiers, he had come upon a woman lying dead between two trees. There wasn't a wound on her. She was young. Dark haired. She looked as if she had lain down for a nap. He reached down and touched her. She was still warm.

One of his comrades, a soldier, had suggested they all take turns mounting her before she got cold. It was a joke, but Deel had pointed his rifle at him and run him off. Later, in the trenches he had been side by side with the same man, a fellow from Wisconsin, who like him had joined the Great War by means of Canada. They had made their peace, and the Wisconsin fellow told him it was a poor joke he'd made, and not to hold it against him, and Deel said it was all right, and then they took positions next to each other and talked a bit about home and waited for the war to come.

During the battle, wearing gas masks and firing rifles, the fellow from Wisconsin had caught a round and it had knocked him down. A moment later the battle had ceased, at least for the moment.

Deel bent over him, lifted his mask, and then the man's head. The man said, 'My mama won't never see me again.'

'You're gonna be okay,' Deel said, but saw that half the man's head was missing. How in hell was he talking? Why wasn't he dead? His brain was leaking out.

'I got a letter inside my shirt. Tell Mama I love her . . . Oh, my god, look there. The stars are falling.'

Deel, responding to the distant gaze of his downed companion, turned and looked up. The stars were bright and stuck in place. There was an explosion of cannon fire and the ground shook and the sky lit up bright red; the redness clung to the air like a veil. When Deel looked back at the fellow, the man's eyes were still open, but he was gone.

Deel reached inside the man's jacket and found the letter. He realized then that the man had also taken a round in the chest, because the letter was dark with blood. Deel tried to unfold it, but it was so damp with gore it fell apart. There was nothing to deliver to anyone. Deel couldn't even remember the man's name. It had gone in one ear and out the other. And now he was gone, his last words being, 'The stars are falling.'

While he was holding the boy's head, an officer

came walking down the trench holding a pistol. His face was darkened with gunpowder and his eyes were bright in the night and he looked at Deel, said, 'There's got to be some purpose to all of it, son. Some purpose,' and then he walked on down the line.

Deel thought of that night and that death, and then he thought of the dead woman again. He wondered what had happened to her body. They had had to leave her there, between the two trees. Had someone buried her? Had she rotted there? Had the ants and the elements taken her away? He had dreams of lying down beside her, there in the field. Just lying there, drifting away with her into the void.

Deel felt now as if he were lying beside that dead woman, blond instead of dark haired, but no more alive than the woman between the trees.

'Maybe we ought to just sleep tonight,' Mary Lou said, startling him. 'We can let things take their course. It ain't nothin' to make nothin' out of.'

He moved his hand away from her. He said, 'That'll be all right. Of course.'

She rolled on her side, away from him. He lay on top of the covers with his hands against his lower belly and looked at the log rafters.

A couple of days and nights went by without her warming to him, but he found sleeping with her to be the best part of his life. He liked her sweet smell and he liked to listen to her breathe. When she was deep asleep, he would turn slightly, and carefully, and rise up on one elbow and look at her shape in the dark. His homecoming had not been what he had hoped for or expected, but in those moments when he looked at her in the dark, he was certain it was better than what had gone before for nearly four horrible years.

The next few days led to him taking the boy into the woods and finding the right wood for a bow. He chopped down a bois d'arc tree and showed the boy how to trim it with an axe, how to cut the wood out of it for a bow, how to cure it with a fire that was mostly smoke. They spent a long time at it, but if the boy enjoyed what he was learning, he never let on. He kept his feelings close to the heart and talked less than his mother. The boy always seemed some yards away, even when standing right next to him.

Deel built the bow for the boy and strung it with strong cord and showed him how to find the right wood for arrows and how to collect feathers from a bird's nest and how to feather the shafts. It took almost a week to make the bow, and another week to dry it and to make the arrows. The rest of the time Deel looked out at what had once been a plowed field and was now twenty-five acres of flowers with a few little trees beginning to grow, twisting up among the flowers. He tried to imagine the field covered in corn.

Deel used an axe to clear the new trees, and

that afternoon, at the dinner table, he asked Mary Lou what had happened to the mule.

'Died,' Mary Lou said. 'She was old when you left, and she just got older. We ate it when it died.'

'Waste not, want not,' Deel said.

'Way we saw it,' she said.

'You ain't been farmin', how'd you make it?'

'Tom brought us some goods now and then, fish he caught, vegetables from his place. A squirrel or two. We raised a hog and smoked the meat, had our own garden.'

'How are Tom's parents?'

'His father drank himself to death and his mother just up and died.'

Deel nodded. 'She was always sickly, and her husband was a lot older than her . . . I'm older than you. But not by that much. He was what? Fifteen years? I'm . . . Well, let me see. I'm ten.'

She didn't respond. He had hoped for some kind of confirmation that his ten-year gap was nothing, that it was okay. But she said nothing.

'I'm glad Tom was around,' Deel said.

'He was a help,' she said.

After a while, Deel said, 'Things are gonna change. You ain't got to take no one's charity no more. Tomorrow, I'm gonna go into town, see I can buy some seed, and find a mule. I got some muster-out pay. It ain't much, but it's enough to get us started. Winston here goes in with me, we might see we can get him some candy of some sort.'

'I like peppermint,' the boy said.

'There you go,' Deel said.

'You ought not do that so soon back,' Mary Lou said. 'There's still time before the fall plantin'. You should hunt like you used to, or fish for a few days . . . You could take Winston here with you. You deserve time off.'

'Guess another couple of days ain't gonna hurt nothin'. We could all use some time gettin' re-acquainted.'

Next afternoon when Deel came back from the creek with Winston, they had a couple of fish on a wet cord, and Winston carried them slung over his back so that they dangled down like ornaments and made his shirt damp. They were small but good perch and the boy had caught them, and in the process, shown the first real excitement Deel had seen from him. The sunlight played over their scales as they bounced against Winston's back. Deel, walking slightly behind Winston, watched the fish carefully. He watched them slowly dying, out of the water, gasping for air. He couldn't help but want to take them back to the creek and let them go. He had seen injured men gasp like that, on the field, in the trenches. They had seemed like fish that only needed to be put in water.

As they neared the house, Deel saw a rider coming their way, and he saw Mary Lou walking out from the house to meet him.

Mary Lou went up to the man and the man

leaned out of the saddle, and they spoke, and then Mary Lou took hold of the saddle with one hand and walked with the horse toward the house. When she saw Deel and Winston coming, she let go of the saddle and walked beside the horse. The man on the horse was tall and lean with black hair that hung down to his shoulders. It was like a waterfall of ink tumbling out from under his slouched, gray hat.

As they came closer together, the man on the horse raised his hand in greeting. At that moment the boy yelled out, 'Tom!' and darted across the field toward the horse, the fish flapping.

They sat at the kitchen table. Deel and Mary Lou and Winston and Tom Smites. Tom's mother had been half Chickasaw, and he seemed to have gathered up all her coloring, along with his Swedish father's great height and broad build. He looked like some kind of forest god. His hair hung over the sides of his face, and his skin was walnut colored and smooth and he had balanced features and big hands and feet. He had his hat on his knee.

The boy sat very close to Tom. Mary Lou sat at the table, her hands out in front of her, resting on the planks. She had her head turned toward Tom.

Deel said, 'I got to thank you for helpin' my family out.'

'Ain't nothin' to thank. You used to take me

huntin' and fishin' all the time. My daddy didn't do that sort of thing. He was a farmer and a hog raiser and a drunk. You done good by me.'

'Thanks again for helpin'.'

'I wanted to help out. Didn't have no trouble doin' it.'

'You got a family of your own now, I reckon.'

'Not yet. I break horses and run me a few cows and hogs and chickens, grow me a pretty good-size garden, but I ain't growin' a family. Not yet. I hear from Mary Lou you need a plow mule and some seed.'

Deel looked at her. She had told him all that in the short time she had walked beside his horse. He wasn't sure how he felt about that. He wasn't sure he wanted anyone to know what he needed or didn't need.

'Yeah. I want to buy a mule and some seed.'

'Well, now. I got a horse that's broke to plow. He ain't as good as a mule, but I could let him go cheap, real cheap. And I got more seed than I know what to do with. It would save you a trip into town.'

'I sort of thought I might like to go to town,' Deel said.

'Yeah, well, sure. But I can get those things for you.'

'I wanted to take Winston here to the store and get him some candy.'

Tom grinned. 'Now, that is a good idea, but so happens, I was in town this mornin', and—'

139

Tom produced a brown paper from his shirt pocket and laid it out on the table and carefully pulled the paper loose, revealing two short pieces of peppermint.

Winston looked at Tom. 'Is that for me?'

'It is.'

'You just take one now, Winston, and have it after dinner,' Mary Lou said. 'You save that other piece for tomorrow. It'll give you somethin' to look forward to.'

'That was mighty nice of you, Tom,' Deel said.

'You should stay for lunch,' Mary Lou said. 'Deel and Winston caught a couple of fish, and I got some potatoes. I can fry them up.'

'Why that's a nice offer,' Tom said. 'And on account of it, I'll clean the fish.'

The next few days passed with Tom coming out to bring the horse and the seed, and coming back the next day with some plow parts Deel needed. Deel began to think he would never get to town, and now he wasn't so sure he wanted to go. Tom was far more comfortable with his family than he was and he was jealous of that and wanted to stay with them and find his place. Tom and Mary Lou talked about all manner of things, and quite comfortably, and the boy had lost all interest in the bow. In fact, Deel had found it and the arrows out under a tree near where the woods firmed up. He took it and put it in the smokehouse. The air was dry in there and it would cure better, though he was uncertain the boy would ever have anything to do with it.

Deel plowed a half-dozen acres of the flowers under, and the next day Tom came out with a wagonload of cured chicken shit, and helped him shovel it across the broken ground. Deel plowed it under and Tom helped Deel plant peas and beans for the fall crop, some hills of yellow crook-neck squash, and a few mounds of watermelon and cantaloupe seed.

That evening they were sitting out in front of the house, Deel in the cane rocker and Tom in a kitchen chair. The boy sat on the ground near Tom and twisted a stick in the dirt. The only light came from the open door of the house, from the lamp inside. When Deel looked over his shoulder, he saw Mary Lou at the washbasin again, doing the dishes, wiggling her ass. Tom looked in that direction once, then looked at Deel, then looked away at the sky, as if memorizing the positions of the stars.

Tom said, 'You and me ain't been huntin' since well before you left.'

'You came around a lot then, didn't you?' Deel said.

Tom nodded. 'I always felt better here than at home. Mama and Daddy fought all the time.'

'I'm sorry about your parents.'

'Well,' Tom said, 'everyone's got a time to die, you know. It can be in all kinds of ways, but sometimes it's just time and you just got to embrace it.'

141

'I reckon that's true.'

'What say you and me go huntin'?' Tom said, 'I ain't had any possum meat in ages.'

'I never did like possum,' Deel said. 'Too greasy.'

'You ain't fixed 'em right. That's one thing I can do, fix up a possum good. 'Course, best way is catch one and pen it and feed it corn for a week or so, then kill it. Meat's better that way, firmer. But I'd settle for shootin' one, showin' you how to get rid of that gamey taste with some vinegar and such, cook it up with some sweet potatoes. I got more sweet potatoes than I know what to do with.'

'Deel likes sweet potatoes,' Mary Lou said.

Deel turned. She stood in the doorway drying her hands on a dish towel. She said, 'That ought to be a good idea, Deel. Goin' huntin'. I wouldn't mind learnin' how to cook up a possum right. You and Tom ought to go, like the old days.'

'I ain't had no sweet potatoes in years,' Deel said.

'All the more reason,' Tom said.

The boy said, 'I want to go.'

'That'd be all right,' Tom said, 'but you know, I think this time I'd like for just me and Deel to go. When I was a kid, he taught me about them woods, and I'd like to go with him, for old times' sake. That all right with you, Winston?'

Winston didn't act like it was all right, but he said, 'I guess.'

★　★　★

142

That night Deel lay beside Mary Lou and said, 'I like Tom, but I was thinkin' maybe we could somehow get it so he don't come around so much.'

'Oh?'

'I know Winston looks up to him, and I don't mind that, but I need to get to know Winston again . . . Hell, I didn't ever know him. And I need to get to know you . . . I owe you some time, Mary Lou. The right kind of time.'

'I don't know what you're talkin' about, Deel. The right kind of time?'

Deel thought for a while, tried to find the right phrasing. He knew what he felt, but saying it was a different matter. 'I know you ended up with me because I seemed better than some was askin'. Turned out I wasn't quite the catch you thought. But we got to find what we need, Mary Lou.'

'What we need?'

'Love. We ain't never found love.'

She lay silent.

'I just think,' Deel said, 'we ought to have our own time together before we start havin' Tom around so much. You understand what I'm sayin', right?'

'I guess so.'

'I don't even feel like I'm proper home yet. I ain't been to town or told nobody I'm back.'

'Who you missin'?'

Deel thought about that for a long time. 'Ain't nobody but you and Winston that I missed, but I need to get some things back to normal . . . I need to make connections so I can set up some credit at the store, maybe some farm trade for things we need next year. But mostly, I just want to be here with you so we can talk. You and Tom talk a lot. I wish we could talk like that. We need to learn how to talk.'

'Tom's easy to talk to. He's a talker. He can talk about anything and make it seem like somethin', but when he's through, he ain't said nothin' . . . You never was a talker before, Deel, so why now?'

'I want to hear what you got to say, and I want you to hear what I got to say, even if we ain't talkin' about nothin' but seed catalogs or pass the beans, or I need some more firewood or stop snoring. Most anything that's got normal about it. So, thing is, I don't want Tom around so much. I want us to have some time with just you and me and Winston, that's all I'm sayin'.'

Deel felt the bed move. He turned to look, and in the dark he saw that Mary Lou was pulling her gown up above her breasts. Her pubic hair looked thick in the dark and her breasts were full and round and inviting.

She said, 'Maybe tonight we could get started on knowing each other better.'

His mouth was dry. All he could say was, 'All right.'

His hands trembled as he unbuttoned his union suit at the crotch and she spread her legs and he climbed on top of her. It only took a moment before he exploded.

'Oh, God,' he said, and collapsed on her, trying to support his weight on his elbows.

'How was that?' she said. 'I feel all right?'

'Fine, but I got done too quick. Oh, girl, it's been so long. I'm sorry.'

'That's all right. It don't mean nothin'.' She patted him stiffly on the back and then twisted a little so that he'd know she wanted him off her.

'I could do better,' he said.

'Tomorrow night.'

'Me and Tom, we're huntin' tomorrow night. He's bringin' a dog, and we're gettin' a possum.'

'That's right . . . Night after.'

'All right, then,' Deel said. 'All right, then.'

He lay back on the bed and buttoned himself up and tried to decide if he felt better or worse. There had been relief, but no fire. She might as well have been a hole in the mattress.

Tom brought a bitch dog with him and a .22 rifle and a croaker sack. Deel gathered up his double barrel from out of the closet and took it out of its leather sheath coated in oil and found it to be in very good condition. He brought it and a sling bag of shells outside. The shells were old, but he had no cause to doubt their ability. They had been stored along with the gun, dry and contained.

The sky was clear and the stars were out and the moon looked like a carved chunk of fresh lye soap, but it was bright, so bright you could see the ground clearly. The boy was in bed, and Deel

145

and Tom and Mary Lou stood out in front of the house and looked at the night.

Mary Lou said to Tom, 'You watch after him, Tom.'

'I will,' Tom said.

'Make sure he's taken care of,' she said.

'I'll take care of him.'

Deel and Tom had just started walking toward the woods when they were distracted by a shadow. An owl came diving down toward the field. They saw the bird scoop up a fat mouse and fly away with it. The dog chased the owl's shadow as it cruised along the ground.

As they watched the owl climb into the bright sky and fly toward the woods, Tom said, 'Ain't nothin' certain in life, is it?'

'Especially if you're a mouse,' Deel said.

'Life can be cruel,' Tom said.

'Wasn't no cruelty in that,' Deel said. 'That was survival. The owl was hungry. Men ain't like that. They ain't like other things, 'cept maybe ants.'

'Ants?'

'Ants and man make war 'cause they can. Man makes all kinds of proclamations and speeches and gives reasons and such, but at the bottom of it, we just do it 'cause we want to and can.'

'That's a hard way to talk,' Tom said.

'Man ain't happy till he kills everything in his path and cuts down everything that grows. He sees something wild and beautiful and wants to hold it down and stab it, punish it 'cause it's wild. Beauty draws him to it, and then he kills it.'

'Deel, you got some strange thinkin',' Tom said.
'Reckon I do.'

'We're gonna kill so as to have somethin' to eat, but unlike the owl, we ain't eatin' no mouse. We're having us a big, fat possum and we're gonna cook it with sweet potatoes.'

They watched as the dog ran on ahead of them, into the dark line of the trees.

When they got to the edge of the woods the shadows of the trees fell over them, and then they were inside the woods, and it was dark in places with gaps of light where the limbs were thin. They moved toward the gaps and found a trail and walked down it. As they went, the light faded, and Deel looked up. A dark cloud had blown in.

Tom said, 'Hell, looks like it's gonna rain. That came out of nowhere.'

'It's a runnin' rain,' Deel said. 'It'll blow in and spit water and blow out before you can find a place to get dry.'

'Think so?'

'Yeah. I seen rain aplenty, and one comes up like this, it's traveling through. That cloud will cry its eyes out and move on, promise you. It ain't even got no lightnin' with it.'

As if in response to Deel's words it began to rain. No lightning and no thunder, but the wind picked up and the rain was thick and cold.

'I know a good place ahead,' Tom said. 'We can

get under a tree there, and there's a log to sit on. I even killed a couple possums there.'

They found the log under the tree, sat down and waited. The tree was an oak and it was old and big and had broad limbs and thick leaves that spread out like a canvas. The leaves kept Deel and Tom almost dry.

'That dog's done gone off deep in the woods,' Deel said, and laid the shotgun against the log and put his hands on his knees.

'He gets a possum, you'll hear him. He sounds like a trumpet.'

Tom shifted the .22 across his lap and looked at Deel, who was lost in thought. 'Sometimes,' Deel said, 'when we was over there, it would rain, and we'd be in trenches, waiting for somethin' to happen, and the trenches would flood with water, and there was big ole rats that would swim in it, and we was so hungry from time to time, we killed them and ate them.'

'Rats?'

'They're same as squirrels. They don't taste as good, though. But a squirrel ain't nothin' but a tree rat.'

'Yeah? You sure?'

'I am.'

Tom shifted on the log, and when he did Deel turned toward him. Tom still had the .22 lying across his lap, but when Deel looked, the barrel was raised in his direction. Deel started to say somethin', like, 'Hey, watch what you're doin','

148

but in that instant he knew what he should have known all along. Tom was going to kill him. He had always planned to kill him. From the day Mary Lou had met him in the field on horseback, they were anticipating the rattle of his dead bones. It's why they had kept him from town. He was already thought dead, and if no one thought different, there was no crime to consider.

'I knew and I didn't know,' Deel said.

'I got to, Deel. It ain't nothin' personal. I like you fine. You been good to me. But I got to do it. She's worth me doin' somethin' like this . . . Ain't no use reaching for that shotgun, I got you sighted; twenty-two ain't much, but it's enough.'

'Winston,' Deel said, 'he ain't my boy, is he?'

'No.'

'He's got a birthmark on his face, and I remember now when you was younger, I seen that same birthmark. I forgot but now I remember. It's under your hair, ain't it?'

Tom didn't say anything. He had scooted back on the log. This put him out from under the edge of the oak canopy, and the rain was washing over his hat and plastering his long hair to the sides of his face.

'You was with my wife back then, when you was eighteen, and I didn't even suspect it,' Deel said, and smiled as if he thought there was humor in it. 'I figured you for a big kid and nothin' more.'

'You're too old for her,' Tom said, sighting down the rifle. 'And you didn't never give her no real attention. I been with her mostly since you left. I just happened to be gone when you come home. Hell, Deel, I got clothes in the trunk there, and you didn't even see 'em. You might know the weather, but you damn sure don't know women, and you don't know men.'

'I don't want to know them, so sometimes I don't know what I know. And men and women, they ain't all that different . . . You ever killed a man, Tom?'

'You'll be my first.'

Deel looked at Tom, who was looking at him along the length of the .22.

'It ain't no easy thing to live with, even if you don't know the man,' Deel said. 'Me, I killed plenty. They come to see me when I close my eyes. Them I actually seen die, and them I imagined died.'

'Don't give me no booger stories. I don't reckon you're gonna come see me when you're dead. I don't reckon that at all.'

It had grown dark because of the rain, and Tom's shape was just a shape. Deel couldn't see his features.

'Tom—'

The .22 barked. The bullet struck Deel in the head. He tumbled over the log and fell where there was rain in his face. He thought just before he dropped down into darkness: It's so cool and clean.

★   ★   ★

150

Deel looked over the edge of the trench where there was a slab of metal with a slot to look through. All he could see was darkness except when the lightning ripped a strip in the sky and the countryside lit up. Thunder banged so loudly he couldn't tell the difference between it and cannon fire, which was also banging away, dropping great explosions near the breast works and into the zigzagging trench, throwing men left and right like dolls.

Then he saw shapes. They moved across the field like a column of ghosts. In one great run they came, closer and closer. He poked his rifle through the slot and took half-ass aim and then the command came and he fired. Machine guns began to burp. The field lit up with their constant red pops. The shapes began to fall. The faces of those in front of the rushing line brightened when the machine guns snapped, making their features devil red. When the lightning flashed they seemed to vibrate across the field. The cannons roared and thunder rumbled and the machine guns coughed and the rifles cracked and men screamed.

Then the remainder of the Germans were across the field and over the trench ramifications and down into the trenches themselves. Hand-to-hand fighting began. Deel fought with his bayonet. He jabbed at a German soldier so small his shoulders failed to fill out his uniform. As the German hung on the thrust of Deel's blade, clutched at the rifle barrel, flares blazed along the length of the trench,

151

and in that moment Deel saw the soldier's chin had bits of blond fuzz on it. The expression the kid wore was that of someone who had just realized this was not a glorious game after all.

And then Deel coughed.

He coughed and began to choke. He tried to lift up, but couldn't, at first. Then he sat up and the mud dripped off him and the rain pounded him. He spat dirt from his mouth and gasped at the air. The rain washed his face clean and pushed his hair down over his forehead. He was uncertain how long he sat there in the rain, but in time, the rain stopped. His head hurt. He lifted his hand to it and came away with his fingers covered in blood. He felt again, pushing his hair aside. There was a groove across his forehead. The shot hadn't hit him solid; it had cut a path across the front of his head. He had bled a lot, but now the bleeding had stopped. The mud in the grave had filled the wound and plugged it. The shallow grave had most likely been dug earlier in the day. It had all been planned out, but the rain was unexpected. The rain made the dirt damp, and in the dark Tom had not covered him well enough. Not deep enough. Not firm enough. And his nose was free. He could breathe. The ground was soft and it couldn't hold him. He had merely sat up and the dirt had fallen aside.

Deel tried to pull himself out of the grave, but was too weak, so he twisted in the loose dirt and lay with his face against the ground. When he was strong enough to lift his head, the rain had passed, the clouds had sailed away, and the moon was bright.

Deel worked himself out of the grave and crawled across the ground toward the log where he and Tom had sat. His shotgun was lying behind the log where it had fallen. Tom had either forgotten the gun or didn't care. Deel was too weak to pick it up.

Deel managed himself onto the log and sat there, his head held down, watching the ground. As he did, a snake crawled over his boots and twisted its way into the darkness of the woods. Deel reached down and picked up the shotgun. It was damp and cold. He opened it and the shells popped out. He didn't try to find them in the dark. He lifted the barrel, poked it toward the moonlight, and looked through it. Clear. No dirt in the barrels. He didn't try to find the two shells that had popped free. He loaded two fresh ones from his ammo bag. He took a deep breath. He picked up some damp leaves and pressed them against the wound and they stuck. He stood up. He staggered toward his house, the blood-stuck leaves decorating his forehead as if he were some kind of forest god.

It was not long before the stagger became a walk. Deel broke free of the woods and onto the path that crossed the field. With the rain gone it was bright again and a light wind had begun to blow. The earth smelled rich, the way it had that night in France when it rained and the lightning flashed and the soldiers came and the damp smell of the earth blended with the biting smell of gunpowder and the odor of death.

He walked until he could see the house, dark like blight in the center of the field. The house appeared extremely small then, smaller than before; it was as if all that had ever mattered to him continued to shrink. The bitch dog came out to meet him but he ignored her. She slunk off and trotted toward the trees he had left behind.

He came to the door, and then his foot was kicking against it. The door cracked and creaked and slammed loudly backward. Then Deel was inside, walking fast. He came to the bedroom door, and it was open. He went through. The window was up and the room was full of moonlight, so brilliant he could see clearly, and what he saw was Tom and Mary Lou lying together in mid-act, and in that moment he thought of his brief time with her and how she had let him have her so as not to talk about Tom anymore. He thought about how she had given herself to protect what she had with Tom. Something moved inside Deel and he recognized it as the core of what man was. He stared at them and they saw him and froze in action. Mary Lou said, 'No,' and Tom leaped up from between her legs, all the way to his feet. Naked as nature, he stood for a moment in the middle of the bed, and then plunged through the open window like a fox down a hole.

Deel raised the shotgun and fired and took out part of the windowsill, but Tom was out and away. Mary Lou screamed. She threw her legs to the side of the bed and made as if to stand, but couldn't. Her legs were too weak. She sat back down and started yelling his name. Something called from deep inside Deel, a long call, deep and dark and certain. A bloody leaf dripped off his forehead. He raised the shotgun and fired. The shot tore into her breast and knocked her sliding across the bed, pushing the back of her head against the wall beneath the window.

Deel stood looking at her. Her eyes were open, her mouth slightly parted. He watched her hair and the sheets turn dark.

He broke open the shotgun and reloaded the double barrel from his ammo sack and went to the door across the way, the door to the small room that was the boy's. He kicked it open. When he came in, the boy, wearing his nightshirt, was crawling through the window. He shot at him, but the best he might have done was riddle the bottom of his feet with pellets. Like his father, Winston was quick through a hole.

Deel stepped briskly to the open window and looked out. The boy was crossing the moonlit field like a jackrabbit, running toward a dark stretch of woods in the direction of town. Deel climbed through the window and began to stride after the boy. And then he saw Tom. Tom was off to the right, running toward where there used to be a deep ravine

155

and a blackberry growth. Deel went after him. He began to trot. He could imagine himself with the other soldiers crossing a field, waiting for a bullet to end it all.

Deel began to close in. Being barefoot was working against Tom. He was limping. Deel thought that Tom's feet were most likely full of grass burrs and were wounded by stones. Tom's moon shadow stumbled and rose, as if it were his soul trying to separate itself from its host.

The ravine and the blackberry bushes were still there. Tom came to the ravine, found a break in the vines, and went over the side of it and down. Deel came shortly after, dropped into the ravine. It was damp there and smelled fresh from the recent rain. Deel saw Tom scrambling up the other side of the ravine, into the dark rise of blackberry bushes on the far side. He strode after him, and when he came to the spot where Tom had gone, he saw Tom was hung in the berry vines. The vines had twisted around his arms and head and they held him as surely as if he were nailed there. The more Tom struggled, the harder the thorns bit and the better the vines held him. Tom twisted and rolled and soon he was facing in the direction of Deel, hanging just above him on the bank of the ravine, supported by the blackberry vines, one arm outstretched, the other pinned against his abdomen, wrapped up like a Christmas present from nature, a gift to what man and the ants liked to do best. He was breathing heavily.

Deel turned his head slightly, like a dog trying to distinguish what it sees. 'You're a bad shot.'

'Ain't no cause to do this, Deel.'

'It's not a matter of cause. It's the way of man,' Deel said.

'What in hell you talkin' about, Deel? I'm askin' you, I'm beggin' you, don't kill me. She was the one talked me into it. She thought you were dead, long dead. She wanted it like it was when it was just me and her.'

Deel took a deep breath and tried to taste the air. It had tasted so clean a moment ago, but now it was bitter.

'The boy got away,' Deel said.

'Go after him, you want, but don't kill me.'

A smile moved across Deel's face. 'Even the little ones grow up to be men.'

'You ain't makin' no sense, Deel. You ain't right.'

'Ain't none of us right,' Deel said.

Deel raised the shotgun and fired. Tom's head went away and the body drooped in the clutch of the vines and hung over the edge of the ravine.

The boy was quick, much faster than his father. Deel had covered a lot of ground in search of him, and he could read the boy's sign in the moonlight, see where the grass was pushed down, see bare footprints in the damp dirt, but the boy had long reached the woods, and maybe the town beyond. He knew that. It didn't matter anymore.

He moved away from the woods and back to

157

the field until he came to Pancake Rocks. They were flat, round chunks of sandstone piled on top of one another and they looked like a huge stack of pancakes. He had forgotten all about them. He went to them and stopped and looked at the top edge of the pancake stones. It was twenty feet from ground to top. He remembered that from when he was a boy. His daddy told him, 'That there is twenty feet from top to bottom. A Spartan boy could climb that and reach the top in three minutes. I can climb it and reach the top in three minutes. Let's see what you can do.'

He had never reached the top in three minutes, though he had tried time after time. It had been important to his father for some reason, some human reason, and he had forgotten all about it until now.

Deel leaned the shotgun against the stones and slipped off his boots and took off his clothes. He tore his shirt and made a strap for the gun, and slung it over his bare shoulder and took up the ammo bag and tossed it over his other shoulder, and began to climb. He made it to the top. He didn't know how long it had taken him, but he guessed it had been only about three minutes. He stood on top of Pancake Rocks and looked out at the night. He could see his house from there. He sat cross-legged on the rocks and stretched the shotgun over his thighs. He looked up at the sky. The stars were bright and the space between them was as deep as forever. If man could, he would tear the stars down, thought Deel.

Deel sat and wondered how late it was. The moon had moved, but not so much as to pull up the sun. Deel felt as if he had been sitting there for days. He nodded off now and then, and in the dream he was an ant, one of many ants, and he was moving toward a hole in the ground from which came smoke and sparks of fire. He marched with the ants toward the hole, and then into the hole they went, one at a time. Just before it was his turn, he saw the ants in front of him turn to black crisps in the fire, and he marched after them, hurrying for his turn, then he awoke and looked across the moonlit field.

He saw, coming from the direction of his house, a rider. The horse looked like a large dog because the rider was so big. He hadn't seen the man in years, but he knew who he was immediately. Lobo Collins. He had been sheriff of the county when he had left for war. He watched as Lobo rode toward him. He had no thoughts about it. He just watched.

Well out of range of Deel's shotgun, Lobo stopped and got off his horse and pulled a rifle out of the saddle boot.

'Deel,' Lobo called. 'It's Sheriff Lobo Collins.'

Lobo's voice moved across the field loud and clear. It was as if they were sitting beside each other. The light was so good he could see Lobo's mustache clearly, drooping over the corners of his mouth.

'Your boy come told me what happened.'

'He ain't my boy, Lobo.'

'Everybody knowed that but you, but wasn't no cause to do what you did. I been up to the house, and I found Tom in the ravine.'

'They're still dead, I assume.'

'You ought not done it, but she was your wife, and he was messin' with her, so you got some cause, and a jury might see it that way. That's something to think about, Deel. It could work out for you.'

'He shot me,' Deel said.

'Well now, that makes it even more different. Why don't you put down that gun, and you and me go back to town and see how we can work things out.'

'I was dead before he shot me.'

'What?' Lobo said. Lobo had dropped down on one knee. He had the Winchester across that knee and with his other hand he held the bridle of his horse.

Deel raised the shotgun and set the stock firmly against the stone, the barrel pointing skyward.

'You're way out of range up there,' Lobo said. 'That shotgun ain't gonna reach me, but I can reach you, and I can put one in a fly's asshole from here to the moon.'

Deel stood up. 'I can't reach you, then I reckon I got to get me a wee bit closer.'

Lobo stood up and dropped the horse's reins. The horse didn't move. 'Now don't be a damn fool, Deel.'

Deel slung the shotgun's makeshift strap over his shoulder and started climbing down the back of the stones, where Lobo couldn't see him. He came down quicker than he had gone up, and he didn't even feel where the stones had torn his naked knees and feet.

When Deel came around the side of the stone, Lobo had moved only slightly, away from his horse, and he was standing with the Winchester held down by his side. He was watching as Deel advanced, naked and committed. Lobo said, 'Ain't no sense in this, Deel. I ain't seen you in years, and now I'm gonna get my best look at you down the length of a Winchester. Ain't no sense in it.'

'There ain't no sense to nothin',' Deel said, and walked faster, pulling the strapped shotgun off his shoulder.

Lobo backed up a little, then raised the Winchester to his shoulder, said, 'Last warnin', Deel.'

Deel didn't stop. He pulled the shotgun stock to his hip and let it rip. The shot went wide and fell across the grass like hail, some twenty feet in front of Lobo. And then Lobo fired.

Deel thought someone had shoved him. It felt that way. That someone had walked up unseen beside him and had shoved him on the shoulder. Next thing he knew he was lying on the ground looking up at the stars. He felt pain, but not like the pain he had felt when he realized what he was.

A moment later the shotgun was pulled from his hand, and then Lobo was kneeling down next to him with the Winchester in one hand and the shotgun in the other.

'I done killed you, Deel.'

'No,' Deel said, spitting up blood. 'I ain't alive to kill.'

'I think I clipped a lung,' Lobo said, as if proud of his marksmanship. 'You ought not done what you done. It's good that boy got away. He ain't no cause of nothin'.'

'He just ain't had his turn.'

Deel's chest was filling up with blood. It was as if someone had put a funnel in his mouth and poured it into him. He tried to say something more, but it wouldn't come out. There was only a cough and some blood; it splattered warm on his chest. Lobo put the weapons down and picked up Deel's head and laid it across one of his thighs so he wasn't choking so much.

'You got a last words, Deel?'

'Look there,' Deel said.

Deel's eyes had lifted to the heavens, and Lobo looked. What he saw was the night and the moon and the stars. 'Look there. You see it?' Deel said. 'The stars are fallin'.'

Lobo said, 'Ain't nothin' fallin', Deel,' but when he looked back down, Deel was gone.

JUVENAL NYX

WALTER MOSLEY

1.

She named me Juvenal Nyx and made me a child of the night.

I was attending a Saturday-night meeting at Splinter – the Radical Faction Bookstore, presenting the Amalgamation of Black Student Unions' stand on when and how we would agree to work with white radical organizations. For too long, we believed, had our systems, movements, and ultimate liberation been co-opted by white groups pretending, maybe even believing, that they were our friends and allies. But in the end we were saddled with goals outside our communities, diverted into pathways that abandoned our people's needs and ends.

The speech went very well, and the people there, both black and white, seemed to take my words seriously. I felt that the articulation of our goals was in itself a victory, a line drawn in the quick-drying cement that had been poured into the frame of the coming revolution.

I was very young.

She approached me after the series of speakers had made their comments, pleas, pledges, and calls for solidarity. She was short and white, pale actually, wearing loose-fitting jeans and a faded blue T-shirt. She wasn't pretty and didn't do much in the way of make-up. Only her eyes were arresting. They were very dark, maybe even black, with a patina of silver glowing underneath now and then.

'I like what you had to say,' she told me. 'Any man must stand on his own before relying on the help of others.'

Her use of the word *man* made me curious. I assumed, from the way she dressed, that she'd be a feminist.

'That's right,' I said. 'The black man doesn't need Mr Charlie to pave the way. It's the white man who wants our power.'

'Everyone wants your strength,' she said.

With that she looked into my eyes and touched my left wrist. Her fingers were cold.

'Will you have coffee with me?' she asked.

No, was in my throat but 'Yes' came out of my mouth. 'Only for just a bit,' I added awkwardly. 'I have to get back to my people and report.'

'I am from Rumania,' she told me at the café across the street from the bookstore. 'My parents have died and I am alone in the world. I work sometimes doing freelance copyediting and I go to meetings at night.'

'Political meetings?' I asked, wondering at the moonlight that emanated from behind her eyes.

'No kind in particular,' she said, dismissing all content with the shrug of a shoulder. 'I go to readings and lectures, art openings and the like. I just want to be around people, to belong for a while.'

'You live alone?'

'Yes. I prefer it that way. Relationships seem to lose their meaning, and after a few weeks I crave solitude again.'

'How old are you?' I asked, wondering at the odd way in which she spoke.

'I am young,' she said, smiling as if there was a joke hidden among her words. 'Come home with me for the night.'

'I don't chase after white girls, Julia,' I said, because that was the name she'd given me.

'Come home with me,' she said again.

'I'll walk you to your door,' I said, reluctantly, 'but after that I have to get back to Central House.'

'What is Central House?'

'The officers and senior members of the BSUs around the city have rented a brownstone in Harlem. We live together and prepare for whatever's coming.'

She smiled at my words and stood.

'Julia,' a man said when we were halfway down the block from the café. 'Wait up.'

He was tall and brawny, white and blond.

He might have been a football player at some university, maybe the one I was attending.

'Martin,' she said by way of a tepid greeting.

'Where you going?' He had a thick gauze wad taped to his left forearm.

When she didn't answer he gave me an evil look.

'This is my, my girlfriend, dude,' he said.

I didn't reply. Instead I was preparing for a fight I didn't think I could win. He was very big and I am, at best, a middleweight.

'Just walk away and you won't get hurt,' the footballer added.

His tone had a pleading quality to it. This made him seem all the more dangerous.

'Hey, man,' I said. 'I just met the lady, but you aren't gonna make me go anywhere.'

He reached for me and I got ready to throw the hardest punch I could. I wasn't about to let that white boy make me turn tail and run.

'Martin, stop,' Julia said. Each syllable was the sound of a hammer driving a nail.

Martin's fingers splayed out like a fan and he drew the hand back as if it had been burned.

'Go away,' she said, 'and don't bother me again.'

Martin was well over six feet tall and weighed maybe two-forty, most of which was muscle. He shook like a man resisting a strong wind. The muscles of his neck bunched up and corded and he grimaced, exposing his teeth in a skull-like grin. After a minute or so of this strain, Martin turned his back to us and staggered from the sidewalk into the street and away. Cowering as he stumbled off, he gave the impression of a man reeling from a beating.

'You were ready to fight him,' Julia said.

I didn't answer.

'He would have hurt you,' she stated.

With that she took my arm and walked me across downtown Manhattan to the pedestrian entrance of the Brooklyn Bridge. I didn't question our walk. There was a buildup of energy in my blood and muscles from the fight I'd almost had, from fear of the pounding I would have surely received.

On the way she told me about her life in Rumania, her escape from the Communists to Munich where she lived with Gypsies for a time. It was a cool October evening and I listened, feeling no need to respond. For her part, she held on to my arm happily prattling about a life that seemed like a story out of a book.

When we got to the other side, she walked me to where there were many warehouses and few residences. We came to a stairwell leading down to a doorway below the surface of the street. She pushed the door open without using a key.

We went down a long hallway until coming to stairs that took us down at least three more levels. There we came to another hall and then to a door that she produced a key for.

★   ★   ★

It was a small, dimly lit room with a maple table in one corner and a single mattress on the floor. There were no windows, of course, and the room smelled dry and stale, like a tomb that had been sealed for centuries.

The door closed behind me and I turned to look Julia in the eye. The moons there were luminescent and her smile took my breath away. She shucked the blue T-shirt, stepped out of the loose pants, and she was naked. I realized as I lunged for her that this uncontrolled sexuality had been coming on ever since Martin had threatened me. I pulled down my pants and Julia started laughing. I dragged her to the small bed and we were together. My pants were around my ankles. My shoes were still on my feet but I couldn't take the time to remove them. I had to be in her. I had to fuck her and to keep on fucking. Nothing could stop me. Even my orgasm only slowed down the gyrating urgency for a moment or two.

All the while Julia was laughing and talking to me in some foreign tongue. Now and again she'd pull my hair back and examine my eyes with those eerie lights in hers.

I writhed on top of her while she entwined me with her cold legs and arms. I could not stop. I could not pull away. For the first time in my life, I felt, I knew what freedom was. I understood that this passion was the only thing that touched the core of my being.

★　　★　　★

I awoke not remembering having lost consciousness, yet I must have passed out, because I was now in another room in a bed with a frame. My wrists and ankles were chained to the four corners of the bed and I was naked.

This room was also windowless and stale. It felt as if I was far underground, but I yelled anyway. I screamed and hollered until my throat was raw, but no one came. No one heard me.

As hours went past I thrashed and called out, but the chains were strong and the walls thick. There was a columnlike yellow candle burning for the little light Julia had left me, and I wondered if I was meant to die in that underground tomb.

At times I worried that this was some white supremacist plot against the BSU of New York. Had they captured me to make a statement? Were they going to lynch me or burn me? Would I be a martyr for the cause?

It was many hours later when the door came open and Julia walked in. I yelled for all I was worth before she could close the door, but she wasn't bothered. She smiled and came to sit next to me on the bed.

She was wearing a red velvet robe that flowed all the way down to her bare feet. There was a hood, but it hung down behind her head.

'This is a room within a room that is itself within a larger room,' she said. 'We are far underground and no one can hear you.'

'Why you got me chained down like this?' I asked, trying to keep the fear out of my voice.

In answer, she stood up, letting the sumptuous robe fall to the floor. She was as naked as I. The breath left my lungs, but I don't know if it was her nakedness or those eyes that left me stunned.

She smiled again and knelt down at my side. She moved her head quickly and bit into my left forearm.

I have spent many days over the next few paragraphs of description.

How can I explain a feeling completely foreign, a feeling that pushed every emotion I could possibly experience past the threshold of my ability to bear it? The pain was a song that I cried out to in cracked harmony. The flow of blood was not only my life but the lives of all who came before me. Her quivering joy was a wild animal in my chest clawing and ripping to escape my silly so-called civilized existence.

My back arched upward and I cried out for release – and for the pain to continue. I wanted to bleed into Julia more than I had craved sex. I was an infant again – so excited by the new sensations of life that I needed the chains to contain my ecstasy.

When I slumped back to the mattress, I no longer existed. I was the husk of the cocoon of a moth that had transformed itself from worm to flight. I was filled with nothing, surrounded by nothing. I was not dead because I had never truly lived. The flailing larvae and the fluttering bug had used my inert being merely for the transition, leaving me nothing but emptiness, like the transient aftermath of a weak smile.

'Juvenal Nyx,' a voice whispered.

'What?' I rasped.

'That is your name.'

I drifted for many hours that seemed like weeks or months. I was not unconscious or asleep but neither was I aware of the world around me. In this limbolike ether I was approached by various entities representing sentients that claimed no race, sex, or species.

'You are in danger of knowledge,' one such being, who seemed to be a yellow nimbus with no origin, said.

'Of being found out?' I asked in some fashion other than speech.

'Of knowing,' the empty halo of light replied.

'I don't understand.'

'Then there is still hope.'

'Juvenal,' a human voice said.

I opened my eyes and saw Julia, again in jeans and T-shirt, sitting at the foot of the bed. She was staring at me in a way that I can only describe as hungry.

'Julia.'

The smile did not leaven her rapacious eyes.

'You are a sweet man.' Though she whispered these words I heard them as a shout down a long, echoing hallway. 'I scented your sweetness before I entered the bookstore. I came there for you.'

'You let Martin go after biting his arm,' I said, 'didn't you?'

'I let them all go after the first bite,' she said. 'Hundreds of them . . . thousands.'

I, the old me, sighed in relief.

'And I want to let you go too,' she said, 'but your blood sings to me.'

She touched my inner right thigh halfway between knee and groin. Her cold fingers rubbed that spot. Just the touch caused an echo of dark delight.

She bent over me and hovered an inch away from the place she'd touched, her lunar eyes gazing into mine.

'Bite it,' I said in spite of the panic in my chest.

Over the next four days she drank from my other arm and leg, and finally from my abdomen just above the naval. I was in constant ecstasy and dread. I didn't eat, sleep, or feel the need to relieve myself. My body was in a state of total repose except when she fed on my blood.

'We never drink much,' she told me one evening after having feasted. She was lying back with her head against my thigh, savoring her perversion. 'It doesn't take much to keep us alive. We aren't like your people who need to kill and squander to keep themselves going. Just a cupful of fresh blood and we can live for many days.'

'Then why do you bite me every day?' I asked. There was no fear in my question. Just after the bite I felt drugged, yielding. I simply wanted to understand what she was saying.

She sat up. Her once-black eyes were now white with that strange light.

'We cannot multiply like you,' she said. 'We must create our progeny. Our bite contains a drug that would quickly become a poison to most people. To some, however, those that are sweet, we can pass on the trait that makes us unique. These we call our lovers.'

'You love me?'

'I love your taste.'

'You mean like I love a good steak?'

A wave of disgust passed over her face.

'No, not death, but the life that lives in you and in me simultaneously. The feeling of being that I carry in me that is you. This, this taste is the most exquisite experience that any living creature can know.'

'What about Martin?' I asked when I got the feeling she might leave. I hated it when she left after biting me. It was as if I needed her there with me to keep the darkness away.

'Our bite, like I said, is a drug. It makes those we feed on want us. Usually they forget or remember us as a dream, but sometimes they stalk us. This is one possible consequence of the symbiosis between us. I made the mistake of taking you to the place where Martin had met me. His hunger is strong, but if I were to bite him again he would certainly die.'

'How long ago did you bite him?'

'Two years.'

'And the wound still needed a bandage?'

'Probably not. Sometimes they wear the dressing as a reminder.'

'Do you . . . ,' I began, but she put her cold hand on my forehead and I passed out.

When I awoke, the morning after the last bite, the chains had been removed. On a single straight-backed chair I found my clothes – neatly folded. Lying across the soft pile was a cream-colored envelope with the name JUVENAL NYX printed on it. The room was quiet and I knew somehow that Julia was gone for good.

My bites throbbed but didn't hurt.

I rushed out of the door that led into a hallway that completely encompassed my cell. There was a door from that hall into another corridor that surrounded the first hallway. There was no furniture or even a carpet in the two buffering halls. The only other room I found was a small toilet. Seeing this I realized that my body was coming back to me and I had to go.

Dear Juvenal,
You are mine from now until the far-off day when either you or I cease to exist. That may not be for many years, even centuries. You will

discover many things about yourself over the next weeks and months. Do not fear them. Do not despair. You are mine as if you came from my own womb and I am yours, though we cannot see each other for a long time. Trust in your instincts and your urges. Give in to your hungers and passions. One day we will be together again – when it is safe for both of us. These rooms are now yours. Use them as I have. I love you,
Julia

The letter was written with a fountain pen and each word was wrought for me.

I went back into the cell and looked around. The floors were bare, unfinished pine. The bed was simple. There was only the one chair. That room could have been a poem about Julia's life and now mine.

I sat down hearing far-off music, like cellos, in the distance. After a while I realized that this music was the singing in my blood.

After a long time of sitting there, wondering what drug she put in her mouth before biting me, I stood up and walked away from her subterranean chamber, never intending to return.

The day was bright, glaring. Everything sounded crisp and loud. I had been in darkness for so long that my eyes hurt and the sun burned against my skin.

But there was also a crystalline quality to the air and vistas. I crossed the bridge feeling light, weightless. The people around me seemed burly and somewhat bumbling. I felt friendly toward them. I was halfway across the Brooklyn Bridge before I realized that I hadn't thought about race once that day. White, black, and brown, they all seemed the same to me.

I chided myself to snap out of it and see the political and racial landscape as I knew it was. I tried to tell myself that my imprisonment had damaged my sense of reality, that Julia had robbed me of my ability to see clearly.

But try as I might I couldn't find fault with the men and women going on their way. And Julia . . . her moony eyes and slight accent brought no anger or fear, recrimination or desire for revenge.

I walked on feeling lighter and happier with each step. The world seemed to be singing some joyous hymn to its own life and destiny. The birds and bugs and even the chemical scents in the air made me feel nostalgic for something that had passed away but lived on in sense memory.

I laughed and did a little jig as I went.

I decided to walk all the way up to Harlem and Central House.

I felt like some kind of prince walking up crowded Fifth Avenue. The people were my unwitting subjects and I was beneficent royalty. In amongst them, now and again, I saw bright-colored coronas reminding me of the yellow halo that had warned me about knowledge.

When I got to Central Park, the song in the sky turned strident. It was howling, but I didn't mind it. The trees whispered of their age and gravity. They had gone one way while I had taken the opposite direction. There was a thrumming in my blood and I was so light-headed that I had to take a seat on a park bench.

I was grinning at the people going past. Some glanced at me with worried looks on their faces. Long ago, last week, I would have said that it was because I was a black man, filled with the purpose of my race, but then I thought that they couldn't possibly understand the experience that flowed in my veins.

The sun was screaming at me and I decided to stand. It was only then that I realized how weak I was. I fell face forward to the pavement. It didn't hurt because I was unconscious before I hit the ground.

Somewhere the sun was setting. Its final shout over the horizon was followed by a silence so profound that I was yanked out of sleep, as if someone had dumped a hundred pounds of ice on my bare skin. I leaped up from the hospital bed and gazed out of the window into the burgeoning darkness of twilight.

'What's wrong with you, guy?' a man said.

I turned to see him. He was one of six other

men in beds around the room, a white man with a gray beard and a darker, though still somewhat gray, mustache.

'How did I get here?' I asked.

'They just dragged you in. We thought you was dead.'

I was still dressed. The excitement of the day was replaced by the certainty of night. The thrill that filled me was dark and dangerous.

I was in the street before I realized that I had no shoes on my feet. But I wasn't bothered by the touch of my skin on the concrete and asphalt.

I headed back to the park. Once there I searched out my prey.

She was a young brown-skinned woman walking down a quiet lane. There was no fear emanating from her. I headed in her direction and, while passing, I put an arm around her waist, pulled her to me, and bit, with a lower tooth I'd never had before, into her neck. It was a pinprick, a small wound that would heal quickly. She fought me for all of eight seconds and then I felt her hand caress the back of my neck.

'Who are you?' she whispered. 'What are you doing to me?'

Her blood flowed slowly into my mouth. It was the richest, most sumptuous meal I'd ever had. It was steak and butter and thick red wine that gods ate on the high holidays of their divinity.

'Please,' she whispered in a wavering voice.

'What's happening to me? I feel it everywhere,' and she rubbed her body against mine.

I drank more and more.

She told me things in that park while people wandered past thinking that we were lovers who couldn't wait for closed doors.

As I tasted her rich bounty, she whispered the secrets of her life. Her desires and disappointments, loves and mistakes flowed as her blood. I realized somewhere in the back of my mind that I was somehow feeding on her soul as well as the serum of her life.

This delightful experience lasted for a quarter hour and then suddenly the tooth retracted painfully into my lower gum. I pulled back from her and she reached out for me.

'Who are you?' she asked.

'Juvenal Nyx,' I said.

'What did you do to me?' She brought the fingers of her right hand to her neck.

'It's a drug.'

'I,' she hesitated, 'I want more.'

'Meet me here tomorrow at the same time and I will bring it to you.'

She was about to say something else, but I put a finger to her lips.

'Go,' I said and she obeyed immediately.

I was running through the park with all the fleet lightness of a young deer or the quick-footed predator on its trail. I was laughing and uncontainable.

My first prey would forget me. If she didn't, if she came back, I would not return to that spot for many weeks. I knew, somehow, that the drug of my bite would turn toxic in her veins if I ever bit her again.

I sped all the way to Harlem, but when I got to the street where Central House stood I balked. For the first time I understood, in my intellect, that things had changed. I had been going on my senses up until that block. But then I realized that I couldn't just walk into the political commune in bare feet, with blood on my breath.

I went into the alley of the building across the street and scaled the wall with little difficulty. When I reached the rooftop I hunkered down, black skin in gathering darkness, to spy on my friends.

Cecil Bontemps and Minerva Jenkins walked out of the front door of the house late in the evening. I concentrated on them with all of my senses. They talked about the meeting they'd just quit. It was a summit about me, my disappearance. They mentioned a white girl I was seen leaving with.

'Jimmy was always a flake,' Cecil said. 'Prob'ly shacked up and high as a kite with that chick.'

An animal growled and I started, looking around the empty roof. It was only then that I realized the bestial noise had come from the anger in me.

'Jimmy don't get high,' Minnie said. 'You know that. Something's happened to him. We should do like Troy says and go to the police.'

'We cain't have the police rummagin' around Central,' he said. 'What if they found our weapons?'

We had been stockpiling rifles and ammunition for the coming revolution. We kept them in a trunk in the basement, ready for the day that martial law was declared on the Black Man.

'We got to do something, Cecil.'

'Okay. Yeah. All right. Let's go down to that bookstore again.'

I stayed on that roof for three days eavesdropping on my onetime comrades. In the day, the sun would rise, bellowing across the sky, and I'd fall into a coma after a while. At night I roused and watched my friends as if they were prey.

On the fourth evening I chased a young man down an alley three blocks north of Central House. I yoked him in a doorway and bit into his shoulder. He whimpered and cried as I drank of the serum of his life. It felt uncomfortably sexual. I realized that unless it was necessary, I'd prefer the blood of women.

'What did you do to me?' His speech was slurred, but he was still afraid.

'Go,' I said in a deep voice that was alien to me. He ran.

I'd forgotten about Central House by that time. For the rest of the night I prowled the streets, looking but not wanting, a danger but not a threat.

At dawn I returned to the Brooklyn warehouse

where Julia had taken me. Two floors below the room she'd first taken me to was the tomblike chamber that would be home from then on. She'd left the key to the door in my pocket.

In the darkness, far below the street, I could hear the faraway singing of the sun. I felt safe in my vault – dangerous too.

2.

That was thirty-three years ago, October 1976. Since then I've inhabited the underground chamber that Julia somehow owned. The title had been signed over to me, and I lived there, sleeping in that bed or sitting on the straight-backed chair, going out now and again for a cupful of blood from some unwary pedestrian. Sometimes I'd bite them just enough to introduce the drug into their system, then use their money to let a hotel room where slowly, over the course of the evening, I would lick their necks and growl like a great wolf.

I have killed no one and discovered many things about my mutation.

One very important detail is that I heal very quickly.

I found this out one evening when a gang of young men decided to attack me and the woman I was feeding on in Prospect Park. There were eight of them, but I was at full strength and so fought them off after some effort. I realized later that I had been stabbed three times in the chest.

Certainly my lung was pierced and possibly I'd sustained damage to my heart.

I considered going to the hospital, but something kept me from human company when I was wounded and so I went home to die.

For many days I lay on the floor of my chamber feeling the pain in my chest. But after a week or so I revived enough so that I could go out and feed. Now all that's left of my fatal wounds are three whitish scars on my chest.

I don't read books or go to movies, watch television or follow the news. The only human contact I've had up until quite recently has been primarily limited to the whispering euphoria of my victims. I've fed every few days or so and have lived on the sustenance of human blood and the soul seepage when they are under my sway. I can sit for days in my underground chamber savoring the soft murmurings of my victims. Their words about secret desires and unfulfilled dreams imbue me with the possibilities of a life that has been denied me. Sometimes I drift for hours in the secrets told me from swooning lips. I can see the images that they remember and feel the emotions they have hidden from everyone else.

For the first few years I only went after women because of the intimate nature of my bite. But as time has gone by I have also preyed upon some men. My taste for blood has been refined and I seek out certain flavors and scents. Some nights I go out and there is no one for me. And though

I prefer young women, there are others who demand notice.

I have discovered other things about my nature. I am, for instance, allergic to the full moon. Those nights, if I am exposed to lunar regency, I develop a fever and a headache so powerful that I am blinded by its potency. If I go out in the full moon, I remain incapacitated for over a week.

This is how I found out another quirk in my physical characteristics. When the fever is upon me I am weak, so much so that most normal people can fend off my attack. And because the malady lasts for so long I am further weakened by the subsequent lack of sustenance. In this diminished state I am forced to seek out quarry that is likewise incapacitated.

After the first time I was weakened by the lunar allergy, I came upon an old woman confined to a wheelchair who had been left for a while by an unprofessional attendant. The attendant had gone down to the water not far from my crypt and was talking at a phone booth. While she was there I snuck up behind the old woman and bit.

Her dreams were fragmented and her blood thin, but it was all I could do. I hoped that she would not die from my attack. I find that since my transformation I have an instinctual reverence for life in all its myriad forms. Spiders and roaches, rats and human beings all have a right to life in my eyes. I drank half a dram of the old woman's tasteless blood and hurried away to revive.

Four weeks later I saw the woman walking with a new nurse. She was healthy for a woman her age and chattering happily with the new helper. I realized then that my bite has certain curative properties. I remember smiling at my elderly prey as I walked past. She looked as if she recognized something about me, though that should have been impossible seeing that I'd attacked her from behind.

Another part of my life has been the coronas, empty circles of light that are seemingly invisible to the human eye. They come in every color and have a variety of natures. Some are predatory, attacking and destroying others of their kind. Some are able to communicate with me. Not many approve of my being. I don't know if it is that they don't want to be seen or if they are repulsed by my urges and needs. Regardless – we exist on different planes and cannot touch or affect each other in any physical way.

The only corona I recognize is the yellow being that approached me while Julia was making me into Juvenal Nyx. It appears to me at times, imparting cryptic messages about knowledge and perception.

'You are on the path to knowing what should be secret,' it has said more than once – not in words but the meaning has crossed the void between us and settled on my mind.

I paid little attention to these messages until nine months ago.

I was down on Water Street watching the old woman who had been wheelchair bound before I bit her. By now she no longer had a nurse and was herself looking after what might have been a toddler grandchild.

I felt paternal toward the old woman and ancient in my bones. It was a summer evening and the sun was far enough behind the horizon that I didn't have to worry about light-headedness.

'Come,' a voice in my head said.

I turned and saw the jagged yellow corona floating in the air behind me.

I stood to follow, but the strange piping voice then said, 'Later.'

'Come later?' I asked the empty air.

The corona disappeared and I went back to my subterranean home to wait for it to reappear. I had eaten quite recently and so had no need to hunt.

Late that night the yellow light appeared in my chamber. It did not speak but led the way up and out of my home. It brought me to the pedestrian entrance of the Brooklyn Bridge and faded from sight.

I walked out on the pathway. It was late in the evening and unseasonably cool, so I was one of the few people out strolling. When I had just passed the first pylon of the bridge, I caught sight of a woman who had climbed out on a girder and was now about to jump.

My condition makes me quite agile and strong.

I ran straight out across the girder and caught the woman by her wrist just as she was falling over the side. I pulled her up and held her around the waist in case she wanted to try again.

'This is not a good idea,' I said. My voice was dry and cracked, as I rarely spoke out loud.

'What's wrong with your eyes?' she replied.

For some reason this made me smile.

'You were going to kill yourself,' I said.

'That's not going to happen now,' she said, 'obviously.' She looked back over the side a little wistfully. 'You want to buy me some coffee?'

Her name was Iridia Lamone. She'd been born and raised in northern California and had come to New York to study painting.

'I married my high school boyfriend, but we don't really get along anymore,' she told me at the Telltale Bean in Brooklyn Heights.

There was no hint in her demeanor that she'd just tried to kill herself.

My senses were in such a heightened state from the corona and saving a life that it took me a while to identify the potency of her scent. There was a bouquet to her blood that I had never experienced before. It drew me on a primal level. I found myself having to hold back from biting her right there in the coffee shop.

'Is that why you tried to kill yourself?' I asked.

'Tarver is always depressed,' she said. 'He mopes around the house when he's not working and he's

187

jealous of my painting. Whenever I'm working he finds some way to interfere. Either he needs my attention or finds something wrong with the house. He comes in with plumbing problems and unpaid bills – anything to distract me, anything so he doesn't have to feel bad about me living my life.'

'That's not really an answer,' I said.

'I don't owe you an answer, Juvenal. What kind of name is that anyway?'

'I was very sick once,' I said. 'A woman saved my life and after that she suggested that I go by the name Juvenal Nyx.'

'Why?'

'It means "child of the night."'

'It's like you were named after a poem.'

'The disease left me with certain allergies to natural light. If I go out in the sun, I get weak. If I stay out long enough, I lose consciousness.'

'And do you get a rash?' she asked. She was smiling, less than an hour out from her attempted suicide.

'No, but I get a kind of allergy to bright moon-light too.'

'Wow. And you call this better?'

'It is best. I know the parameters of my exist-ence and experience ecstasy every night.'

This was true though I had never spoken it. I wasn't cursed or debilitated. I didn't miss my family or friends. The life I had known decades before seemed to me like a rat trapped in a researcher's maze. My sex, my race, my repetitious existence – these were the chains of mortality, the bonds that I had shrugged.

'Ecstasy?' she uttered.

The look in her eyes told me that I loved her. The scent on her breath was the odor of procreation.

'Why did you try to jump?' I asked.

'It just all came together,' she said in a matter-of-fact tone. 'I didn't want to go home to Tarver and I was sure that I'd never paint again.'

'Why not just leave him?'

'Because that would kill him and then I'd have his death on my head.'

'And so you'll do it again?'

'I don't think so,' she mused.

Iridia had dark bronze skin and large almond-shaped eyes. Her gold-brown hair was long and thick, tied back into a braid that was reminiscent of a broad rope.

'Why not?' I asked.

'Because I believe in fate and you saved me at the last possible moment, when I had given up.'

'Because I saved you, you won't try to kill yourself again?'

'Not just because you saved me,' she said. She reached across the table and took my cold hand in hers. 'I had already jumped. I could feel the gravity give way beneath me. I had given myself up to death and then you caught me and held me.'

We gazed into each other's eyes and I was lost.

'Would you ever give up the sun?' I asked.

'Never,' she said. 'I'm a watercolorist and I need it to feed my heart.'

'But you were willing to die,' I argued.

'Not anymore.'

It was at that moment I came into control of my life. All that had gone before was immediately obvious and clear. I had existed as human being for twenty-two years following the pathways that were prescribed. I had a race and gender, nationality and language. I was what the world made me. And then, when Julia came, I was what she made me. So tenuous was my existence that the transformation she wrought tore apart the paper-thin fabric of my identity. I hadn't even been able to maintain my name. I had, for fifty-five years, never made a choice on my own. I was always led, always formed by others' hands. Even my school politics came from a knee-jerk desire to belong.

Iridia had found her identity with a simple gesture, had changed her direction when she saw a new light.

'Will you come home with me tonight?' I asked.

'But I have to go back to Tarver in the morning.'

'All right.'

I wanted more than anything to bite Iridia, to change her from human being to predator child. The fang in my lower jaw throbbed as we kissed, as we made love, but I would not bring it out.

I knew, instinctively, that if I turned her, we

190

would have to separate. That is why Julia left me before I awakened to my powers. The scent of love for us is fatal. Once we make our children, we are compelled to devour them.

This hunger yawned in me like the chasm under Iridia when she leaped from the Brooklyn Bridge; it is why I had never come across a being like myself. We are very rare. Our love is truly a hunger, and we, like our human forebears, are our own best prey.

'What's your real name, Juvenal Nyx?' she asked in the early hours of the morning after we'd made love for hours.

I had to think for a few moments before saying, haltingly, 'James Tremont of Baltimore.'

'You don't sound sure,' she said before kissing my naval.

'It's been so long.'

'You're not that old.'

'I'm older than I look.'

Her nostrils flared and the gland under my jaw swelled with venom. I pressed against it and kissed her left nipple.

'Bite it,' she whispered.

'A little later,' I said.

'I want it now.'

'How will I ever get you to come back if I don't make you wait?'

She sat up in the bed, in the empty underground room.

'I've never met a man like you,' she said.

'Then we're even,' I replied, thinking that I hadn't talked so much in decades.

'You really don't need music or books or even paintings on the wall?'

'For a long time I thought that the only things I needed were food and sleep.'

'And now?'

'So much more that I can't even begin to articulate it.'

'I'll have to tell Tarver about tonight,' she said softly.

'Yeah.'

'I won't leave him.'

I wanted to tell her that the love wrenching my chest could never live with her – my hunger for her soul was too great.

'Will we see each other again?' I asked.

'I won't leave you either,' she said with certainty.

'Why not? You hardly know me.'

'I know you better than I've known any man,' she said. 'You saved my life. And I think that's what you were made for – saving lives.'

3.

I took an office on the top floor of the Antwerp Building and put up a sign that read: JUVENAL NYX: PROBLEM SOLVER.

I fastened little business cards to phone booths and bulletin boards around the city, had Iridia's

192

brother, Montrose, make me a small Web site, and took out an ad in two free papers. I *borrowed* the money for these investments from some of my wealthier victims. I plan to pay them back and so have chosen to overlook the undue influence I had over them.

I decided on the path of self-employment because this is against the nature of my being. Creatures like me are supposed to be hidden in the night, secreted away from the world in general. We're supposed to live off humanity, not aid people with their real and imagined plights.

It was time for me to go against the tide of my fate.

My business hours are from sunset to dawn, and I will listen to any problem, any problem at all – from severe acne to the threat of death or imprisonment. I accept and reject jobs, collect fees based on the client's ability to pay, and spend every weekend with Iridia.

I find missing persons, cure a variety of minor illnesses, and even save a life now and then.

Tarver Lamone hates me, but I don't worry about him. I can usually sense danger when it's near and it's pretty hard to do me harm. I worry about Iridia sometimes, but she is so certain about right and wrong, and her own indecipherable path, that I have not figured out how to say no to her.

And I am addicted to her nearness. Once, when she had to go home to California for three weeks, I fell into a state of near catatonia that lasted for almost a month. It took Iridia and Montrose breaking into my subterranean condo and her sitting with me for hours to bring me back to consciousness.

It doesn't sound like the good life, I know, but it has its bright sides. Every day I get calls from people who need someone like me. I've helped children with their homework and ladies shake their stalkers. I cured one man of acrophobia and permanently paralyzed a serial killer who wanted to stop his trade.

Everything was going fine until one early morning, at six minutes past twelve, when a woman walked into my office.

I'm six feet and one half inch in height. She was quite a bit taller than I, with skin whiter than maggots' flesh. Her hair was luxurious, long and black. She might have been beautiful if it hadn't been for the intensity of her laser green eyes. The gown she wore was either black or green, maybe both, and her high-heeled shoes seemed to be made from red glass.

'Mr Nyx?' she asked.

'Yes,' I said, feeling an unfamiliar wave of fear.

'You're young.'

'I'm older than I look.'

She glanced around my office. The décor was much like my underground home. There were three straight-backed oak chairs and a small round oak table under the window that looked out on

Brooklyn. The only decoration that hung on the wall was a watercolor of a patch of weeds in the bright sun.

'May I sit?' she asked. Her voice was neither masculine nor feminine, hardly was it human, it sounded so rich and deep.

'Certainly,' I said.

She lowered herself into the closest chair and I sat across from her. She looked into my eyes and I concentrated on not looking away. This made her smile. It was a predatory smile – on this subject I consider myself an expert.

She was beautiful in the way that fire is, dangerous and untouchable.

Her nostrils flared and then, after a minute had passed, she handed me a card that read MAHEY X. DEMOLA in red lettering at the lower left-hand corner.

That was all, no job title, profession, address, or phone. There was no e-mail or emblem. If you didn't know what that name meant, then you didn't know anything.

'How can I help you, Ms Demola?'

She smiled and stared for another spate of seconds.

'The painting surprises me,' she said at last.

'Why?'

'Your hours, your profession. You don't seem like a sun worshipper.'

'My girlfriend's a painter. She gave me that for an office-warming present.'

'Serious?' she said.

'Come again?'

'Is it serious between you?'

'Why are you here, Ms Demola?'

'I've lost my pet.' Her smile would seduce emperors and frighten children.

'Dog?'

'A rare breed, large and quite vicious.'

'I don't know . . .'

'I worry that Reynard may be dangerous.'

The light in her eyes shifted, and either I was made to pay attention or the words themselves moved me.

'Dangerous how?'

'He's a carnivore and he's large,' she said in way of explanation.

'If a dog's attacking people in the city, I'm sure animal control will be out after it.'

'Reynard is a sewer rat in spite of his size. I believe that he's found his way into the abandoned subway tunnels under the city. There are, I believe, people living down there, people who might not be on the radar of your animal control.'

I'd spent some time in the various abandoned catacombs beneath the city. I've hunted there and spent some relaxing days deep under the ground, away from the sounds of the city.

'How big are we talking?'

'Big.'

Mahey carried a large white bag that looked to be made of some kind of naked flesh. From the sack she took a blue velvet roll, maybe a foot and a half in length. This she handed to me.

I unfurled the cloth, revealing a simple black knife, somewhat less than a foot long. The handle was part and parcel of the metal blade.

'Carry this with you,' she said.

'I didn't say I was taking the job.'

'Don't let's be coy, Mr Nyx.'

I wanted to argue further, but instead I rolled the dark metal blade back up and stood.

'I guess I better be getting to work then.'

'You can see me to my car downstairs,' she said, a little less formal than she had been.

When we got into the close quarters of the elevator, I was assailed by the odor of deep woods. It wasn't a sweet smell, but there was lightness and dark, decay and new growth. It was almost overpowering.

On the street there was a cherry red Lincoln Town Car parked at the front door. A short, porcine man in a bright green suit stood at the ready, waiting for Ms Demola.

As we approached him, someone shouted, 'Hey, Nyx!'

He was jogging across the street, coming right at me. It was Tarver Lamone wearing white exercise pants and a gray sweatshirt. He was moving pretty quickly when he pulled a pistol out of the pouch of the sweatshirt. I was so surprised that I didn't move immediately. The chauffeur was taken off guard also, but Mahey was anything but slow. She reached out and put four fingers on the forearm of Tarver's gun hand. The whole arm turned to spaghetti and hung down, lifeless.

'He is not yours to kill,' she said in an almost matter-of-fact tone. 'Not tonight.'

Tarver dropped the pistol and screamed. He turned and ran away. His gait was odd because the right arm was still hanging loosely at his side.

I turned away from him to stare at my Amazonian client.

'What was that?' I asked.

'You were not made for love, Mr Nyx,' she said. 'Its spikes and spines will stake you as certainly as Reynard's great teeth.'

With those words she moved toward the car door, now held open by the piggish driver.

I watched them drive away and wondered, for the first time, if this rebellion against my nature was a good thing.

Grand central station was pretty much empty at one in the morning. I moved to the entrance of the IRT and made it to the downtown platform, populated with a few midnight commuters: young lovers and drunks, street punks and the homeless. A local train came and almost everyone got on.

I went to the far end of the platform and jumped down to the track. I was moving pretty fast, and so even if anyone saw anything, they wouldn't have been able to stop me.

Half a mile north there was a metal ladder that

led down to a network of sub-subterranean tunnels and corridors. One of these led to a crawl space that took me even farther down, to another set of passageways and access tunnels. Some of these paths led to offices and utility stockrooms used by subway workers for storage and relaxation. There were forgotten conduits also, some of which brought underground travelers to places that made up a city below the city.

I had been walking down a completely darkened tunnel for half an hour when a sudden stench almost brought me to my knees. I lit a match. Usually I can move in the dark with no light at all. It's one of the abilities I developed after meeting Julia. But though I can move without bumping into things, I can't really see.

The match revealed a rotting, decimated corpse. It had been human, but I couldn't tell if it was man or woman. The groin, belly, and chest had been ripped out and the face was chewed off completely. Much of the flesh was gone. Only the hands were somewhat intact, but they were gnarled and filthy.

Whoever it was, they hadn't been dead for long, but down under the subway there was lots of life that sought out dead flesh. Roaches, rats, and flies swarmed around the corpse. I staggered away wondering about Mahey X. Demola's pet.

Along the path I discovered six more corpses. The odor was cloying. The scuttling sounds in the darkness were upsetting, even for me.

I was headed for the underground commune called the City of Light, named for the electric hookup a man named Nathan Charles had connected years before. There were lamps, fans, video players, and even computers in the cavern down under East Seventy-Third Street. I had been down here before during my nocturnal wanderings, had gotten to know some of the people who inhabited this strange place.

As I made my way toward the underground cooperative, I feared that there would be more bodies – many more.

'Who's there?' a man asked and a bright light shone in my night eyes.

All my senses were temporarily blinded by the glare, but I'd recognized the voice.

'It's me, Lester, Juvenal.'

'Juvy?' The light moved away. 'What you doin' down here, son?'

'I heard that there was some kinda dog down here attacking your people. I thought I'd come down and help.'

'Help yourself an' get your ass outta here,' one of my few friends told me. 'Whatever it is down here attackin' us, it ain't no dog. It's a fuckin' monster, man. Shit. It ripped off Lonnie Bingham's arm wit' just one swipe. He died screamin'.'

With the light out of my face, I could see my friend Lester. He was my age (and therefore looked much older), tall like me, black, and bald. I'd met him on one of my sojourns in the underground caverns. I liked him because he hadn't been to the surface in thirty years. He ran the City of Light, a beneficent mayor of the out crowd.

'How many people have died?' I asked.

'There's a dozen missin'. We made us a bunker in the north quarter. Everybody's there right now. The thing cain't get in, but we ain't been able to get out to bring down food and supplies. We need a big gun too.'

There came a howl through the vast network of tunnels, caves, and caverns. The sound entered all of my senses: a sour taste and acrid smells assailed me, my skin ached, and visions of violent screams danced before me. My entire body tingled, then suddenly my attention was drawn to a spot up ahead.

'That's it,' Lester said. 'That's the beast.'

'It's up ahead,' I said. 'You go on, L. Go get your supplies and weapons. I'm gonna take care of this here dog.'

'You crazy, Juvy? You just a kid, man. You cain't hurt that thing. I shot it point-blank wit' my twenty-two pistol an' he hardly even slowed down.'

Lester grabbed my arm and I pushed him away. I'm much stronger than normal men. Lester hit the ground and rolled a few feet. I turned my back on him and kept going.

The thing wailed again. This cry brought on hallucinations. I could see people running from beasts of all sorts. I smelled death and the stars themselves began to cry. I saw men and women

201

being raped then slaughtered – then eaten. Their attackers were vicious beings who looked like children but who were older than the oldest trees in the forest.

When the vision ended I found myself on my knees with a pain like a spike through my brain.

I got up and moved quickly toward the City of Light.

It was less than even a shantytown in a hollowed-out grotto of stone. There were tents and lean-tos, fire cans and furniture under the electric light that had christened the town of eighty or so. At the far end from the entrance was a huge metal door. No one knew what the vault was for. Now it held the remainder of Lester's people.

Above it on a natural stone ledge crouched Mahey X. Demola's *pet*. He was covered with golden fur except for the snout, which was a striped black and blood red. His paws were nearly hands, and though he squatted down on all fours I believed that he could stand upright and tall.

A growl sounded in my throat. All rational thought fled my mind. A rage, deep and frightening, sang through my muscles, and the beast above me howled.

I saw an eye in the darkness above Mahey's *dog*. It stared at me and wondered while the creature leaped from its ledge.

I saw the golden blur coming. I wanted to dive and roll, then grab and rend and bite and tear.

But instead I was dazzled by that eye, wondering what it could mean . . .

Reynard slammed into me and I went flying. He was hard as stone, and I was, for the first time in decades, merely human. Reynard swiped at me, raking his claws first across my face and then on my chest.

I hit him with both fists and had no effect whatever. He bit into my arm then butted me with his high crown. I fell to the ground, senseless but still hating. Reynard hovered above me, his mouth a stench-filled yawn of hunger, hatred, and vicious anticipation.

There came seven small pops. I thought for an instant that it was the sound of Reynard ripping off one of my limbs, but then I heard a gurgling cry. It was my name being spoken.

Juvenal.

The thoughts cascading at that moment didn't have a linear progression. Lester's face was there and his .22 pistol – that had made the pops. He used his weapon to try to save me, dooming us both in the process. The small-caliber gun was his only weapon.

The black iron knife, shoved in my belt, was mine.

I didn't try to unroll the blue velvet. While Reynard looked up to see what was stinging his face, I plunged the blue roll into his chest.

His howl was what I can only call a cacophony of exploding stars. I was falling, careening through an emptiness that was unending. I was impossible and so was the idea of me. I was bleeding and hating, killing . . .

'Juvy, stop!' Lester yelled. He was trying to pull me off the beast's corpse. I was plunging the knife into its inert body again and again. I was outraged by the visions he'd shown me. I wanted him to take them back.

'He's dead, man!' Lester cried and he managed to pull me back.

I was weakened by the wounds and loss of blood, but the rage still filled me.

The knife pulsed in my grip and I turned away.

'Juvenal,' Lester called.

'Not now, man,' I said. 'Not now.'

I staggered away down tunnel after tunnel, having no idea where I was going. The iron knife thrummed in my hand. It felt good. It felt diseased. It felt alive and angry, like a bumblebee clenched in your fist.

I came across an abandoned campsite in a recess in a wall. There I pulled out a soiled trench coat. I put it on to hide my bloody wounds and held the blade up in the sleeve of the coat.

I climbed up into the subway and made it to the Twenty-Eighth Street stop. I climbed out and staggered into the gathering dawn.

'Mr . Nyx,' a gruff voice, which maybe shouldn't have spoken in words at all, called.

It was Mahey's piggish chauffeur standing next to the cherry red limo.

He held the back door open and I didn't have the strength to refuse.

'Hello, Mr. Nyx,' Mahey said when I fell into the seat beside her.

I didn't respond.

'Did you find Reynard?'

'Yeah. You didn't say what you wanted me to do, so I killed him.'

'Just so. Do you have the knife?'

It was throbbing against my forearm. I didn't want to give it up. But those green lights would not be denied. I pulled out the blade and handed it to her. She took a plastic sheet from her skin purse and took the thing without actually touching it.

She placed the knife in the bag and gave me a smile that was supposed to be friendly. Then she produced a wad of cash and handed it to me.

'Where can I drop you, Mr. Nyx?'

I slept on my office floor for more than sixty hours.

My small suite of offices has a bathroom with a change of clothes hanging in the closet. After two and a half days of comatose sleep, I washed off at the sink and dressed. Then I went to sit in a chair at the window and thanked the night that I was still alive.

My physical wounds were almost healed, but the memories still pained me. Reynard and I had something in common. He was a creature like me. His howls carried knowledge and his stench spoke

205

of an alternate history to the evolutionary blunderings of known life.

And Mahey also was part of my hidden lineage. I was sure of this. And what was that black blade that she wouldn't touch? And that eye which I imagined but am also sure of its existence?

There came a knock on the door.

I wondered for a moment if it was Tarver with his gun or maybe Mahey, or one of her henchmen, with a pulsating black knife.

A creature like Reynard would not knock.

'Who is it?'

'Eerie,' she said.

I opened the door and the woman I loved all the way down to the molecular level stood there before me dressed in yellow and white.

She looked me in the eye and I looked back.

'We have to talk,' she said.

I ushered her in.

Perched in chairs across from each other, it was the first time in months that we'd come together without a kiss.

'Yes?' I said.

'Tarver's in a mental ward, out of his head and with his right arm completely paralyzed.'

'Uh-huh?'

'He goes in and out, but at one point he said that you did this to him.'

'Oh. Well, you see—'

'What's going on?' Iridia asked.

'Tarver came here with a pistol,' I said.

'What?'

'He came up to me and pulled it out, but before he could shoot, the woman I was with, a client, blocked his arm. He screamed and ran away, but as far as I could see she didn't cut him or anything.'

'But then how did he get paralyzed and crazy?'

I hesitated. Up until that moment, my identity, my abilities were secret. Secrets are like the night: they hide from sight that which we suspect and fear. But I no longer wanted to live in darkness. Iridia, the love of my being, was not someone I wanted to hide from. And even if the truth made me lose her, at least she would know me, if only for a while.

'I want to tell a story about a woman named Julia,' I said. 'She named me Juvenal Nyx and made me a child of the night.'

THE KNIFE

RICHARD ADAMS

All that is narrated in this story took place in 1938.

It was not until Philip actually saw the knife lying in the bushes that his life changed its nature, as it were, from a fantasy to a frightening possibility. He stopped, turned his head for a glance and then took a couple of steps back, stared and remained staring, as though he needed to make sure that the knife was real.

Yes, it was real all right. It was the only thing for some time that had been able to break through the palisade of his dismal, all-absorbing dread.

Before that, his thoughts had been dominated by his horrible apprehension, the prospect of severe physical pain, inescapable and coming soon. It was as though his mind had been running a tape again and again. For its starting point it had Stafford's final words to him yesterday. 'So I shall see you in the library after prayers tomorrow night, and you've got no one to thank but your-self.' Next came Stafford's turning away and his own imprisonment, as it were, within those words, surrounding him like the bars of a cage. And then the intervening time; and so back to Stafford's words.

Ever since the beginning of this term and Stafford's appointment as head prefect of the house, he had become – not only in his own eyes, but in everyone else's – Stafford's principal victim. 'Stafford doesn't like you, does he?' Jones had said. 'And *can* you blame him?' added Brown, at which both of them had roared with laughter.

All through the term his offences had accumulated, earning themselves on the way a whole series of petty punishments, which had climaxed last week in his being beaten by Stafford in the house library. The pain had been severe – the worst he had ever undergone – and now it was apparently going to be repeated.

Last night he had hardly slept. He couldn't eat breakfast and could hardly eat lunch. Jones and Brown were the only people he had told.

And now here he was, trudging through the wet woods alone on a half-holiday afternoon. And now, here was the knife. It burst in upon his thoughts, which surrendered and came to a stop.

It was very like the knives he had seen on television, the knives which scores of people had handed in to the police as the result of a public appeal.

He stooped and picked it up. It was a good foot long in its fancy sheath and it had a very sharp point. And now, straight on cue, came the fantasy.

The knife had been sent to him by a mysterious

Power, and he was under orders to use it. He was always entertaining fantasies. There was no end to them: revenge fantasies, sexual fantasies, supreme-power fantasies. To a considerable extent, he lived in solitude with his fantasies.

Under orders to use it. When and where? 'My lord, I shall use it in the middle of the night, and no one will be able to tell—' He broke off. Deliberately changed his thoughts. However, the first thoughts returned. But of course he wasn't really going to use it, was he?

If he did, what would happen then? For once he couldn't imagine. However, one thing was clear. There would be a tremendous row; the most tremendous row ever. But suppose no one could tell it was him?

He wouldn't be beaten again, would he? The beating would be swallowed up in the awful row. Everything would change. Yes, that was the real point. Everything would change, including his life.

No one knew he had a knife. And no one would want to claim it after he'd used it as he meant to. Before house prayers that evening he had thought out exactly what he was going to do.

Going upstairs to bed he was so much preoccupied that he stumbled into someone without noticing who. 'Oh, damn you, Jevons, why can't you look where you're going?' 'Sorry, er – sorry, er—'

Most of the senior boys had single rooms. He had had one now for two terms. That night after lights out he lay silently in the dark, willing himself to keep awake.

But he fell asleep. When he woke it was two in the morning by his watch. Last chance to say no. But yes, he was still determined to do it. What had he to lose?

Got the knife? Got the torch? Got someone else's bath towel he'd pinched from the changing room? He opened the door of his room, stepped into the passage and stood listening. Not a sound anywhere. It wasn't far to the door of Stafford's room (mind, no fingerprints).

And now he was standing beside Stafford's bed, listening to his steady breathing as he lay on his back. He turned on the torch, shone it on Stafford's throat and all in one movement plunged in the knife. The point was so sharp that he hardly felt it pierce. He let go of the hilt and all in one movement spread the towel over throat, knife and all, ran back to his room, shut the torch in a drawer and got back into bed.

All this he remembered clearly. And the aftermath? Well, the tremendous row. The shock throughout the school. The shock throughout the country. The newspapers, the headmaster, the police, the finger-printing. (To what purpose? He had readily given his own.)

Apparently, no one had told the police that he was a boy on the wrong side of Stafford. So many boys were.

His parents had not been hard to persuade when

he had asked them if he could leave at the end of the term.

I'm his godfather, and I've always kept up a friendly interest in him. We've been close friends for many years.

One night last week, after he'd come to dinner with me, he told me everything and said that he'd often had a mind to give himself up. I've told him to dismiss that notion altogether and assured him that his secret is entirely safe with me. I wouldn't let on to a living soul.

Well, would you?

WEIGHTS AND MEASURES

JODI PICOULT

The loudest sound in the world is the absence of a child. Sarah found herself waiting for it, the moment she opened her eyes in the morning: that satin ribbon of a giggle, or the thump of a jump off the bed – but instead all she heard was the hiss of the coffeemaker that Abe must have preset in the kitchen last night, spitting angrily as it finished its brewing. She glanced at the clock over the landscape of Abe's sleeping body. For a moment, she thought about touching that golden shoulder or running her hand through his dark curls, but like most moments, it was gone before she remembered to act on it. 'We have to get up,' she said.

Abe didn't move, did not turn toward her. 'Right,' he said, and from the pitch of his voice she knew that he hadn't been asleep either.

She rolled onto her back. '*Abe.*'

'Right,' he repeated. He pushed off the bed in one motion and closeted himself in the bathroom, where he ran the shower long before he stepped inside, incorrectly assuming the background noise would keep anyone outside from hearing him cry.

★　　★　　★

213

The worst day of Abe's life had not been the one you'd imagine, but the one after that, when he went to choose his daughter's coffin. Sarah begged him to go; said she could not sit and talk about what to do with their daughter as if she were a box of outgrown clothing that had to be stored somewhere safe and dry. The funeral director was a man with a bad comb-over and kind, gray eyes, and his first question to Abe was whether he'd seen his daughter . . . afterward. Abe had – once the doctors and nurses had given up and the tubes had been removed and the crash carts pulled away, he and Sarah were given a moment to say good-bye. Sarah had run out of the hospital room, screaming. Abe had sat down on the edge of the bed with the plastic mattress that crinkled beneath his weight, and had threaded his fingers with his daughter's. For a brief, heart-stopping moment, he thought he'd felt her move, but it turned out to be his own sobbing, jarring the bed. He'd sat like that for a while, and then somehow managed to pull her onto his lap and crawl onto the cot himself, as if he were the patient.

What he remembered was not how still she was, or how her skin grew ashen under his touch, but how she had weighed just the tiniest bit less than she had that morning, when he'd carried her through the double doors of the emergency room. It wasn't remarkable to think that he – a man who lived by weights and measures – would be sensitive to this even at a moment as overwhelming as that one. Abe recalled hearing medical examiners say a person who died lost twenty-one grams of weight – the measure of a human soul. He realized, though, holding his daughter in his arms, that the scale was all wrong. Loss should have been measured in leagues: the linear time line he would not spend with her as she lost her first tooth, lost her heart over a boy, lost the graduation cap she tossed into a silvered sky. Loss should have been measured circularly, like angles: the minutes between the two of them, the degrees of separation.

We suggest that you dress your daughter the way she would have wanted, the funeral director had said. *Did she have a favorite party dress, or a pair of over-alls she always wore to climb trees? A soccer uniform? A T-shirt from a favorite vacation?*

There were other questions, and decisions to be made, and finally, the funeral director took Abe into another room to choose a coffin. The samples were stacked against the wall, jet and mahogany sarcophagi gleaming at such a high polish he could see his own ravaged features in their reflections. The funeral director led Abe to the far end of the room, where three stunted coffins were propped like brave soldiers. They ranged from some that came up as high as his hip to one that was barely bigger than a bread box.

Abe picked one painted a glossy white, with gold piping, because it reminded him of his daughter's bedroom furniture. He kept staring at it. Although the funeral director assured him that it was the right size, it did not seem large enough to Abe to hold a girl as full of life as his daughter. It was certainly not large enough, he knew, to pack inside the turtle shell of grief that he'd armored himself in this past day. Which meant, of course, that even after his daughter was gone, the sorrow would remain behind.

The funeral was held at a church neither Abe nor Sarah attended, a service arranged by Sarah's mother, who in spite of this still managed to believe in God. At first, Sarah had fought it – how many idealistic discussions had she and Abe had about religion being akin to brainwashing; about letting their child choose her own rainbow of beliefs? – but Sarah's mother put her foot down, and Sarah – still reeling – was weak enough to be toppled. *What kind of parent*, Felicity had said tearfully, *doesn't want a man of God to say a few words over her daughter?* Now, Sarah sat in the front pew as this pastor spoke, words that flowed over the crowd like an anesthetic breeze. In her hand was a small teal green Beanie Baby, a dog that had gone everywhere with her child, to the point where it was hairless and frayed and barely even recognizable in its animalhood. Sarah squeezed it in her fist so tight that she could feel its seeded stuffing start to push at the seams.

Try to remember, as we celebrate her short and glorious life, that sadness comes out of love. Sadness is a kind of terrible privilege.

Sarah wondered why the pastor hadn't mentioned the truly important things: like the fact that her daughter could take a toilet paper roll and turn it into a pretend video camera that occupied her imagination for hours. Or that the only songs that made her stop crying when she had colic as an infant were tracks from *Sgt. Pepper's Lonely Hearts Club Band.* She wondered why he hadn't told the people who'd come here that her daughter had only just learned how to do a round off in gymnastics and that she could pick the Big Dipper out of any night sky?

Oh, Lord, receive this child of Yours into the arms of Your mercy, into the blessed rest of everlasting peace, and into the company of angels.

At that, Sarah lifted her head. *Not Your child*, she thought. *Mine.*

Ten minutes later, it was over. She remained stone still while everyone else left to get into their cars and drive to the cemetery. But she had worked out something special with Abe; the one request, really, she'd had for this funeral. She felt Abe's hand come onto her shoulder and his lips move against her ear. 'Do you still—'

'Yes,' she interrupted, and then he was gone too.

She walked up to the coffin, surrounded by an embarrassment of flowers. Fall flowers, like the ones she'd had in her wedding bouquet. She forced herself to glance down at her daughter – who looked, well, perfectly normal, which was the great irony here.

'Hey, baby,' Sarah said softly, and she tucked the small green dog underneath her daughter's arm. Then she opened up the large purse she'd brought with her to the funeral service.

It had been critical for her to be the last one to see her daughter before that casket was closed. She wanted to be the last one to lay eyes on her girl, the same way – seven years ago – she had been the first.

The book she pulled out of her purse was so dog-eared and worn that its spine had cracked and some of its pages were only filed in between others, instead of glued into place. '"In a great green room,"' she began to read, '"there was a fireplace, and a red balloon, and a picture of . . ."'

She hesitated. This was the part where her daughter would have chimed in: *the cow jumping over the moon*. But now, Sarah had to say the words for her. She read through to the end, going by heart when the tears came so furiously that she could not see the words on the page. '"Goodnight stars,"' she whispered. '"Goodnight air. Goodnight noises everywhere."' Then she drew in a ragged breath and touched her finger to her daughter's lips. 'Sleep tight,' Sarah said.

In the gathering hall at the church, Abe thought there were obscene amounts of food, as if pastries and deviled eggs and casseroles could make up for the fact that nobody really knew what to say to him. He stood holding a plate piled high that someone had brought him, although he hadn't taken a single bite. From time to time, a friend or a relative would come up to him and say something stupid: *How are you doing? Are you holding up okay? It won't hurt as much, in time.* Things like that only made him want to put down his plate and punch the speaker until his hand bled, because that kind of pain he could understand better than the empty ache in his chest that wouldn't go away. No one said what they all were truly thinking, when they furtively glanced over at Abe with his bad-fitting black suit and his Styrofoam plate: *I'm so glad it happened to you, and not me.*

'Excuse me.'

Abe turned around to find a woman he'd never met before – middle-aged, with wrinkles around her eyes that made him think she had smiled, often, in her youth. Maybe one of Felicity's church ladies, he thought. She was holding a box of daffodil bulbs. 'I'm so sorry for your loss,' she said, and she held out the box.

He set down the plate on a chair beside him so that he could take the bulbs. 'Plant these now,' she said, 'and when they come up in the spring, think of her.'

She touched his arm and walked off, leaving Abe holding on to this hope.

Sarah had met Abe when she was new to Los Angeles, and some friends had taken her to a cigar club that was so exclusive you had to enter through a corporate office building and give the doorman the password to be let into the correct elevator bank. The club was on the roof of the building, and Sarah's friends had tried to cure her East Coast homesickness by showing off Mel Gibson's humidor. It was a dark place, one where actors who fancied themselves to be musicians were likely to pick up a guitar and jam with the band; one that only made Sarah even more aware of how much she hated this city, this new job, this departure from where she really wanted to be.

They sat at the bar, pulling up stools beside a good-looking guy with hair as dark as ink and a smile that made Sarah feel like she was caught in a whirlpool. Sarah's friends ordered cosmos and tried to outflirt each other – getting him to reveal that he was the drummer in the band, and that his name was Abe. When one of the girls came back from the bathroom and exclaimed, *Have you seen all the stars?* Abe leaned over and asked Sarah to dance. They moved like smoke over the empty dance floor, to a canned jazz track. 'Why me?' Sarah asked simply.

His hand, resting on the small of her back, pulled her just that much closer. 'Because,' Abe said, 'when your friend started talking about stars, you were the only one in this whole fucking place who looked up at the sky.'

Three months later, they moved to Massachusetts together. Six months later, they got married, amid many toasts and jokes about Abraham and Sarah and their destiny to create a tribe. But like their biblical counterparts, it took years for them to have a child – eight, to be exact. Just long enough for Sarah to believe it was time to give up trying. Just short enough for her to be overwhelmed with the news of her pregnancy; to never give a second thought to the fact that this might not be the end of the struggle, but instead, the beginning.

On the way home from the church, Sarah turned to Abe and told him to stop at the grocery store. 'There's nothing in the house,' she said, as if this wasn't obvious on so many levels. They were too numb to think about how they looked, at one in the afternoon, moving through the frozen foods aisle in coat and tie and pearls and heels. They wandered through the store, picking out the items that seemed to scream normal: eggs and bread and cheese and milk; things any family could use. In the cereal aisle, Abe started to automatically reach for the berry Kix, her favorite, until he realized that they didn't need it anymore; and he covered gracefully by taking instead the cereal box beside it, some god-awful bran thing that looked like straw and that he knew he'd never eat.

They went to the line with their favorite checkout girl, the one who didn't mind when their daughter helped scan the bar codes on the soup cans and the frozen peas. She smiled when she saw them. 'Wow, look at you two!' she said, glancing at their clothes and winking. 'Don't tell me food shopping is what passes for a date without the kids nowadays . . .'

Abe and Sarah froze. This woman wouldn't know – how *could* she? She thought, as would any other stranger, that their daughter was home with a babysitter, watching *The Princess Diaries* for the six hundredth time or pretending the Tupperware was a drum set. As Abe signed the credit card receipt, the checkout clerk reached beneath her cash register and pulled out a lollipop. 'She likes blue, right? Tell her I missed her.'

'Yes,' Abe said, grasping it so tightly that the stick curved. 'Yes, I will.'

He followed Sarah as she pushed the cart outside, where the sun was so bright it brought tears to his eyes. Sarah turned to him, speechless and staring. 'What?' Abe said, his voice raw. 'What did I do wrong?'

Three days later, Sarah woke up and pulled on her favorite sweater only to realize that her arms now stretched a good three inches past the ends of the sleeves. Annoyed – did Abe shrink it in the wash? – she pulled out another only to realize that she'd outgrown that one, too. She stared at herself in the mirror for a moment and then pushed the sleeves up to her elbows, where she could not see anything wrong.

She tried to pretend that she didn't notice when she unloaded the dishwasher and could, for the first time in her life, reach the top shelf of the cabinets without having to stand on a stool or ask Abe for his help.

On his last day of paid bereavement leave, Abe remembered sitting in the hospital with his daughter. There were starfish painted on the window glass, and while they waited for the doctor and Sarah read a waiting-room magazine from the turn of the century, his daughter had wanted to play I spy. It had gotten to the point, in the past seven years, where Abe could almost do this semi-conscious – since his daughter had a habit of changing midstream what her target object was, anyway, the game didn't make any linear sense. He guessed the exit sign over the door, the bath-room knob, the starfish on the far right, getting more and more impatient, and wishing the doctor would just come in already so that he didn't have to play one more damn round.

It had only been a sore throat. Her fever wasn't more than 101. That was the criteria – you weren't supposed to worry about a fever until it spiked past 102, something Sarah had learned the hard way when she'd call the pediatrician early on, freaking out over everything from hangnails to cradle cap. But over the course of their daughter's life, they'd weaned themselves into health care confidence. They didn't rush her into the office at the sign of the first cough; they made her sleep overnight on an earache to make sure it was present the next morning before they went to get it checked.

And this time, Sarah had kept her home from school waiting to see if it was a virus, or strep throat. They'd done what they were supposed to do as parents; they'd listened to the doctors; they'd played by the rules – and by dinnertime, the rules didn't apply. Children weren't supposed to die of strep throat, but then again, you did not have to look far for the *shouldn'ts*. All over this world there were tsunamis sweeping entire countries out to sea; there were Eskimo women with breast milk full of mercury; there were wars being fought that had been started for the wrong reasons. All over this world impossible things were happening that never should have.

Abe realized he would play I spy for a thousand years, if he could.

The next day, when Abe left for work, Sarah cleaned. Not just a cursory vacuum and floor mop, mind you, but toilets scrubbed by hand and radiator registers being dusted and the washing of the walls. She went into her drawers and bagged all the sweaters that did not fit, and the new pile of pants that ended above her ankles. She got rid of the travel coffee mugs and gravy boats and cherry pitters she never used, weeding through the kitchen drawers. She organized Abe's clothes by color grouping; she threw out all the medicine bottles past their expiration date. She wiped down the shelves of the refrigerator and tossed the capers and the mustard and the horseradish that hadn't been used except for that one recipe months ago.

She began to organize the closets in the house – the front one, with the winter coats still in hibernation and the boots tossed like gauntlets into a Rubbermaid bin on the floor – and then the hall closet with its piles of snowy towels and heady potpourri. It was in that one that she found herself reaching to the rear of the top shelf – the hiding spot she'd never been able to reach herself without a struggle, before, and that therefore became her cache of Christmas gifts bought and saved all year for her daughter. One by one, Sarah pulled out a remote-control robot, an art set to make flower fairies, a dress-up kit – treasures she'd found in January or March or May and had known, in that instant, that her daughter would love. She stood immobile for a long moment, holding this bounty in her elongated arms, paralyzed by the most concrete evidence she'd found yet that her daughter was Not. Coming. Home.

Sarah sat down in the middle of the hall. She opened up the plastic shrink-wrapped robot, installed its batteries, and sent him careening into the bathroom. She opened the dress-up kit and wrapped a pink boa around her own neck; peered into the tiny heart-shaped mirror to apply the fuchsia lipstick and glittery blue eye shadow, a whore's version of happiness.

When the phone rang, she ran into the bedroom

to pick up an extension. 'How are you doing?' Abe asked.

'Fine,' Sarah said. In the bedroom mirror, she could still see the clown-red cheeks, the garish mouth. 'I'm fine.'

She hung up the phone and went into the kitchen for a large black trash bag, big enough to hold a yard's worth of leaves, or a closet full of the future. She scooped all the unused toys for her daughter into the trash bag and carried it over her shoulder out to the garage. Because it was not trash day, Sarah drove all the way to the municipal dump, where she let the attendant punch her ticket once for the privilege of hauling the sack over the ravine's edge. She waited, until this bag full of what she'd lost nestled itself between other bags stuffed with the things people actually chose to give away.

Pharmacists live in minutiae, which is why Abe had learned a whole system of measurement in college that most educated folks don't even know exists. Ask anyone who has ever filled the innards of a tiny gelatin capsule with a drug, and they will know that twenty grains equals one scruple. Three scruples equal one dram apothecaries. Eight drams apothecaries equal one ounce apothecaries, which equals four hundred eighty grains, or twenty-four scruples.

Abe was trying to count the twenty-four scruples, but they had nothing to do with the pills he had spilled before him on the little rubber mat from Pfizer, a freebie he'd gotten at some conference in Santa Fe. It was funny – a scruple, by itself, was a misgiving; make it plural and it suddenly was a set of principles, of ethics. It *was* that simple, he understood now. You only had to survive one of your regrets, and it was enough to make you realize you'd been living your life all wrong.

He regretted telling his daughter to clean up her room the day before she died. He regretted the fact that he hadn't hugged her in front of her friends after her fall concert at school, because he thought her embarrassment was more important than his pride. He regretted not taking his family to Australia, when they were still a family. He regretted not having been given the chance to meet a grandchild. He regretted having seven years, instead of seventy-seven.

Abe pushed aside these thoughts and began to recount the pills. But he had to keep hiking up his pants – they were riding that low on his hips. Finally, ducking behind a wall of meds, he unbuttoned his white coat and notched his belt tighter. It would make sense that he was losing weight – he hadn't been eating, really – but the belt suddenly didn't fit at all. There simply wasn't a notch where he needed it to be; he'd grown that thin, that fast.

Frustrated, he unwound some twine in the back room used for shipments and took off his belt, looping the rope in its place. He thought of going back inside and finishing the order, but instead he walked out through the back receiving door of the pharmacy and kept walking – around the block, and then down three more, and through the traffic light, until he came to a bar he passed every day when he drove home. Olaf's, it was called, and it was open, even though it was only eleven A.M.

He was aware, as he walked through the door, that he looked like a poor man's Charlie Chaplin, with a rope holding up his pants. He was aware that he hadn't been to a bar during the day since he'd been a drummer a lifetime ago. There were five people at the bar, even this morning, and they weren't the sort of folks you found in bars at night. These were the hard-luck cases, the ones who needed whiskey (a dram!) to get through another few hours of an ordinary workday; or the call girls who needed to forget before they went home to sleep off last night's memories; or the old men who only wanted to find their youth in the bottom of a bottle of gin.

Abe climbed onto a stool – and climbed was the word; he must have been more exhausted than he thought, for all the effort that it took to get onto it. 'Have you got Jameson?' he asked the bartender, and the guy looked at him with a smile as crooked as lightning.

'Nice try, kid,' he said.

'Excuse me?'

The bartender shook his head. 'You got any ID?'

Abe was forty-two years old, and he could not remember the last time he'd been carded. He had gray hair at the temples, for God's sake. But he reached for his wallet, only to realize that it was back at work, in his locker, like usual. 'I don't,' he said.

'Well, then,' the bartender said. 'I ain't got Jameson. Come on back when you turn twenty-one.'

Abe stared at him, confounded. He jumped off the stool, landing hard. The whole way back to work, he searched for his reflection in the shiny hoods of Buicks, in plate-glass windows of bakeries, in puddles. When you lost a child, did you lose the years you'd spent with her, too?

A week after their daughter's death, Sarah could not stop thinking about her. She would taste the skin of the little girl, a kiss, the moment before the chicory of the coffee kicked in, or the sweetness of the muffin blossomed on her tongue. She would pick up a newspaper and feel instead the rubbery band of small socks between her fingers as she folded them over after doing the wash. She'd be in one room and hear the music of her daughter's voice, the way grammar leaped through her sentences like a frog.

Abe, on the other hand, was starting to lose her. He would close his eyes and try to conjure up his daughter's face, and he still could, but it was unraveled at the edges a little more each day. He found himself spending hours in her bedroom, inhaling the smell of her strawberry-mango shampoo still trapped in the fibers of the pillow-case, or poring through the books on her shelves and trying to see them through her eyes. He went so far as to open her finger paints, stand stripped to the waist in front of her tiny mirror, draw her heart on his chest.

Although Sarah's Mo was usually to do the opposite of whatever her mother told her to do, this time, she took her advice. She showed up at the church, shuddering as she remembered the hymns that had been played at her daughter's funeral, steeling herself for the absence of the coffin at the altar. She knocked on the pastor's office door, and he ushered her inside and gave her a cup of tea. 'So,' the pastor said, 'your mother's worried about you.'

Sarah opened up her mouth to say something snippy and typically awful, but she caught herself in time. Of *course* her mother was worried. That was the job description, wasn't it? That was why she had come.

'Can I ask you something?' Sarah said. 'Why *her*?'

'I don't understand . . .'

'I get the whole God thing. I get the kingdom of heaven. But there are millions of seven year olds out there. Why did God take *mine*?'

The pastor hesitated. 'God didn't take your daughter, Sarah,' he said. 'Illness did.'

Sarah snorted. 'Sure. Pass the buck when it's

convenient.' She could feel herself dangerously at the edge of breaking down, and wondered why on earth she'd thought it was a good idea to come here.

The pastor reached for her hand. His were warm and papery, familiar. 'Heaven's an amazing place,' he said softly. 'She's up there, and she's looking down on us, right now, you know.'

Sarah felt her throat tighten. 'My daughter,' she said, 'can't ride a ski lift without hyperventilating. She panics in elevators. She doesn't even like bunk beds. She's terrified of heights.'

'Not anymore.'

'How do you know that?' Sarah exploded. 'How do you know that there's anything afterward? How do you know it doesn't just . . . end?'

'I don't know,' the pastor said. 'But I can hope. And I truly believe that your daughter is in heaven, and even if she does still get scared, Jesus will be there to keep her safe.'

She turned away as a tear streaked down her cheek. 'She doesn't know Jesus,' Sarah said. 'She knows me.'

Abe found himself defying gravity. He'd be standing in the kitchen, getting a glass of water, and he'd find himself rising to the balls of his feet. He could not walk fast down the street without starting to float between strides. He started to put stones in the pockets of his pants, which were all too long for him now.

He was sitting on his daughter's bed one Saturday, remembering a conversation they'd had. *Can I still live here when I get married?* she'd asked, and he'd grinned and said that would be perfectly fine.

But what about your husband? he'd asked.

His daughter had considered this carefully. *Well, we could set up the cot, like when I have a sleepover.*

The doorbell rang, and when Abe went downstairs, he found the little girl his daughter had considered her best friend – the last one who'd used that cot, actually – standing red eyed beside her mother. 'Hi, Abe,' the woman said. 'I hope this isn't too much of an imposition.'

'No!' he said, too brightly. 'No! Not at all!'

'It's just that Emily's having some trouble, with, well, *you know*. She drew a picture, and wanted to bring it here. She thought maybe you could hang it up.' The little girl thrust out a piece of paper toward Abe: a crayon drawing of two little girls – one dark-haired, like his daughter, one fair, like Emily. They were holding hands. There was a melting sun overhead, and grass beneath their feet.

Abe realized he was nearly at a level with Emily; he barely had to crouch down to look her in the eye. 'This is beautiful, honey,' he said. 'I'm going to put it up right over her bed.' He reached out as if to touch the crown of her head, but realized that this might hurt him more than it would offer comfort, and at the last minute pulled his arm back to his side.

232

'Are you all right?' Emily's mother whispered. 'You look . . .' Her voice trailed off as she tried to find the right word, and then she just gave up and shook her head. 'Well. Of *course* you're not all right. I'm so sorry, Abe. I truly am.' With one last look, she took Emily's hand and started to walk down the driveway.

Abe held the crayon picture in his hand so tightly that it crumpled. He watched Emily kick the unraked leaves along the sidewalk, setting up small tornadoes as her mother looked straight ahead, not even aware that she was missing this one small, wonderful thing.

Sarah and Abe did not really speak to each other, not until Abe walked into their daughter's room and found Sarah taking the books off the shelves and putting them into boxes. 'What are you doing?' he asked, stricken.

'I can't move past this,' Sarah said, 'knowing it's all right down the hall.'

'No,' Abe answered.

Sarah hesitated. 'What do you mean, *no?*'

Abe reached into one of the boxes and took out a fistful of picture books, jammed them back onto the shelf. 'Just because you're ready to give her up,' he said, 'doesn't mean I am.'

Sarah's face bloomed with color. 'Give her up?' she whispered. 'Is that what you think I'm doing? For God's sake, Abe, all I want to do is *function* like a normal human being again.'

'But you're not normal. *We're* not normal.' His eyes filled with tears. 'She *died*, Sarah.'

Sarah winced, as if she had taken a blow. Then she turned on her heel and walked out of the room.

Abe sank onto the floor, his fingers speared through his hair. After a half hour, he stood up and walked down the hall to their bedroom. He found Sarah lying on her side, staring at the sun as it shamefully scuttled off the horizon. Abe lay down on the bed, curling his body around hers. 'I lost her,' he whispered. 'Please don't tell me I've lost you.'

Sarah turned to him, and rested her palm on his cheek. She kissed him, all the words she could not say. They began to comfort each other – a touch here, a brush of lips there, a kindness. But when their clothes had dissolved into pools on the floor, when Abe braced himself over his wife and took hold of her body and tried to settle her curves against his canyons, they did not come together seamlessly, the way they used to. They were off, just enough to make it uncomfortable; just enough for her to say, *Let me try this* and for him to say, *Maybe this way*.

Afterward, when Sarah had fallen asleep, Abe sat up and stared down at the end of the bed, at his wife's feet hanging long and white over its edge.

The next morning, Abe and Sarah lay in the dark. 'Maybe I need to be alone for a while,' Sarah said, although it wasn't what she'd hoped to say.

'Maybe you do,' Abe replied, although it was the opposite of what he meant. It was as if, in this new world, where the impossible had actually happened, nothing fit anymore: not language, not reason, not even the two of them.

When Sarah got out of bed, she took the sheet with her – a modesty she hadn't needed for fifteen years of marriage. It prevented Abe from seeing what he would have noticed, in an instant: that the growth Sarah had experienced was exactly the same amount Abe himself had diminished; and that, if you could measure anything as insubstantial as that, it would have been exactly the same size and scope as the daughter they'd lost.

Sarah reached the suitcase, even though it was stored in the top rafters of the attic. Abe watched her pack. At the door, they made promises they both knew they would not keep. 'I'll call,' Sarah said, and Abe nodded. 'Be well,' he answered.

She was going to stay with her mother – something that, in all the years of their marriage, Abe never would have imagined coming to pass; and yet he considered this a positive sign. If Sarah was choosing Felicity, in spite of their rocky relationship, maybe there was hope for all children to return to their parents, regardless of how impossible the journey seemed to be.

He had to pull a chair to the window, because he was no longer tall enough to see over its sill. He stood on the cushion and watched her put her suitcase into the car. She looked enormous to him, a giantess – and he considered that this is what motherhood does to a woman: make her larger than life. He waited until he could not see her car anymore, and then he climbed down from the chair.

He could not work anymore; he was too short to reach the counter. He could not drive anywhere, the pedals were too far from his feet. There was nothing for Abe to do, so he wandered through the house, even emptier than it had been. He found himself, of course, in his daughter's room. Here, he spent hours: drawing with her art kit; playing with her pretend food and cash register; sifting through the drawers of her clothing and playing a game with himself: can you remember the last time she wore this? He put on a Radio Disney CD and forced himself to listen to the whole of it. He lined up her stuffed animals, like witnesses.

Then he crawled into her dollhouse, one he'd built for her last Christmas. He closed the door behind himself. He glanced around at the carefully pasted wallpaper, the rich red velvet love seat, the kitchen sink. He climbed the stairs to the bedroom, where he could stare out the window to his heart's content. The view, it was perfect.

GOBLIN LAKE

MICHAEL SWANWICK

I n 1646, shortly before the end of the Thirty Years' War, a patrol of Hessian cavalrymen, fleeing the aftermath of a disastrous battle to the north wherein a botched flanking maneuver had in an hour turned certain victory to object rout, made camp at the foot of what a local peasant they had captured and forced to serve as a guide assured them was one of the highest mountains in the Spessart region of Germany. Among their number was a young officer named Johann von Grimmelshausen, a firebrand and habitual liar who was known to his comrades as Jurgen, which in English translates as Jack.

As the front lines were distant and the countryside unwary, the patrol had picked up a great deal of food and several casks of Rhine wine on their way. So that night they ate and drank well. When the food was done, they called upon their guide to tell them of the countryside in which they found themselves. He, having slowly come to the opinion that they did not intend to kill him when they were done with his services (and, possibly, having plans of lulling them with his servility and then slipping away under cover of darkness when they were all asleep), was only too happy to oblige them.

'Directly below us, not a quarter of a mile's distance away, is the Mummelsee –' in the local dialect the name meant Goblin Lake – 'which is bottomless, and which has the peculiar property that it changes whatever is thrown into it into something else. So that, for example, if any man were to tie up a number of pebbles in a kerchief and let it down into the water on a string, when he pulled it up the pebbles would have turned into peas or rubies or the eggs of vipers. Furthermore, if there were an odd number of pebbles, the number of whatever they became should invariably be even, but if they were even they would come out odd.'

'That would be a very pretty way of making a living,' Jack observed. 'Sitting by the banks of a lake, turning pebbles into rubies.'

'What they become is not predictable,' the peasant cautioned. 'You could not rely on them turning to gemstones.'

'Even if they did so only one time in a hundred . . . Well, I have spent many a day fishing with less to show for it.'

By now, several of the cavalrymen were leaning forward, listening intently. Even those who stared loftily way into the distance, as if they did not care, refrained from speaking lest they miss something profitable. So, seeing too late that he had excited their avarice, the peasant quickly said, 'But it is a very dangerous place! This was the very lake which Luther said was cursed and that if you threw a stone into it a terrible storm immediately blows up, with hail and lightning and great winds, for there are devils chained up in its depths.'

'No, that was in Poltersberg,' Jack said negligently.

'Poltersberg!' the peasant spat. 'What does Poltersberg know of terrors? There was a farmer hereabout who had to kill his best plow horse when it broke a leg. Being of an inquiring turn of mind, he hauled its carcass to the lake and threw it in. Down it sank, and up it rose again, alive – but transformed horribly, so that it had teeth like knives, two legs rather than four, and wings like those of an enormous bat. It screamed in agony and flew away into the night, no man knows where.

'Worse, when the carcass hit the water, some of it was splashed over the farmer's face, erasing his eyes completely, so that from that instant onward, he was blind.'

'How did he know the horse was transformed, then?' Jack asked with a sardonic little smile.

The peasant's mouth opened and then closed again. After a bit, he said, 'It is also said that there were two cutthroats who brought the body of a woman they had—'

Jack cut him off. 'Why listen to your stories when we can find out for ourselves?'

There was a general murmur of agreement and, after a little prodding with a knife, the peasant led them all downward.

The way down to the Mummelsee was steep and roadless, and the disposition of the soldiers was considerably soured by the time they reached it. Their grumblings, moreover, were directed as much toward Jack as toward the rascally peasant guide, for on reflection it was clear to them all that he had insisted on this journey not from any real belief that he would end up rich – for what experienced military man believes that? – but from his innate love of mischief.

Oblivious to their mood, Jack sauntered to the end of a crumbling stone pier. He had brought along a double handful of fresh cherries, which he carried in his cap, and was eating them one by one and splitting their stones into the water. 'What is that out there?' he asked, gesturing negligently toward what appeared to be a large, submerged rock, roughly rectangular in shape and canted downward to one side. It was easily visible, for the moon was full and unobscured and its light seemed to render the nighttime bright as day.

'In my grandfather's time,' the peasant said eagerly, as if anxious to restore his good reputation, 'the Duke of Württemberg caused a raft to be made and put out onto the lake to sound its depths. But after the measure had been led down nine thread cables with a sinking lead and yet had found no bottom – why, then the raft, contrary to the nature of wood, began to sink. So that all made haste for the land, fearing greatly. Nor did any escape without a soaking, and terrible diseases were said to have afflicted them in their old age.'

'So that's the raft, you say?'

'If you look closely, you can see where the arms of Württemberg were carved into the wood. Worn, perhaps, but clear to see.' The peasant pointed earnestly at some faint markings that a credulous man might convince himself were as described.

Jack rounded on him savagely. 'You scoundrel! I have been watching the cherry stones as they sank in the water, and nothing happened to them. One did not become two, two were not transformed into seventeen, and none of them – not a one! – showed the least tendency to become rubies or emeralds or vipers or oxen or even fish.'

Protesting wildly, the peasant tried to scuttle around Jack and so off the pier. Jack, for his part, was equally determined not to allow him to do so. Thus it was that a game of rat-and-mastiff took place, with the peasant playing the part of the rat and the cavalrymen the mastiffs. And though the numbers were all on one side, all the desperation and cunning were on the other.

At the last, Jack made a lunge for the peasant and, just as the man escaped his enclosing arms, found himself seized by two of his laughing comrades, hoisted up into the air, and thrown into the Mummelsee.

★   ★   ★

Down, down, down, Jack sank, choking. The water was as clear as crystal, and yet far down in the distance as black as coal, for the monstrousness of its depth. So filled with anger at his comrades was he that at first he did not notice when he stopped choking. Then, before he could properly marvel at this strange turn of circumstance, he was suddenly distracted by movements in the depths of the lake. At a distance, the creatures looked like so many frogs, flitting to and fro, but as they grew closer they seemed very much like human beings, save that their skin was green and their clothes, though fine and flowing, were clearly woven of seaweeds and other underwater plants.

More and more of these water spirits rose up like diving birds and quickly surrounded Jack. So great was their number that he had no choice but to go with them when, by gestures and frowns, the sylphs indicated he was to descend to the very bottom of the Mummelsee. Like a flock of birds circling as they descend from the sky, they guided him down.

When finally Jack lightly touched one foot to the floor of the lake, pushing up a gentle puff of silt, and then with the other creating a second puff, he found there waiting for him a sylph or nix (for the taxonomy of lake spirits was not a subject he was conversant in) clad in raiment of gold and silver, by which token he took this being to be the king of the Mummelsee.

'A good day to you, Jack,' said the king. 'I trust you are well?'

'God save us from hurt and harm, friend!' Jack cried. 'But however could you possibly know my name?'

'As for that, my dear fellow, I have been reading about your adventures, most recently with those scoundrelly false comrades who threw you into this lake.' The king's Vandyke and mustachios waved lightly in the water and this made Jack clutch his throat in sudden apprehension that he was breathing a medium for which mortal men were unsuited. But then the king laughed and his laugh was so natural and warmhearted that Jack could not help but join it. So, realizing that a man who could still laugh was neither dead nor in any sense lacking breath, he put aside his fears.

'What place is this,' Jack asked, 'and what manner of people live here?'

'Why, as the saying goes, "As above, so below." We have our farms and cities and churches, though the god we worship in it may not have the same name as yours. Salt hay is harvested to thatch our roofs. Sea horses pull plows in our fields, and sea cows are milked in our barns. Catfish chase mice fish, and water gnomes drive shafts through the muck in search of mussels and precious stones. The maidens here may have scales, but they are no less beautiful nor any more slippery than those in your above-water world.'

So talking, the king of the Mummelsee led Jack along a pleasant road to what destination he did not yet reveal, and all the nixies who had guided

Jack down formed themselves into a casual procession behind them, laughing and talking among themselves, and flashing from side to side as they went, so that they resembled nothing so much as a great school of minnows. Above a winding road they swam and then through a forest of giant kelp, which abruptly opened up upon a shining white city.

Great were the wonders of that submarine metropolis. The walls of its buildings were so white they glowed, for they were plastered (so explained the king) with powdered pearls. While the streets were not paved with gemstones, many a fresco set into the exterior walls was made of nothing else, and the scenes they depicted were not of warfare but of children at play and lovers chastely courting. The architecture was a happy blend of Moorish and Asian influences, with minarets and pagodas existing in easy harmony, and entrances on all the upper floors as well as the bottommost. Nor did it escape Jack's attention that there were neither locks on the doors nor guards at the entrances to the palace – and this was far from the least of the wonders that he saw.

But the greatest wonder of all, so far as Jack was concerned, was the sylph maiden Poseidonia, the king's daughter, who came out to greet her father on his return to the city. The instant he clapped eyes on her slim and perfect form, Jack was determined to win her. Nor was that a difficult task, as he was a well-made man with a soldier's straight bearing, and his frank admiration drew from her a happy blush and no protests whatsoever. Further, the mer-people being a Heathen folk and not bound by Christian standards of propriety, their mutual infatuation quickly found physical expression.

Time went by. It may have been days or it may have been months.

Late one afternoon, lying in the princess's bed, with the sheets and pillows all in sensuous disarray and a greenish-blue noontide light flowing through her bedroom windows, Jack cleared his throat and hesitantly said, 'Tell me something, oh my best and belovedest.'

'Anything!' replied that passionate young sylph.

'One thing continues to bother me – a small thing, perhaps, but it nitters and natters at the back of my mind, and I cannot rid myself of it, however I try. When first I arrived in this rich and splendid land, your father told me he had been reading of my adventures. By what magic? In what unimaginable book?'

'Why, in this one, dearest of scoundrels.' (It was the sylph's single most endearing quality that she loved Jack for exactly what he was and not one whit through any misapprehension of his char- acter.) 'What other book could it possibly be?'

Jack looked from one end of the room to the other, and replied, 'I see no book.'

'Well, of course not, silly. If it were *here*, how could you be in it?'

'I cannot say, oh delight of my eyes, for your answer makes absolutely no sense to me.'

'Trust me, he read of you in this book, nor have you ever left it.'

Now Jack began to feel the stirrings of anger. '*This* one you say – *which* one? The devil take me if I can make heads or tails of your answers!'

Then the laughter died in Poseidonia's throat, and she exclaimed, 'You poor thing! You truly do not understand, do you?'

'If I understood, would I be at this very instant begging you like a fool for a simple and straight-forward answer?'

She regarded him with a sad little smile. 'I think it is time you talked with my father,' she said at last.

'Is my Lissome young daughter not energetic enough to please you?' asked the king of the Mummelsee.

'That and more,' said Jack, who had long grown used to the sylphs' shockingly direct manner of speaking.

'Then be content with her and this carefree existence you lead, and do not seek to go questing out beyond the confines of these ever-so-pleasant pages.'

'Again you speak in riddles! Majesty, this business is driving me mad. I beg of you, for this once, speak to me plain and simply, even as if I were but a child.'

The king sighed. 'You know what books are?'

'Yes, of course.'

'When was the last time you read one?'

'Why, I—'

'Exactly. Or that anybody you know read one?'

'I have been in the company of rough-and-tumble soldiers, whose response to coming upon a library might typically be to use its contents to start their campfires, so this is not terribly surprising.'

'You must have read books in your youth. Can you tell me the plot of any of them?'

Jack fell silent.

'You see? Characters in books do not read books. Oh, they snap them shut when somebody enters the room, or fling them aside in disgust at what they fancy is said within, or hide their faces in one which they pretend to peruse while somebody else lectures them on matters they'd rather not confront. But they do not *read* them. 'Twould be recursive, rendering each book effectively infinite, so that no single one might be finished without reading them all. This is the infallible method of discovering on which side of the page you lie – have you read a book this year?' The king arched an eyebrow and waited.

After a very long silence, Jack said, 'No. I have not.'

'Then there you are.'

'But . . . how can this be? How can we possibly . . . ?'

'It is the simplest thing imaginable,' replied the

king. 'I, for example, dwell within chapters eleven through seventeen of book five of something called *Simplicissimus*. It is, I assure you, a good life. So what if the walls of my palace are as thin as paper, the windows simply drawn on by pen, and my actions circumscribed by the whimsy of the artist? I neither age nor die, and when you, taking a brief rest from your romantic gymnastics with my daughter, care to visit me, I always find our little conversations diverting.'

Glumly, Jack stared out through a window paned with nacre polished so smooth as to be transparent. 'It is a hard thing,' he said, 'to realize that one is not actually real.' Then, after a long moment's thought, 'But this makes no sense. Granted that my current surroundings and condition are hardly to be improved upon. Yet I have seen things in the war that . . . Well, it doesn't bear thinking upon. Who on earth would create such a world as ours? Who could possibly find amusement in such cruelties as, I grant you, I have sometimes been a part of?'

'Sir,' said the king, 'I am not the artist, and he, I suspect, is nobody of any great esteem in his unimaginably larger world. He might pass you on the street unnoticed. In conversation, it is entirely possible, he would not impress you favorably. Why, then, should you expect more from him than he – or, as it may be, she – might reasonably expect from his or her vastly more potent creator?'

'Are you saying that our author's world is no better than our own?'

'It is possible it is worse. From his work we can infer certain things about the world in which he lives. Our architecture is ornate and romantic. His therefore is plain and dull – sheets of gray concrete, perhaps, with each window the exact twin of all the others – or he would not have bothered to imagine ours in such delightful detail.'

'Then, since our world is so crude and violent, it stands to reason that his must be a paragon of peace and gentility?'

'Say rather that ours has an earthy vigor while his is mired down in easy hypocrisy.'

Shaking his head slowly, Jack said, 'How is it that you know so much about the world we live in, and yet I know so little?'

'There are two types of characters, my son. Yours is forever sailing out of windows with his trousers in his hand, impersonating foreign dignitaries with an eye to defrauding uncharitable bishops, being ambushed in lightless alleys by knife-wielding ruffians, and coming home early to discover his newlywed bride in bed with his mistress's husband.'

'It is as if you had been reading my diary,' Jack said wonderingly. 'Had I a diary to read.'

'That is because you are the active sort of character, whose chief purpose is to move the plot along. I am, however, more the reflective sort of character, whose purpose it is to expound upon and thus reveal the inner meaning of the narrative. But I see you are confused – let us step briefly out of my story.'

And, as simply as one might turn a page, Jack found himself standing in a pleasant garden, awash in the golden light of a late-afternoon sun. The king of the Mummelsee was seated in a chair which, though plain and simple, suggested a throne – indeed, such a throne as a philosopher-king might inhabit.

'That is very well observed of you,' the king said in response to Jack's unspoken observation. 'It is possible that, with encouragement, you could be converted to a reflective character yet.'

'Where are we?'

'This is my dear friend Dr .Vandermast's garden in Zayana, where it is eternally afternoon. Here, he and I have had many a long discussion of entelechy and epistemology and other such unimportant and ephemeral nothings. The good doctor has discreetly made himself absent that we may talk in private. He himself resides in a book called – but what matters that? This is one of those magical places where we may with equanimity discuss the nature of the world. Indeed, its aspect is such that we could scarce do otherwise if we tried.'

A hummingbird abruptly appeared before Jack, hanging in the air like a frantic feathered jewel. He extended a finger and the bird hovered just above it, so that he could feel the delicate push of air from its madly pumping wings upon his skin. 'What marvel is this?' he asked.

'It is just my daughter. Though she does not appear in this scene, still she desires to make her wishes known – and so she expresses herself in imagery. Thank you, dear, you may leave now.' The king clapped his hands and the hummingbird vanished. 'She will be heartbroken if you depart from our fictive realm. But doubtless another hero will come along and, being fictional, Poseidonia neither learns from her experiences nor lets them embitter her against their perpetrator's gender. She will greet him as openly and enthusiastically as she did you.'

Jack felt a perfectly understandable twinge of jealousy. But he set it aside. Hewing to the gist of the discussion, he said, 'Is this an academic argument, sir? Or is there a practical side to it?'

'Dr .Vandermast's garden is not like other places. If you were to wish to leave our world entirely, then I have no doubt it could be easily arranged.'

'Could I then come back?'

'Alas, no,' the king said regretfully. 'One miracle is enough for any life. And more than either of us, strictly speaking, deserves, I might add.'

Jack picked up a stick and strode back and forth along the flower beds, lashing at the heads of the taller blossoms. 'Must I then decide based on no information at all? Leap blindly into the abyss or remain doubtful at its lip forever? This is, as you say, a delightful existence. But can I be content with this life, knowing there is another and yet being ignorant of what it might entail?'

'Calm yourself. If that is all it takes, then let us see what the alternative might be.' The king of the Mummelsee reached down into his lap and turned the page of a leather-bound folio that Jack had not noticed before.

'Are you going to be sitting there forever, wool-gathering, when there are chores to be done? I swear, you must be the single laziest man in the world.'

Jack's fat wife came out of the kitchen, absently scratching her behind. Gretchen's face was round where once it had been slender, and there was a slight hitch in her gait, where formerly her every movement had been a dance to music only she could hear. Yet Jack's heart softened within him at the sight of her, as it always did.

He put down his goose quill and sprinkled sand over what he had written so far. 'You are doubtless right, my dear,' he said mildly. 'You always are.'

As he was stumping outdoors to chop wood, draw water, and feed the hog they were fattening for Fastnacht, he caught a glimpse of himself in the mirror that hung by the back door. An old and haggard man with a beard so thin it looked moth eaten glared back at him in horror. 'Eh, sir,' he murmured to himself, 'you are not the fine young soldier who tumbled Gretchen in the hayloft only minutes after meeting her, so many years ago.'

A cold wind blew flecks of ice in his face when he stepped outside, and the sticks in the wood-pile were frozen together so that he had to bang them with the blunt end of the axe to separate them so that they might be split. When he went to the well, the ice was so thick that breaking it raised a sweat. Then, after he'd removed the rock from the lid covering the bucket of kitchen slops and started down toward the sty, he slipped on a patch of ice and upended the slops over the front of his clothing. Which meant not only that he would have to wash those clothes weeks ahead of schedule – which in wintertime was an ugly chore – but that he had to gather up the slops from the ground with his bare hands and ladle them back into the bucket, for come what may the pig still needed to be fed.

So, muttering and complaining to himself, old Jack clomped back into the house, where he washed his hands and changed into clean clothing and sat back down to his writing again. After a few minutes, his wife entered the room and exclaimed, 'It is so cold in here!' She busied herself building up the fire, though it was so much work carrying wood up to his office that Jack would rather have endured the cold to save himself the extra labor later on. Then she came up behind him and placed her hands on his shoulders. 'Are you writing a letter to Wilhelm again?'

'Who else?' Jack growled. 'We work our fingers to the bone to send him money, and he never writes! And when he does, his letters are so brief! He spends all his time drinking and running up debts with tailors and chasing after—' He caught himself in time, and coughed. 'Chasing after inappropriate young women.'

'Well, after all, when you were his age—'

'When I was his age, I never did any such thing,' Jack said indignantly.

'No, of course not,' his wife said. He could feel the smile he did not turn around to see. 'You poor foolish dear.'

She kissed the top of his head.

The sun emerged from behind a cloud as Jack reappeared, and the garden blazed with a hundred bright colors – more of Poseidonia's influence, Jack supposed. Its flowers turned their heads toward him flirtatiously and opened their blossoms to his gaze.

'Well?' said the king of the Mummelsee. 'How was it?'

'I'd lost most of my teeth,' Jack said glumly, 'and there was an ache in my side that never went away. My children were grown and moved away, and there was nothing left in my life to look forward to but death.'

'That is not a judgment,' the king said, 'but only a catalog of complaints.'

'There was, I must concede, a certain authenticity

to life on the other side of the gate. A validity and complexity which ours may be said to lack.'

'Well, there you are, then.'

The shifting light darkened and a wind passed through the trees, making them sigh. 'On the other hand, there is a purposefulness to this life which the other does not have.'

'That too is true.'

'Yet if there is a purpose to our existence – and I feel quite certain that there is – I'll be damned if I know what it is.'

'Why, that is easily enough answered!' the king said. 'We exist to amuse the reader.'

'And this reader – who exactly is he?'

'The less said about the reader,' said the king of the Mummelsee fervently, 'the better.' He stood. 'We have talked enough,' he said. 'There are two gates from this garden. One leads back whence we came. The second leads to . . . the other place. That which you glimpsed just now.'

'Has it a name, this "other place"?'

'Some call it Reality, though the aptness of that title is, of course, in dispute.'

Jack tugged at his mustache and chewed at the inside of his cheek. 'This is, I swear, no easy choice.'

"Yet we cannot stay in this garden forever, Jack. Sooner or later, you must choose.'

'Indeed, sir, you are right,' Jack said. 'I must be resolute.' All about him, the garden waited in hushed stillness. Not a bullfrog disturbed the glassy surface of the lily pond. Not a blade of grass stirred in the meadow. The very air seemed tense with anticipation.

He chose.

So it was that Johann von Grimmelshausen, sometimes known as Jurgen, escaped the narrow and constricting confines of literature, and of the Mummelsee as well, by becoming truly human and thus subject to the whims of history. Which means that he, of course, died centuries ago. Had he remained a fiction, he would still be with us today, though without the richness of experience which you and I endure every day of our lives.

Was he right to make the choice he did? Only God can tell. And if there is no God, why, then we will never know.

MALLON THE GURU

PETER STRAUB

Near the end of what he later called his 'developmental period,' the American guru Spencer Mallon spent four months traveling through India with his spiritual leader, Urdang, a fearsome German with a deceptively mild manner. In the third of these months, they were granted an audience with a yogi, a great holy man who lived in the village of Sankwal. However, an odd, unsettling thing happened as soon as Mallon and Urdang reached the outskirts of the village. A carrion crow plummeted out of the sky and landed, with an audible thump and a skirl of feathers, dead on the dusty ground immediately in front of them. Instantly, villagers began streaming toward them, whether because of the crow or because he and Urdang were fair-skinned strangers, Mallon did not know. He fought the uncomfortable feeling of being surrounded by strangers gibbering away in a language he would never understand, and in the midst of this great difficulty tried to find the peace and balance he sometimes experienced during his almost daily, generally two-hour meditations.

An unclean foot with tuberous three-inch nails flipped aside the dead bird. The villagers drew closer, close enough to touch, and leaning in and jabbering with great intensity, urged them forward by tugging at their shirts and waistbands. They, or perhaps just he, Spencer Mallon, was being urged, importuned, begged to execute some unimaginable service. They wished him to perform some kind of *task*, but the task remained mysterious. The mystery became clearer only after a rickety hut seemed almost to materialize, miragelike, from the barren scrap of land where it squatted. One of the men urging Mallon along yanked his sleeve more forcefully and implored him, with flapping, birdlike gestures, to go into the hut, evidently his, to enter it and *see* something – the man indicated the necessity for vision by jabbing a black fingernail at his protuberant right eye.

I have been chosen, Mallon thought. *I, not Urdang, have been elected by these ignorant and suffering people.*

Within the dim, hot enclosure, he was invited to gaze at a small child with huge, impassive eyes and limbs like twigs. The child appeared to be dying. Dark yellow crusts ringed its nostrils and its mouth.

Staring at Mallon, the trembling villager raised one of his own hands and brushed his fingertips gently against the boy's enormous forehead. Then he waved Mallon closer to the child's pallet.

'Don't you get it?' Urdang said. 'You're supposed to touch the boy.'

Reluctantly, unsure of what he was actually being asked to do and fearful of contracting some hideous disease, Mallon extended one hand and lowered his extended fingers toward the boy's skeletal head as if he were about to dip them for the briefest possible moment into a pail of reeking fluid drawn from the communal cesspit.

Kid, he thought, *for the sake of my reputation, I hope we're going to see a miracle cure.*

At the moment of contact, he felt as though a tiny particle of energy, a radiant erg as quick and flowing as mercury, passed directly from his hand through the fragile wall of the boy's skull.

In the midst of this extremely interesting and in fact amazing phenomenon, the father collapsed to his knees and began to croon in gratitude.

'How do these people know about me?' he asked.

'The real question is, what do they think you did?' Urdang said. 'And how do they think they know it? Once we have had our audience, I suggest we put on our skates.'

Urdang, Mallon realized, had no idea of what had just happened. It was the restoration of a cosmic balance: a bird died, and a child was saved. He had been the fulcrum between death and the restoration. A perfect Indian experience had been given to him. The great yogi would embrace him as he would a son, he would open his house and his ashram and welcome him as a student of unprecedented capabilities.

Proceeding down a narrow lane in the village

proper, Mallon carelessly extended two fingers and ran them along a foot or two of the mudplastered wall at his side. He had no plan, no purpose beyond just seeing what was going to happen, for he knew that in some fashion his touch would alter the universe. The results of his test were deeply gratifying: on the wall, the two lines traced by his fingers glowed a brilliant neon blue that brightened and intensified until it threatened to sear the eyes. The villagers spun around and waved their arms, releasing an ecstatic babble threaded with high-pitched cries of joy. Along with everybody else, Mallon had stopped moving to look at the marvelous, miraculous wall. An electrical buzz and hum filled all the spaces within his body; he felt as though he could shoot sparks from his fingers.

I should touch that kid all over again, he thought. *He'd zoom right up off the bed.*

In seconds, the vibrant blue lines cooled, shrank, and faded back into the dull khaki of the wall. The villagers thrust forward, rubbed the wall, flattened themselves against it, spoke to it in whispers. Those who kissed the wall came away with mouths and noses painted white with dust. Only Mallon, and perhaps Urdang, had been chagrined to see the evidence of his magic vanish so quickly from the world.

The babbling crowd, not at all disappointed, clustered again around him and pushed him forward. Their filthy, black-nailed hands gave him many a fond pat and awed, stroking caress. Eventually they came to a high yellow wall and an iron gate. Urdang pushed himself through the crowd and opened the gate upon a long, lush flower garden. At the distant end of the garden stood a graceful terra-cotta building with a row of windows on both sides of its elaborately tiled front door. The dark heads of young women appeared in the windows. Giggling, the women retreated backward.

The villagers thrust Mallon and Urdang forward. The gates clanged behind them. Far away, an oxcart creaked. Cattle lowed from behind the creamy-looking terra-cotta building.

I am in love with all of India! Mallon thought.

'Come nearer,' said a dry, penetrating voice.

A small man in a dhoti of dazzling white sat in the lotus position just in front of a fountain placed in the middle of the garden. A moment before, Mallon had noticed neither the man nor the fountain.

'I believe that you, sir, are Urdang,' the man said. 'But who is your most peculiar follower?'

'His name is Spencer Mallon,' Urdang said. 'But, Master, with all due respect, he is not peculiar.'

'This man is a peculiarity entire unto himself,' said the little man. 'Please sit down.'

They sat before him, adjusting themselves into the lotus position as well as they could, Urdang easily and perfectly, Mallon less so. He considered it extremely likely that in some deeply positive way he actually was peculiar. Peculiarity of his kind amounted to a great distinction, as the Master understood and poor Urdang did not.

Before them, the great holy man contemplated them in a silence mysteriously shaped by the harsh angles and shining curves of his shaven head and hard, nutlike face. Mallon gathered from the quality of the silence that the yogi was after all not unreservedly pleased by the homage of their visit. Of course the difficult element had to be Urdang – the presence of Urdang in this sacred place. After something like nine or ten minutes, the yogi turned his head to one side and, speaking either to the flowers or the splashing fountain, ordered sweet tea and honey cakes. These delights were delivered by two of the dark-haired girls, who wore beautiful, highly colored saris and sandals with little bells on the straps.

'Is it true that when you came into our village, a carrion crow came toppling dead from the sky?' asked the holy man.

Urdang and Mallon nodded.

'That is a sign, Urdang. We must consider the meaning of this sign.'

'Let us do so, then,' Urdang said. 'I believe the sign to be auspicious. That which eats death is itself devoured by it.'

'Yet death comes tumbling into our village.'

'Immediately afterward, this young man touched the forehead of a dying child and restored him to good health.'

'No one of this young man's age and position can do this,' said the yogi. 'Such a feat requires great holiness, but even great holiness is not sufficient. One must have spent decades in study and meditation.'

'And yet it happened. Death was banished.'

'Death is never banished, it merely travels elsewhere. Your student greatly distresses me.'

'Dear Master, as the villagers led us toward your house, this man I have brought to you extended one arm and—'

The yogi silenced him with a wave of the hand. 'I am not concerned with such displays. Fireworks do not impress me. Yes, they indicate the presence of a gift, but of what use is this gift, to what purposes will it be turned?'

Mallon had touched a dying child, the Master said, yet had he restored it to health? Even if he had, was the healing truly his work? Mere belief could heal as successfully as other forces, temporarily. Was Mallon well schooled in the sutras? How great was his knowledge of Buddhist teachings?

Urdang replied that Mallon was not a Buddhist.

'Then why have you come?'

Mallon spoke from his heart. 'I come for your blessing, dear Master.'

'You cannot have my blessing. I ask for yours instead.' The holy man spoke as if to an ancient enemy.

'*My* blessing?' Mallon asked.

'Render it unto me as you did to the child.'

Confused and irritated, Mallon scooted forward and extended a hand. Almost, he wished to withhold his blessing, as had the yogi, but he could not behave so childishly in front of Urdang. The holy man leaned forward and permitted his brow to be brushed. If any molten particle of energy flew from his hand into the yogi's brain pan, Mallon did not feel its passage.

The Master's face contracted, no mean trick, and for a moment he closed his eyes.

'Well?' Mallon said. Urdang gasped at his rudeness.

'It is very much as I thought,' said the Master, opening his eyes. 'I cannot be responsible for your Spencer Mallon, and you must not request any more of me. I see it all very clearly. Already, this most peculiar, this most dangerously peculiar man has awakened disorder within our village. He must leave Sankwal immediately, and you who brought him here, Urdang, you must leave with him.'

'If that is your wish, Master,' Urdang said. 'But perhaps—'

'No. No more. You would be wise to separate yourself from this student as soon as you can do so honorably. And as for you, young man . . .'

He turned his sorrowful eyes upon Mallon, and Mallon could feel his spirit hovering near, irate and fearful.

'I advise you to take great, great care in everything

264

you do. But it would be wisest if you did nothing at all.'

'Master, why are you afraid of me?' Mallon asked. 'I want only to love you.' In truth, he had wished to love the Master before he met him. Now, he wanted only to leave the village and its frightened, envious yogi far behind him. And, he realized, if Urdang wanted to leave him, that would be fine, too.

'I am grateful you do not,' the Master said. 'You will go from my village now, both of you.'

When Urdang opened the gates, the lanes were empty. The villagers had fled back to their homes. The air darkened, and rain began to fall. Before they reached open ground, the earth had been churned to mud. A loud cry came from the hut of the poor man with the sick child, whether of joy or pain they could not say.

CATCH AND RELEASE

LAWRENCE BLOCK

When you spent enough time fishing, you got so you knew the waters. You had certain spots that had worked for you over the years, and you went to them at certain times of the day in certain seasons of the year. You chose the tackle appropriate to the circumstances, picked the right bait or lure, and tried your luck.

If they weren't biting, you moved on. Picked another spot.

He was Cruising the interstate, staying in the right-hand lane, keeping the big SUV a steady five miles an hour below the speed limit. As he passed each exit, he let up on the gas pedal while he kept an eye out for hitchhikers. There was a string of four exits where they were apt to queue up, college students looking to thumb their way home, or to another campus, or wherever they felt a need to go. There were so many of them, and they were always going someplace, and it hardly mattered where or why.

He drove north, passed four exits, took the fifth,

crossed over and got on the southbound entrance ramp. Four more exits, then off again and on again and he was once more heading north.

Taking his time.

There were hitchhikers at each exit, but his foot never touched the brake pedal. It would hover there, but he always saw something that made him drive on. There were plenty of girls out there today, some of them especially alluring in tight jeans and braless T-shirts, but they all seemed to have boys or other girls as companions. The only solitary hitchhikers he saw were male. And he was not interested in boys. He wanted a girl, a girl all by herself.

Luke 5:5. *Lord, we fished all night and caught nothing.*

Sometimes you could drive all day, and the only reason you'd have to stop was to fill the gas tank. But the true fisherman could fish all night and catch nothing and not regard the time as ill spent. A true fisherman was patient, and while he waited he gave his mind over to the recollection of other days at the water's edge. He'd let himself remember in detail how a particular quarry had risen to the bait and taken the hook. And put up a game fight.

And sizzled in the pan.

When he stopped for her, she picked up her backpack and trotted up to the car. He rolled down the window and asked her where she was headed, and she hesitated long enough to have a look at him and decide he was okay. She named a town fifty or sixty miles up the road.

'No problem,' he said. 'I can just about take you to your front door.'

She tossed her pack in the back, then got in front beside him. Closed the door, fastened her seat belt.

She said something about how grateful she was, and he said something appropriate, and he joined the stream of cars heading north. What, he wondered, had she seen in that quick appraising glance? What was it that had assured her he was all right?

His face was an unmemorable one. The features were regular and average and, well, ordinary. Nothing stuck out.

Once, years ago, he'd grown a mustache. He had thought it might give his face some character, but all it did was look out of place. What was it doing there on his lip? He kept it there, waiting to get used to it, and one day he realized that wasn't going to happen, and shaved it off.

And went back to his forgettable face. Unremarkable, unthreatening. Safe.

'A Fisherman,' she said. 'My dad likes to go fishing. Once, twice a year he'll go away for the weekend with a couple of his buddies and come back with an ice chest full of fish. And my mom gets stuck with cleaning them, and for a week the house totally smells of fish.'

'Well, that's a problem I'm spared,' he told her. 'I'm what they call a catch-and-release fisherman.'

'You don't come home with a full ice chest?'

'I don't even have an ice chest. Oh, I used to. But what I found over time was that it was the sport I enjoyed, and it was a lot simpler and easier if the game ended with the fish removed from the hook and slipped gently back into the water.'

She was silent for a moment. Then she asked if he thought they enjoyed it.

'The fish? Now that's an interesting question. It's hard to know what a fish does or doesn't enjoy, or even if the word *enjoy* can be applied to a fish. You could make the case that a fish fighting for its life gets to be intensely alive in a way it otherwise doesn't, but is that good or bad from the fish's point of view?' He smiled. 'When they swim away,' he said, 'I get the sense that they're glad to be alive. But I may just be trying to put myself in their position. I can't really know what it's like for them.'

'I guess not.'

'One thing I can't help but wonder,' he said, 'is if they learn anything from the experience. Are they warier the next time around? Or will they take the hook just as readily for the next fisherman who comes along?'

She thought about it. 'I guess they're just fish,' she said.

'Well now,' he said. 'I guess they are.'

★   ★   ★

She was a pretty thing. A business major, she told him, taking most of her elective courses in English because she'd always liked to read. Her hair was brown with auburn highlights, and she had a good figure, with large breasts and wide hips. Built for childbearing, he thought, and she'd bear three or four of them, and she'd gain weight with each pregnancy and never quite manage to lose all of it. And her face, already a little chubby, would broaden and turn bovine, and the sparkle would fade out of her eyes.

There was a time when he'd have been inclined to spare her all that.

'Really,' she said, 'you could have just dropped me at the exit. I mean, this is taking you way out of your way.'

'Less so than you'd think. Is that your street coming up?'

'Uh-huh. If you want to drop me at the corner—'

But he drove her to the door of her suburban house. He waited while she retrieved her backpack, then let her get halfway up the path to her door before he called her back.

'You know,' he said, 'I was going to ask you something earlier, but I didn't want to upset you.'

'Oh?'

'Aren't you nervous hitching rides with strangers? Don't you think it's dangerous?'

'Oh,' she said. 'Well, you know, everybody does it.'

'I see.'

'And I've always been okay so far.'

'A young woman alone—'

'Well, I usually team up with somebody. A boy, or at least another girl. But this time, well . . .'

'You figured you'd take a chance.'

She flashed a smile. 'It worked out okay, didn't it?'

He was silent for a moment, but held her with his eyes. Then he said, 'Remember the fish we were talking about?'

'The fish?'

'How it feels when it slips back into the water. And whether it learns anything from the experience.'

'I don't understand.'

'Not everyone is a catch-and-release fisherman,' he said. 'That's probably something you ought to keep in mind.'

She was still standing there, looking puzzled, while he put the SUV in gear and pulled away.

He drove home, feeling fulfilled. He had never moved from the house he was born in, and it had been his alone ever since his mother's death ten years ago.

He checked the mail, which yielded half a dozen envelopes with checks in them. He had a mail-order business, selling fishing lures, and he spent the better part of an hour preparing the checks for deposit and packing the orders for shipment. He'd make more money if he put his business online and let people pay with credit cards, but he didn't need much money, and he found it easier to let things remain as they were. He ran the same ads every month in the same magazines, and his old customers reordered, and enough new customers turned up to keep him going.

He cooked some pasta, heated some meat sauce, chopped some lettuce for a salad, drizzled a little olive oil over it. He ate at the kitchen table, washed the dishes, watched the TV news. When it ended he left the picture on but muted the sound, and thought about the girl.

Now, though, he gave himself over to the fantasy she inspired. A lonely road. A piece of tape across her mouth. A struggle ending with her arms broken.

Stripping her. Piercing each of her openings in turn. Giving her physical pain to keep her terror company.

And finishing her with a knife. No, with his hands, strangling her. No, better yet, with his forearm across her throat, and his weight pressing down, throttling her.

Ah, the joy of it, the thrill of it, the sweet release of it. And now it was almost as real to him as if it had happened.

But it hadn't happened. He'd left her at her door, untouched, with only a hint of what might have been. And, because it hadn't happened, there was no ice chest full of fish to clean——no body to dispose of, no evidence to get rid of, not even that feeling of regret that had undercut his pleasure on so many otherwise perfect occasions.

Catch and release. That was the ticket, catch and release.

The Roadhouse had a name, Toddle Inn, but nobody ever called it anything but Roy's, after the man who'd owned it for close to fifty years until his liver quit on him.

That was something he would probably never have to worry about, as he'd never been much of a drinker. Tonight, three days after he'd dropped the young hitchhiker at her door, he'd had the impulse to go barhopping, and Roy's was his fourth stop. He'd ordered a beer at the first place and drank two sips of it, left the second bar without ordering anything, and drank most of the Coke he ordered at bar number three.

Roy's had beer on draft, and he stood at the bar and ordered a glass of it. There was an English song he'd heard once, of which he recalled only one verse:

> *The man who buys a pint of beer*
> *Gets half a pint of water;*
> *The only thing the landlord's got*
> *That's any good's his daughter.*

The beer was watery, to be sure, but it didn't matter because he didn't care about beer, good or bad. But the bar held something to interest him, the very thing he'd come out for.

She was two stools away from him, and she was drinking something in a stemmed glass, with an orange slice in it. At first glance she looked like the hitchhiker, or like her older sister, the one who'd gone wrong. Her blouse was a size too small, and she'd tried to cope by unbuttoning an extra button. The lipstick was smeared on her full-lipped mouth, and her nail polish was chipped.

She picked up her drink and was surprised to find that she'd finished it. She shook her head, as if wondering how to contend with this unanticipated development, and while she was working it out he lifted a hand to catch the barman's eye, then pointed at the girl's empty glass.

She waited until the fresh drink was in front of her, then picked it up and turned toward her benefactor. 'Thank you,' she said, 'you're a gentleman.'

He closed the distance between them. 'And a fisherman,' he said.

Sometimes it didn't matter what you had on your hook. Sometimes it wasn't even necessary to wet a line. Sometimes all you had to do was sit there and they'd jump right into the boat.

She'd had several drinks before the one he'd bought her, and she didn't really need the two others he bought her after that. But she thought she did, and he didn't mind spending the money or sitting there while she drank them.

Her name, she told him repeatedly, was Marni. He was in no danger of forgetting that fact, nor did she seem to be in any danger of remembering his name, which she kept asking him over and over. He'd said it was Jack – it wasn't – and she kept apologizing for her inability to retain that information. 'I'm Marni,' she'd say on each occasion. 'With an *i*,' she added, more often than not.

He found himself remembering a woman he'd picked up years ago in a bar with much the same ambience. She'd been a very different sort of drunk, although she'd been punishing the Harvey Wallbangers as industriously as Marni was knocking back the gandy dancers. She'd grown quieter and quieter, and her eyes went glassy, and by the time he'd driven them to the place he'd selected in advance, she was out cold. He'd had some very interesting plans for her, and here she was, the next thing to comatose, and wholly incapable of knowing what was being done to her.

So he'd let himself imagine that she was dead, and took her that way, and kept waiting for her to wake up, but she didn't. And it was exciting, more exciting than he'd have guessed, but at the end he held himself back.

And paused for a moment to consider the situation, and then very deliberately broke her neck. And then took her again, imagining that she was only sleeping.

And that was good, too.

'At least I got the house,' she was saying. 'My ex took the kids away from me, can you imagine that?

Got some lawyer saying I was an unfit mother. Can you imagine that?'

The house her ex-husband had let her keep certainly looked like a drunk lived in it. It wasn't filthy, just remarkably untidy. She grabbed him by the hand and led him up a flight of stairs and into her bedroom, which was no neater than the rest of the place, then turned and threw herself into his arms.

He disengaged, and she seemed puzzled. He asked if there was anything in the house to drink, and she said there was beer in the fridge, and there might be some vodka in the freezer. He said he'd be right back.

He gave her five minutes, and when he returned with a can of Rolling Rock and a half-pint of vodka, she was sprawled naked on her back, snoring. He set the beer can and the vodka bottle on the bedside table, and drew the blanket to cover her.

'Catch and release,' he said, and left her there.

Fishing was not just a metaphor. A couple of days later he walked out his front door into a cool autumn morning. The sky was overcast, the humidity lower than it had been. The breeze was out of the west.

It was just the day for it. He got his gear together, made his choices, and drove to the bank of a creek that was always good on this kind of day. He fished the spot for an hour, and by the time he left he had hooked and landed three trout. Each had put up a good fight, and as he released them he might have observed that they'd earned their freedom, that each deserved another chance at life.

But what did that mean, really? Could a fish be said to earn or deserve anything? Could anyone? And did a desperate effort to remain alive somehow entitle one to live?

Consider the humble flounder. He was a salt-water fish, a bottom fish, and when you hooked him he rarely did much more than flop around a little while you reeled him in. Did this make him the trout's moral inferior? Did he have less right to live because of his genetically prescribed behavior?

He stopped on the way home, had a hamburger and a side of welldone fries. Drank a cup of coffee. Read the paper.

Back home, he cleaned and sorted his tackle and put everything away where it belonged.

That night it rained, and did so off and on for the next three days. He stayed close to home, watched a little television.

Nights, he'd lean back in his recliner and close his eyes, letting himself remember. Once, a few months back, he'd tried to count. He'd been doing this for years, long before his mother died, and in the early years his appetite had been ravenous. It was, he sometimes thought, a miracle he hadn't been caught. Back then he'd left DNA all over the place, along with God knew what else in the way of trace evidence.

Somehow he'd gotten away with it. If they'd ever picked him up, if he'd ever attracted the slightest bit of official attention, he was sure he'd have caved immediately. He'd have told them everything, confessed to everything. They wouldn't have needed trace evidence, let alone DNA. All they'd have needed was a cell to lock him into and a key to throw away.

So there had been many, but he'd ranged far and wide and little of what he did ran to pattern. He'd read about other men who had very specific tastes, in essence always hunting the same woman and killing her in the same fashion. If anything, he'd deliberately sought variety, not for precautionary reasons but because it was indeed the spice of life – or death, as you prefer. *When I have to choose between two evils*, Mae West had said, *I pick the one I haven't tried yet.* Made sense to him.

And after he'd changed, after he had in fact become a catch-and-release fisherman, there'd been a point when it seemed to him as though he'd had a divine hand keeping him safe all those years. Who was to say that there was not a purpose to it all, and a guiding force running the universe? He'd been spared so that he could – do what? Catch and release?

It hadn't taken him long to decide that was nonsense. He'd killed all those girls because he'd wanted to – or needed to, whatever. And he'd stopped killing because he no longer needed or wanted to kill, was in fact better served by, well, catching and releasing.

So how many had there been? The simple answer was that he did not know, and had no way of knowing. He had never taken trophies, never kept souvenirs. He had memories, but it had become virtually impossible to distinguish between recollections of actual events and recollections of fantasies. One memory was as real as another, whether it had happened or not. And, really, what difference did it make?

He thought of that serial killer they'd caught in Texas, the idiot who kept finding new killings to confess to and leading the authorities to more unmarked graves. Except some of the victims turned out to have been killed when he was in custody in another state. Was he conning them, for some inexplicable reason? Or was he simply remembering – vividly, and in detail – acts he had not in actuality committed?

He didn't mind the rain. His had been a solitary childhood, and he'd grown into a solitary adult. He had never had friends, and had never felt the need. Sometimes he liked the illusion of society, and at such times he would go to a bar or restaurant, or walk in a shopping mall, or sit in a movie theater, simply to be among strangers. But most of the time his own company was company enough.

One rainy afternoon he picked a book from the shelf. It was *The Compleat Angler*, by Izaak Walton, and he'd read it through countless times and flipped through it many times more. He always seemed to find something worth thinking about between its covers.

God never did make a more calm, quiet, innocent recreation than angling, he read. The line resonated with him, as it always did, and he decided the only change he could make would be to the final word of it. He preferred fishing to angling, fisherman to angler. Stephen Leacock, after all, had observed that angling was the name given to fishing by people who couldn't fish.

On the first clear day, he made a grocery list and went to the mall. He pushed a cart up one aisle and down the next, picking up eggs and bacon and pasta and canned sauce, and he was weighing the merits of two brands of laundry detergent when he saw the woman.

He hadn't been looking for her, hadn't been looking for anyone. The only thing on his mind was detergent and fabric softener, and then he looked up and there she was.

She was beautiful, not young-pretty like the hitchhiker or slutty available like Marni the barfly, but genuinely beautiful. She could have been an actress or a model, though he somehow knew she wasn't.

Long dark hair, long legs, a figure that was at once athletic and womanly. An oval face, a strong nose, high cheekbones. But it wasn't her beauty he found himself responding to, it was something else, some indefinable quality that suddenly rendered the Tide and the Downy, indeed all the contents of his shopping cart, entirely unimportant.

She was wearing slacks and an unbuttoned long-sleeved canvas shirt over a pale blue T-shirt, and there was nothing terribly provocative about her outfit, but it scarcely mattered what she wore. He saw that she had a long shopping list she consulted, and only a few items already in her cart. He had time, he decided, time enough to wheel his cart to the bank of cashiers and pay cash for his groceries. That was better than simply walking away from the cart. People tended to remember you when you did that.

He loaded the bags of groceries back into his cart, and on the way to his SUV he turned periodically for a look at the entrance. He stowed the bags in back, got behind the wheel, and found a good spot to wait for her.

He sat there patiently with the motor idling. He wasn't paying attention to the time, was scarcely conscious of its passage, but felt he'd be comfortable waiting forever for the doors to slide open and the woman to emerge. The impatient man was not meant for fishing, and indeed waiting, patient passive waiting, was part of the pleasure of the pastime. If you got a bite every time your hook broke the water's surface, if you hauled up one fish after another, why, where was the joy?

Might as well drag a net. Hell, might as well toss a grenade into a trout stream and scoop up what floated to the surface.

Ah. There she was.

'I'm a Fisherman,' he said.

These were not the first words he spoke to her. Those were, 'Let me give you a hand.' He'd pulled up behind her just as she was about to put her groceries into the trunk of her car, and hopped out and offered his help. She smiled, and was about to thank him, but she never had the chance. He had a flashlight in one hand, three C batteries in a hard rubber case, and he took her by the shoulder and swung her around and hit her hard on the back of the head. He caught her as she fell, eased her down gently.

In no time at all she was propped up in the passenger seat of his SUV, and her groceries were in her trunk and the lid slammed shut. She was out cold, and for a moment he thought he might have struck too hard a blow, but he checked and found she had a pulse. He used duct tape on her wrists and ankles and across her mouth, fastened her seat belt, and drove off with her.

And, as patiently as he'd waited for her to emerge from the supermarket, he waited for her to return to consciousness. *I'm a fisherman*, he thought, and waited for the chance to say the words. He kept his eyes on the road ahead, but from time to time he shot her a glance, and her appearance never changed. Her eyes were shut, her muscles slack.

Then, not long after he'd turned onto a secondary road, he sensed that she was awake. He looked at her, and she looked the same, but he could somehow detect a change. He gave her another moment to listen to the silence, and then he spoke, told her that he was a fisherman.

No reaction from her. But he was certain she'd heard him.

'A catch-and-release fisherman,' he said. 'Not everybody knows what that means. See, I enjoy fishing. It does something for me that nothing else has ever done. Call it a sport or a pastime, as you prefer, but it's what I do and what I've always done.'

He thought about that. What he'd always done? Well, just about. Some of his earliest childhood memories involved fishing with a bamboo pole and baiting his hook with worms he'd dug himself in the backyard. And some of his earliest and most enduring adult memories involved fishing of another sort.

'Now I wasn't always a catch and release fisherman,' he said. 'Way I saw it back in the day, why would a man go to all the trouble of catching a fish and then just throw it back? Way it looked to me, you catch something, you kill it. You kill something, you eat it. Pretty clear cut, wouldn't you say?'

Wouldn't you say? But she wouldn't say anything,

couldn't say anything, not with the duct tape over her mouth. He saw, though, that she'd given up the pretense of unconsciousness. Her eyes were open now, although he couldn't see what expression they may have held.

'What happened,' he said, 'is I lost the taste for it. The killing and all. Most people, they think of fishing, and they somehow manage not to think about killing. They seem to think the fish comes out of the water, gulps for air a couple of times, and then obligingly gives up the ghost. Maybe he flops around a little first, but that's all there is to it. But, see, it's not like that. A fish can live longer out of water than you'd think. What you have to do, you gaff it. Hit it in the head with a club. It's quick and easy, but you can't get around the fact that you're killing it.'

He went on, telling her how you were spared the chore of killing when you released your catch. And the other unpleasant chores, the gutting, the scaling, the disposal of offal.

He turned from a blacktop road to a dirt road. He hadn't been down this road in quite a while, but it was as he remembered it, a quiet path through the woods that led to a spot he'd always liked. He quit talking now, letting her think about what he'd said, letting her figure out what to make of it, and he didn't speak again until he'd parked the car in a copse of trees, where it couldn't be seen from the road.

'I have to tell you,' he said, unfastening her seat

belt, wrestling her out of the car. 'I enjoy life a lot more as a catch-and-release fisherman. It's got all the pleasure of fishing without the downside, you know?'

He arranged her on the ground on her back. He went back for a tire iron, and smashed both her kneecaps before untaping her ankles, but left the tape on her wrists and across her mouth.

He cut her clothing off her. Then he took off his own clothes and folded them neatly. Adam and Eve in the garden, he thought. Naked and unashamed. *Lord, we fished all night and caught nothing.*

He fell on her.

Back home, he loaded his clothes into the washing machine, then drew a bath for himself. But he didn't get into the tub right away. He had her scent on him, and found himself in no hurry to wash it off. Better to be able to breathe it in while he relived the experience, all of it, from the first sight of her in the supermarket to the snapped-twig sound of her neck when he broke it.

And he remembered as well the first time he'd departed from the catch-and-release pattern. It had been less impulsive that time, he'd thought long and hard about it, and when the right girl turned up – young, blond, a cheerleader type, with a turned-up nose and a beauty mark on one cheek – when she turned up, he was ready.

Afterward he'd been upset with himself. Was he

regressing? Had he been untrue to the code he'd adopted? But it hadn't taken him long to get past those thoughts, and this time he felt nothing but calm satisfaction.

He was still a catch-and-release fisherman. He probably always would be. But, for God's sake, that didn't make him a vegetarian, did it?

Hell, no. A man still had to have a square meal now and then.

POLKA DOTS AND MOONBEAMS

JEFFREY FORD

He came for her at seven in the Belvedere convertible, top down, emerald green, with those fins in the back, jutting up like goalposts. From her third-floor apartment window, she saw him pull to the curb out front.

'Hey, Dex,' she called, 'where'd you get the submarine?'

He tilted back his homburg and looked up. 'All hands on deck, baby,' he said, patting the white leather seat.

'Give me a minute,' she said, laughed, and then blew him a kiss. She walked across the blue braided rug of the parlor and into the small bathroom with the water-stained ceiling and cracked plaster. Standing before the mirror, she leaned in close to check her make-up – enough rouge and powder to repair the walls. Her eye shadow was peacock blue, her mascara indigo. She gave her girdle a quick adjustment through her dress, then smoothed the material and stepped back to take it all in. Wrapped in strapless black, with a design of small white polka dots, like stars in a perfect universe, she turned in profile and inhaled. 'Good

Christ,' she said and exhaled. Passing through the kitchenette, she lifted a silver flask from the scarred tabletop and shoved it into her handbag.

Her heels made a racket on the wooden steps, and she wobbled for balance just after the first landing. Pushing through the front door, she stepped out into the evening light and the first cool breeze in what seemed an eternity. Dex was waiting for her at the curb, holding the passenger door open. As she approached, he tipped his hat and bent slightly at the waist.

'Looking fine there, madam,' he said.

She stopped to kiss his cheek.

The streets were empty, not a soul on the sidewalk, and save for the fact that here and there in a few of the windows of the tall, crumbling buildings they passed a dim yellow light could be seen, the entire city seemed empty as well. Dex turned left on Kraft and headed out of town.

'It's been too long, Adeline,' he said.

'Hush now, sugar,' she told him. 'Let's not think about that. I want you to tell me where you're taking me tonight.'

'I'll take you where I can get you,' he said.

She slapped his shoulder.

'I want a few cocktails,' she said.

'Of course, baby, of course. I thought we'd head over to the Ice Garden, cut the rug, have a few, and then head out into the desert after midnight to watch the stars fall.'

'You're an ace,' she said and leaned forward to

288

turn on the radio. A smoldering sax rendition of 'Every Time We Say Goodbye,' like a ball of wax string unwinding, looped once around their necks and then blew away on the rushing wind.

She lit them each a cigarette as the car sailed on through the rising night. An armadillo scuttled through the beams of the headlights fifty yards ahead, and the aroma of sage vied with Adeline's orchid scent. Clamping his cigarette between his lips, Dex put his free hand on her knee. She took it into her own, twining fingers with him. Then it was dark, the asphalt turning to dirt, and the moon rose slow as a bubble in honey above the distant silhouette of hills; a cosmic cream pie of a face, eyeing Adeline's décolletage. She leaned back into the seat, smiling, and closed her eyes. Only a moment passed before she opened them, but they were already there, passing down the long avenue lined with monkey-puzzle trees toward the circular drive of the glimmering Ice Garden. Dex pulled up and parked at the entrance. As he was getting out, a kid with red hair and freckles, dressed in a valet uniform, stepped forward.

'Mr Dex,' he said, 'we haven't seen you for a while.'

'Take a picture, Jim-Jim,' said Dex and flipped a silver dollar in the air. The kid caught it and dropped it into his vest pocket before opening the door for Adeline.

'How's tricks, Jim?' she asked as he delivered her to the curb.

'They just got better,' he said and patted his vest.

Dex came around the back of the car, took his date by the arm, and together they headed past the huge potted palms and down a brief tunnel toward a large rectangular patio open to the desert sky and bounded by a lush garden of the most magnificent crystal flora, emitting a blizzard of reflection. At the edge of the high-arching portico, Dex and Adeline stood for a moment, scanning the hubbub of revelers and, at the other end of the expanse of tables and chairs and dance floor, the onstage antics of that night's musical act, Nabob and His Ne'er-do-wells. Above the sea of heads, chrome trombone in one hand, mic in the other, Nabob belted out a jazzed-up version of 'Weak Knees and Wet Privates.'

A fellow in white tux and red fez approached the couple. He was a plump little man with a pencil mustache; a fifty-year-old baby playing dress-up. Dex removed his homburg and reached a hand out. 'Mondrian,' he said.

The maitre d' bowed slightly and, raising his voice above the din of merriment, said, 'Always a pleasure to have you both back.'

Adeline also shook hands.

'You're looking particularly lovely tonight,' he said.

'Table for two,' said Dex and flashed a crisp twenty under the nose of Mondrian. 'Something close to the dance floor.'

The plump man bowed again and in his ascent snatched the bill from Dex's hand. 'Follow me, my friends,' he said, and then turned and made his way slowly in amid the maze of tables and the milling crowd. As they moved through the packed house, Adeline waved hello to those who called her name, and when someone shouted to Dex, he winked, sighted them with his thumb, and pulled an invisible trigger. Mondrian found them a spot at the very front, just to the left of the stage. He pulled out and held Adeline's chair, and once she was seated, he bowed.

'Two gin wrinkles,' said Dex, and in an instant the maitre d' vanished back into the crowd.

Adeline retrieved two cigarettes from her purse and lit them on the small candle at the center of the table. Dex leaned over and she put one between his lips. She drew on the other.

'How does it feel to be back in action?' he asked her.

She smiled broadly, blew a stream of smoke, and nodded. 'It always feels right, the first couple of hours on the loose. I'm not thinking about anything else at this moment,' she said.

'Good,' he said and removed his hat, setting it on the empty chair next to him.

The music stopped then and was replaced by the chatter and laughter of the crowd, the clink of glasses and silverware. Nabob jumped down from the band platform, hit the ground, and rolled forward to spring upright next to Dex.

'Dexter,' he said.

'Still sweating out the hits,' said Dex and laughed as he shook hands with the bandleader.

'Bobby, aren't you gonna give me a kiss?' said Adeline.

'I'm just savoring the prospect,' he said and swept down to plant one on her lips. The kiss lasted for a while before Dex reached his leg around the table and kicked the performer in the ass. They all laughed as Nabob moved around the table and took a seat.

Folding his willowy arms in front of him, the bandleader leaned forward and shook his thin head. 'You two out for the stars tonight?' he asked.

'And then some,' said Adeline.

'So fill me in,' said Dex.

'Well, same old same old as usual, you know. And Killheffer's been waiting for you to return.'

A waitress appeared with two gin wrinkles – liquid pink ice and the Garden's own bathtub blend of gin. The glasses caught the light and revealed tiny bubbles rising from a fat red cherry. Dex slipped the young woman a five. She smiled at him before leaving the table.

'Fuck Killheffer,' said Dex, lifting his drink to touch glasses with Adeline.

'He's been in here almost every night, sitting back in the corner, slapping beads on that abacus of his and jotting numbers in a book,' said Nabob.

'Killheffer's solid fruitcake,' said Adeline.

'A strange fellow,' said Nabob, nodding. 'One slow night a while back, and most nights are slow when you fine folks aren't here, he bought me a drink and explained to me how the world is made of numbers. He said that when the stars fall it means everything is being divided by itself. Then he blew a smoke ring off one of his cigars. "Like that," he said and pointed at the center.'

'Did you get it?' asked Adeline.

Nabob laughed and shook his head. 'Jim-Jim makes more sense.'

'If he shows that shit-eating grin in here tonight, I'll fluff his cheeks,' said Dex.

Adeline took a drag of her cigarette and smiled. 'Sounds like boy fun. I thought you were here to dance and drink.'

'I am, baby. I am,' said Dex and finished the rest of his wrinkle, grabbing the cherry stem between his teeth. When he brought the glass away, the fruit hung down in front of his mouth. Adeline leaned over, put one arm around his shoulder and her lips around the cherry. She ate it slowly, chewing with only her lips before it all became a long kiss.

When they finished, Nabob said, 'You're an artist, Miss Adeline.'

Dex ordered another round of wrinkles. They talked for a few minutes about the old days, distant memories of bright sun and blue skies.

'Break's over,' said Nabob, quickly killing the rest of his drink. 'You two be good.'

'Do "Name and Number,"' called Adeline as the bandleader bounded toward the stage. With a running start, he leaped into the air, did a somersault, and landed, kneeling next to his mic stand. He stood slowly, like a vine twining up a trellis.

Dex and Adeline applauded, as did the rest of the house when it saw the performer back onstage. The willowy singer danced with himself for a moment before grabbing the mic. The Ne'er-do-wells took their places and lifted their instruments.

'Mondrian, my good man. Turn that gas wheel and lower the lights,' said Nabob, his voice echoing through the garden and out into the desert.

A moment later the flames of the candles in the center of each table went dimmer by half. 'Ooooh,' said Nabob and the crowd applauded.

'Lower,' he called to the maitre d'.

Mondrian complied. Whistles and catcalls rose out of the dull amber glow of the Ice Garden. The baritone sax hit a note so low it was like a tumbleweed blowing in off the desert. Then the strings came up, there was a flourish of piccolo and three sliding notes from Nabob's chrome T-bone. He brought the mouthpiece away, snapped his fingers to the music, and sang:

'My dear, you tear my heart asunder
When I look up your name and number
Right there in that open book
My flesh begins to cook
It's all sweetness mixed with dread
And then you close your legs around my head
As I look up your name and number . . .'

As Nabob dipped into the second verse, Dex rose and held his hand out to Adeline. He guided her through the darkness to the sea of swaying couples. They clutched each other desperately, legs between legs, lips locked, slowly turning through the dark. Within the deep pool of dancers there were currents of movement that could not be denied. They let themselves be drawn by the inevitable flow as the music played on.

When the song ended, Adeline said, 'I have to hit the powder room.'

They left the dance floor as the lights came up and walked toward the huge structure that held the casino, the gaming rooms, the pleasure parlors of the Ice Garden. Three stories tall, in the style of a Venetian palace, it was a monster of shadows with moonlight in its eyes. At the portico that led inside, Dex handed her a twenty and said, 'I'll see you back at the table.'

'I know,' she barely managed and kissed him on the cheek.

'You okay?' he asked.

'Same old same old,' she said and sighed.

He was supposed to laugh but only managed a smile. They turned away from each other. As he skirted the dance floor on the return journey, Dex looked up at Nabob and saw the performer, midsong, flash a glance at him and then nod toward the table. There was Killheffer, sporting a tux and his so-called smile of a hundred teeth, smoking a Wrath Majestic and staring into the sky.

Arriving at the table, Dex took his seat across from Killheffer, who, still peering upward, said, 'Gin wrinkles, I presumed.'

Dex noticed the fresh round of drinks, and reached for his.

'The stars are excited tonight,' said Killheffer, lowering his gaze.

'Too bad I'm not,' said Dex. 'What's it gonna be this time, Professor? Russian roulette? One card drawn from the bottom of a deck cut three ways? The blindfolded knife thrower?'

'You love to recall my miscalculations,' said Killheffer. 'Time breaks down, though, only through repetition.'

'I'm fed up with your cockeyed bullshit.'

'Well, don't be, because I tell you I've got it. I've done the math. How badly do you want out?'

'Want out?' said Dex. 'I don't even know how I got in. Tell me again you're not the devil.'

'I'm a simple professor of circumstance and fate. An academic with too strong an imagination.'

'Then why that crazy smile? All your antics? That cigar of yours smells like what I vaguely remember of the ocean.'

'I've always been a gregarious fellow and prized a good cigar. The hundred-tooth thing is a parlor trick of multiplication.'

'I'm so fucking tired,' Dex said.

Killheffer reached into his jacket pocket and brought forth a hypodermic needle. He laid it on the table. 'That's the solution,' he said.

The large hypo's glass syringe contained a jade green liquid.

Dex stared at it and shook his head. Tears appeared in the corners of his eyes. 'Are you kidding? That's it? That's the saddest fucking thing I've ever seen.'

'You have to trust me,' said Killheffer, still smiling.

'If you haven't noticed, we're here again. What is it? Poison? Cough syrup? Junk?'

'My own special mixture of oblivion; a distillation of equations for free will. I call it "Laughter in the Dark,"' said the professor, proudly smoothing back his slick black hair.

Dex couldn't help but smile. 'You're a malicious crackpot, but okay, let's get on with it. What's the deal this time?'

'Mondrian is, right at this moment, upstairs, on the third floor, in Sizzle Parlor number four, awaiting a female associate of mine who has promised him exotic favors, but unfortunately will never deliver. Instead, you will arrive. I want him dead.' Killheffer hurriedly tamped out his cigar and snapped his fingers to the passing cigarette girl. She stopped next to Dex and opened the case that hung by a strap around her shoulders. There were no cigarettes, just something covered by a handkerchief.

'You think of everything,' said Dex and reached in to grab the gun. He stood and slipped it into the waist of his pants. 'How do I collect?'

'The cure will be delivered before the night is

through,' said the professor. 'Hurry, Mondrian can only forgo his beloved tips for so long.'

'What do you have against him?' Dex asked as he lifted his hat off the chair beside him.

'He's a computational loop,' said Killheffer. 'A real zero-sum game.'

At the head of the long, dark hallway on the third floor of the pavilion, Dex was stopped by the night man, an imposing fellow with a bald head and a sawed-off shotgun in his left hand.

'What's news, Jeminy?' said Dex.

'Obviously, you are, Dex. Looking for a room?'

He nodded.

'Ten dollars. But for you, for old times' sake, ten dollars,' said Jeminy and laughed.

'You're too good to me,' said Dex, a ten spot appearing in his hand. 'The lady'll be along any minute.'

'Sizzle Parlor number five,' the big man said, his voice echoing down the long hall. 'Grease that griddle, my friend.'

'Will do,' said Dex and before long slowed his pace and looked over his shoulder to check that Jeminy had again taken his seat facing away, toward the stairwell. He passed door after door, and after every six a weak gas lamp glowed on either wall. As he neared parlor number four, he noticed the door was open a sliver, but it was dark inside. Brandishing the gun, he held it straight up in front of him.

Opening the door, he slipped inside, and shut it quietly behind him. Moonlight shone in through

298

one tall, arched window, but Dex could only make out shadows. He scanned the room, and slowly the forms of chairs, a coffee table, a vanity, and, off to the side of the room, a bed became evident to him. Sitting up on the edge of that bed was a lumpen silhouette, atop it, the telltale shape of the fez.

'Is it you, my desert flower?' came the voice of Mondrian.

Dex swiftly crossed the room. When he was next to the figure, and had surmised where his victim's left temple might be, he cocked the gun's hammer with his thumb and wrapped his index finger around the trigger. Before he could squeeze off the shot, though, the slouched bag of shadow that was Mondrian lunged into him with terrific force. Dex, utterly surprised that the meek little fellow would have the gumption to attack, fell backward, tripping on the rug, the gun flying off into the dark. He tried to get to his feet, but the maitre d' landed on him like nine sandbags, one hand grabbing his throat. No matter how many times Dex managed a punch to Mondrian's face, the shadow of the fez never toppled away. They rolled over and over and then partially into the moonlight. Dex saw the flash of a blade above him, but his arms were now pinned by his assailant's knees. Unable to halt the knife's descent, he held his breath in preparation for pain. Then the lights went on, there was a gunshot, and his attacker fell off him.

Dex scrabbled to his feet and turned to find Adeline, standing next to the open door, the muzzle of the gun still smoking. From down the hall, he heard Jeminy blow his whistle, an alert to the Ice Garden's force of leg breakers.

'Nice shot, baby,' he said. 'Kill the lights and close the door.'

She closed the door behind her, but didn't flip the switch. 'Look,' she said to Dex, pointing with the gun at the floor behind him. He turned and saw the hundred-tooth smile of Killheffer. The fez was secured around the professor's chin by a rubber band. A bullet had left a gaping third eye in his forehead.

'The rat fuck,' said Dex. He leaned over, grabbed his hat where it had fallen, and then felt through Killheffer's jacket pockets. All he came up with was a cigar tube, holding a single Wrath Majestic. He slipped it into his inside jacket pocket.

'They're coming,' said Adeline. She hit the lights. There was the sound of running feet and voices in the hallway. 'They're going door-to-door.'

'We'll shoot our way out,' said Dex.

Adeline was next to him. She whispered in his ear, 'Don't be a jackass, we'll take the fire escape.'

Dex moved toward the window. Adeline slipped off her heels.

Somehow Mondrian had known to call the car up, because when Dex and Adeline arrived in front of the Ice Garden, breathless, scuff marks on their clothes, the Belvedere was there, top down and running, Jim-Jim holding Adeline's door.

'I like your shoes,' said the boy, pointing to her bare feet.

'My new fashion, Jim,' said Adeline.

Dex moved quickly around the car. Mondrian was there to open the door for him. As Dex slid in behind the wheel, he said, 'No hard feelings about tonight,' and flashed a tip to cover the intended homicide. Mondrian bowed slightly and snatched the bill.

'Ever at your service,' said the maitre d'. 'Safe journey.' He shut the car door.

Dex took a silver dollar out of his pocket, hit the gas, and flipped the coin back over the car. *Jim-Jim caught it* and before he could stash it in his vest pocket, the Belvedere was no more than two red dots halfway down the avenue of monkey-puzzle trees.

'My feet are killing me,' said Adeline as they screeched out of the entrance to the Ice Garden and onto the desert highway.

'You are one hell of a shot,' he said.

'Lucky,' she said, her voice rising above the wind.

'I'll cherish the moment.'

'All well and good,' said Adeline, 'but what's his game this time?'

'Laughter in the dark,' said Dex and cut the wheel hard to the right. Adeline slid toward him and he wrapped his arm around her shoulders. The car left the road and raced along an avenue of moonlight, plowing through tumbleweeds, trailing a plume of dust across the desert. Adeline switched on the radio and found Dete Walader, crooning 'I Remember You.'

They lay on a blanket beneath shimmering stars. A light breeze blew over them. Here and there, the dark form of a cactus stood sentry. Ten yards away, the radio in the Belvedere played something with strings. Adeline took a sip from her silver flask and handed it to Dex. He flicked the butt of the Majestic off into the sand, and took a drink.

'What is this stuff?' he asked, squinting.

'My own special mixture of oblivion,' she said.

'That's Killheffer's line,' he said. 'Did you see him tonight?'

She nodded and laid her cheek against his chest. 'In the ladies' room; he was in the stall next to the one I chose, waiting for me.'

'He gets around,' said Dex, ''cause he was at our table when I got back to it.'

'He whispered from the other stall that he wanted me to kill Mondrian. I said I wouldn't, but then he said he had the solution and was willing to trade me for the murder. I told him I wanted to see it. The next thing, the door to my stall flew open and he was standing there. I almost screamed. I didn't know what to do. I was on the toilet, for criminy sake. He had that stupid smile on his face, and he pulled down his zipper.'

Dex rose to one elbow. 'I'll kill him,' he said.

'Too late,' said Adeline. 'He reached into his pants and pulled out this big hypodermic needle with green juice in it. He said, "You see the tip at the end of that needle? Think of that as the period at the end of your interminable story. Do you want out?" I just wanted to get rid of him, so I nodded. He handed me a gun and told me Mondrian was in Sizzle Parlor number four.'

A long time passed in silence.

'But, in the end, you decided to off Mondrian?' said Dex.

'I guess so,' said Adeline. 'What else is there to do when we come to the Ice Garden but fall in with Killheffer's scheme? Mondrian might as well be made of papier-mâché and that's the long and short of it. He's polite, but, sure, I'd clip him for the possibility of a ticket out.'

'I'd miss you,' said Dex.

'I wouldn't leave you here alone,' she said. 'I was getting the needle for you.'

'You didn't think of using it yourself? Baby, I'm touched.'

'Well, maybe once when I realized that if it worked, you wouldn't come for me anymore and I'd spend each go-round in that crappy apartment building back in dragsville watching the plaster crack.'

'I was ready to blow Mondrian's brains out for you too,' he said. 'I can see how stale it's getting for you.'

'You never thought of yourself?' she asked.

Dex sat up and pointed into the distance at a pair of headlights. 'Let's get the guns,' he said. He stood and helped her up. She found her underwear a few feet away and slipped them back on.

'Who do you think it is?' she asked, joining him at the car.

He handed her a pistol. 'Ice Garden thugs,' he said.

When the approaching car came to a halt a few feet from the blanket, Dex reached over the side of the Belvedere and hit the lights, to reveal a very old black car, more like a covered carriage with a steering wheel and no horse. The door opened and out stepped Mondrian. He carried an open umbrella and a small box. Taking three furtive steps forward, he called out, 'Mr Dexter.'

'Expecting rain, Mondrian?' said Dex.

'Stars, sir. Stars.'

Adeline laughed from where she was crouched behind the Belvedere.

'A package for the lady and gentleman,' said Mondrian.

'Set it down at your feet, right there, and then you can go,' said Dex.

Mondrian set the package on the sand, but remained standing at attention over it.

'What are you waiting for?' asked Dex.

Mondrian was silent, but Adeline whispered, 'He wants a tip.'

Dex fired two shots into the umbrella. 'Keep the change,' he called.

Mondrian bowed, said, 'Most generous, sir,' and then got back in the car. As the maitre d' pulled away, Adeline retrieved the package. Dex met her back on the blanket where she sat with the box, an eight-inch cube wrapped in silver paper and a red bow, like a birthday present, on her lap.

'It could be a bomb,' he said.

She hesitated for an instant, and said, 'Oh, well,' and tore the wrapping off. Digging her nails into the seam between the cardboard flaps, she pulled back on both sides, ripping the top away. She reached in and retrieved Killheffer's hypodermic needle. She put her hand back into the box and felt around.

'There's only one,' she said.

'Now you know what his game is,' said Dex.

She held it up in the moonlight, and the green liquid inside its glass syringe glowed. 'It's beautiful,' she said with a sigh.

'Do it,' said Dex.

'No, you,' she said and handed it to him.

He reached for it, but then stopped, his fingers grazing the metal plunger. 'No,' he said and shook his head. 'It was your shot.'

'It probably won't even work,' she said and laid it carefully on the blanket between them, petting it twice before withdrawing her hand.

'We'll shoot dice,' said Dex, running his pinky finger the length of the needle. 'The winner takes it.'

Adeline said nothing for a time, and then she nodded in agreement. 'But first a last dance in case it works.'

Dex got up and went to the car to turn the radio up. 'We're in luck,' he said, and the first notes of

'Polka Dots and Moonbeams' drifted out into the desert. He slowly swayed his way back to her. She smoothed her dress, adjusted her girdle, and put her arms around him, resting her chin on his shoulder. He held her around the waist and they turned slowly, wearily, to the music.

'So, we'll shoot craps?' she whispered.

'That's right,' he said.

Three slow turns later, Adeline said, 'Don't think I don't remember you've got that set of loaded dice.'

Dex put his head back and laughed, and, as if in response, at that very moment, the stars began to fall, streaking down through the night, trailing bright streamers. First a handful and then a hundred and then more let go of their hold on the firmament and leaped. Way off to the west, the first ones hit with a distant rumble and firework geysers of flame. More followed, far and near, and Dex and Adeline kissed amid the conflagration.

'Pick me up at seven,' she said, her bottom lip on his earlobe, and held him more tightly.

'I'll be there, baby,' he promised, 'I'll be there.'

With the accuracy of a bullet between the eyes, one of the million heavenly messengers screeched down upon them, a fireball the size of the Ice Garden. The explosion flipped the Belvedere into the air like a silver dollar and turned everything to dust.

ABOUT THE CONTRIBUTORS

Dublin-born **Roddy Doyle** has written novels, play, and screenplays. His novel *Paddy Clarke Ha Ha Ha* won the Booker Prize in 1993. His Barrytown trilogy has been filmed as *The Commitments*, *The Snapper*, and *The Van*.

Joyce Carol Oates has published more than fifty novels, as well as numerous short story collections and volumes of poetry and nonfiction. Her novel *Them* won the National Book Award.

Joanne Harris is the author of *The Evil Seed* and *Chocolat*, which was a number one bestseller in the London *Sunday Times* and was shortlisted for the 1999 Whitbread Novel of the Year. *Runemarks*, published in 2007, was her first book for children and young adults.

Michael Marshall Smith is a British novelist, screenwriter, and shortstory writer. He has won the British Fantasy, the August Derleth, and the Philip K. Dick awards. His book *The Intruders* was picked up by the BBC for a major new drama series.

Joe R. Lansdale is the author of scores of novels and short stories, including the popular Hap and Leonard mystery series. He is a multiple winner of the Bram Stoker Award. He lives in Nacogdoches, Texas, with his wife and family.

Walter Mosley is the author of more than twenty books in many categories, but is perhaps best known for the highly regarded and popular Easy Rawlins hard-boiled detective novels. Born in Los Angeles, he now lives in New York City.

Richard Adams is the author of *Shardik, The Girl in the Swing*, and many other novels, but is perhaps best known for *Watership Down*, which was a national bestseller, and was awarded the Carnegie Medal and the Guardian Award for Children's Fiction.

Jodi Picoult is a number one bestselling author, with more than 14 million books in print worldwide. She won the New England Bookseller Award for fiction in 2003, and currently lives in Hanover, New Hampshire.

Michael Swanwick began publishing in the early 1980s, and is currently based in Philadelphia. He is the winner of the Hugo, World Fantasy,

Theodore Sturgeon Memorial, and Nebula awards.

Peter Straub's novel *Ghost Story* is generally considered a high point of the modern horror novel. He has won the Bram Stoker, World Fantasy, and International Horror Guild awards. Born in Milwaukee, Wisconsin, he now lives in New York City.

Lawrence Block is the highly acclaimed author of two series set in New York, featuring Private Eye Matthew Scudder and burglar Bernie Rhodenbarr. In 1993 Block was tapped as a Grand Master by the Mystery Writers of America.

Jeffrey Ford is known for his iconoclastic and literary dark fantasy novels. He is the winner of numerous awards for both his short stories and longer works. He lives in southern New Jersey with his wife and family.